THE TELECOM
TAKEOVER

Beverly Winter

For my brother Bob Eldridge, Jr., in memoriam.

Acknowledgments

I am immensely grateful to Trai Cartwright who saw potential in this novel. Her editorial help, sharp insight, and enthusiasm were key to bringing my story to life. Line edits by Shelley Widhalm ensured that my work was the strongest it could be. I appreciate the invaluable assistance of the Northern Colorado Writers community and the Raintree Writers critique group, including Pat Stoltey, Jim Davidson, Gordon MacKinney, Brian Kaufman, Ken Harmon, and Brigitte Dempsey. A special thanks to my cousin Gene Eldridge, an excellent writer, and my sister, Nancy Markey, whose support I can always count on. And my heartfelt gratitude to the many talented writers and storytellers in my family tree.

Contents

Prologue: Monday, April 17

A woman in a pink ruffled top shifted the legal-size sheets to her left arm and pushed the door open with her right. Lifting the stack with both hands, she dropped it onto the oak conference table. The top sheet fluttered to the floor. She snatched it up and slapped it onto the dusty pile. "Hi! I'm Sue. You get to take over the city audit. Here's the workpapers. I made a few calculations on the last page." With a toss of her blond ponytail, she was out the door.

Beth Madison, along with Jim Dennis and Tom Shuler, stared at the heap of papers on the table before them.

"So we get to untangle Sue's audit on our first day," Beth said. "We brought our entire group's workload from Principal Processing Company. We're responsible for the same work we were doing before, plus the jobs of our laid-off coworkers. We can't take on Heenehan's, too!" *Sixty-plus hour workweeks? Over my dead body.*

"I guess we should count ourselves lucky that Heenehan Telecom hired us in this recession," Jim said. "Sue must've stashed that printout under her desk, wishing it would disappear."

Tom flipped through the sheets and studied the calculations. "People like Sue keep us employed. When we were at Principal, I worked with the city. We can handle this one. Sue started out right, but ended up in the weeds." He wiped dust from his hands onto his chair.

Tom passed the workpapers to Beth. She examined the last page and set it in front of Jim. "Look, her analysis is all over the place."

Jim studied the sheet. "I see what you mean. Sue should have consulted with her supervisor when she got lost. Good that Heenehan didn't pay the city's assessment."

"I don't understand why she didn't take the opportunity to manage this important audit herself," Beth said. "She could've asked us to help her get back on track."

Tom said, "Maybe audits aren't her strong suit. After we're settled in our cubicles, I'll sort the file, draft our response, and email the city's audit team."

"I can dig out Heenehan's tax reports," Beth said. *If Sue tries to palm off any more of her work, I'm going to have a word with our manager.*

"I'll pull together the backup documentation," Jim said. "Another new hire named Amber starts work today. She can help us."

"We'll wrap it up in a couple weeks," Tom said.

Morning sunshine streamed through slatted window blinds in the large fourth-floor conference room. Leaning back in a black office chair at the conference table, Amber Wolfe brushed aside a strand of her emerald choppy bob. "I'm already loving this gig." *My dream job. I earned it!*

At the head of the table, Li Chang adjusted his slender frame in the chair. "Amber, the Tech Team is committed to giving this assignment the serious attention it deserves."

Across the table, computer technicians Ludmila Kozlova and Spartak Volkov nodded their heads.

"We will gather every piece of data inside this company. Important people are monitoring our progress. We must operate carefully."

"Sure thing, Li."

"Heenehan Telecom Company is a minor player in the telecommunications world. But their network interfaces with other companies, national banks, the federal government, most states, and many cities. Its tax group is critical to our operation."

"You and the two Russians are pretending to be consultants."

"Our contract with Heenehan guarantees we will detect errors in past tax returns and obtain substantial tax refunds from all states. That is the work Ludmila and Spartak and I claim to do."

"It's really easy for me to play a tax accountant."

"Amber, you are a tax department employee. You have an important role, to distract in every way you can. Keep the group off balance without drawing attention to yourself. It shouldn't be difficult. Continuing mergers and acquisitions confuse workers, leaving them disorganized and in conflict with each other. Your manager, Brad Mitchell, hires underqualified, underclass types. You're going to fit right in."

Underqualified? I'll show him.

"Occupying a room here in their building is risky, but we can move forward faster by mixing with their employees. Do you understand what I'm saying?"

"I get it. I'm gonna have the whole tax group working for us," Amber said, eyeing Chang. Olive skin, crisp, blue button-down shirt, sleek sideburns, deep voice. So fine.

"The new hires from Principal Processing Company could thwart our mission. They must be eliminated. You need to make that happen."

"Will do."

"Amber, your tax skills are sparse. You'd better hope HR doesn't check out your 'master's degree.' Don't antagonize anyone in this company. Our presence here is a delicate matter. Use Hwan Cho only when necessary. Hwan's technical skills are crucial to our operation, but he is not reliable."

"I can make Hwan do anything I tell him. If he don't, I'll, like, yank his visa."

"You're not going to yank anything. And don't say 'like' and 'you know.' You're speaking low-level English. Drop the street lingo. Communicate your ideas clearly. Dress professionally. Did you take the public speaking class I recommended?"

"Yes, I did," Amber said.

"I expect you to pick up on social cues and relate well to your coworkers. Am I making sense to you?"

"Totally! You know, we should lock up all of Heenehan's computers. The employees gonna think the system has a virus. We do our work. When we're done, make Heenehan pay us Bitcoins to unfreeze their computers. My friend overseas pays cash for Bitcoins for a small fee."

"We don't operate that way. Our offshore private foundation gives us plenty of cash. We're not going to work with Bitcoins or any other cryptocurrencies. They're too volatile and too vulnerable to hackers."

"Okay. I just thought of it 'cause the cops can't control it. Maybe in our next job." *A money-spinning idea, and he's thumbs-down. I'll keep after him.*

"Ludmila and Spartak understand more English than they speak. They need employees' passwords to move forward with the computer work. Your most important task will be to ensure that Heenehan's systems are linked to Wong Tel's. I expect regular updates. It's a big job. If it isn't well-handled, there will be consequences for you."

I love it when he shows me who's boss. "Yeah, I know that, Li. I sent out them two emails Ludmila and Spartak wrote. The one from HR's email address is like, so real! I sent that one to all the employees. I got back lots of their passwords. So we can already get into most of Heenehan's network. I sent out the other email from the CEO's email address lookin' like he approved our fees. The accounts payable supervisor set us up as the Consulting Group."

Amber held Chang's eyes. "I always do good work for you. I won't let you down, Li.

Chapter 1: Monday, May 1

Jagged rhythms pulsed through the chill basement. *Electronic jazz, too jarring for my middle-aged ears at this early hour. Mom's going to feel the vibrations upstairs.* From his phone on the nightstand, Jim Dennis switched to another work in progress. Breezy tempo, smooth elements. He scribbled his ideas on a yellow sticky note. *I'll develop this one into a full composition.*

Jim's tabby cat extended her striped legs and tail, stretched, and jumped onto the gray bathroom sink countertop. Hannah sat with paws tucked under her ginger body, a furry pom-pom watching Jim with wide green eyes and emitting tiny meows.

After brushing his teeth, Jim filled his rinsing cup with water and swallowed an Adderall capsule. He split a Prozac tablet, swallowed half, and dropped the other half back into the bottle. The few sips of last night's vodka should be undetectable. He swished with mouthwash to be sure. Classic shirt and a trendy haircut, a light brown rinse covering the emerging gray. Business casual, with style. A dark jolt of panic popped through the anxiety rumbling under his skin.

Hannah jumped to the floor and rubbed against his leg, leaving cinnamon-colored fur on his black pants. Jim stroked her soft back and gently scratched behind her upright ears. "See you this evening, sweetie." He pulled open the window curtains, gathered his phone, keys, and an energy bar, and climbed the stairs to the main floor of his house.

Rose stood at the landing, hands on hips, uncombed gray hair skimming a navy flowered bathrobe. "You're not going out in that pink shirt, Jimmy! Put on your blue one."

My dear old, feisty mother. "It's salmon, not pink. It's a popular color."

"Not for a man. Go back downstairs and change!"

"Love you, Mom, running late." Jim brushed past Rose and exited through the kitchen door to the attached garage. He got into his red Outback and went to work.

Beth plunged her hands into icy water streaming from the shiny chrome faucet into the porcelain sink. She splashed her face. *Now I'm awake!* She squeezed her gray-blonde hair section by section, making smooth, wet waves. A few drops of water bloomed on her tan slacks. Her aqua, geometric-patterned blouse hung low on one side. She re-buttoned her blouse and clipped an unruly gray hair from one of her eyebrows.

Having escaped the fate of Principal Processing Company "expendables," Beth found her new position at Heenehan a painful reversal. Long days. Difficult coworkers. Fatigue that used to be a temporary energy drag, resolved by a little caffeine, had become a knockout punch. By late afternoon, creeping brain fog often left her searching for her thoughts and words and speaking in fragments.

On her home office desk, an official letter stating her future monthly retirement benefit portended a seismic shift in her lifestyle. Managing on a tight budget would be a given. No travel money, but more than enough for basic needs. *I did it when I was raising Jason. I can do it again. I want to get strong and healthy. Invite my grandkids over for pizza and a movie. Have some fun! Maybe think like an artist again. In the meantime, things can happen. What if my health fails? What if my retirement account takes a nosedive?*

I don't have far to fall. I need this job until my full monthly retirement benefit kicks in.

Beth pushed through her normal two miles on the living room exercise bike. In the kitchen, she gulped down a small bowl of whole grain cereal and washed her bowl in the sink. Returning to the bathroom, she dropped her toothbrush on the floor. She tossed it into the trashcan, found a new toothbrush, tore open the packaging with stiff fingers, and brushed her teeth.

This messy crash pad will become my sanctuary. I know just how to fix it up.

Beth hit the remote to open her garage door. A warm spring breeze carried a delicate fragrance of pink sweet peas, winding through a wrought iron trellis next to her condo. She slid behind the wheel of her blue Civic and tuned to her favorite classic rock station.

Beth arrived at the suburban office park in twenty minutes. She cut through the vast parking lot and walked down a sidewalk along freshly cut grass. A bluebird arced across a brilliant orange sunrise fading into coral. Fuzzy-headed cattails with flat leaf blades spiked along the edge of the pond, offsetting lime green leaves sprouting from tree buds. Deep purple violas stood out in the landscape design. Yellow, white, and red pansies shimmered from early morning sprinklers. Distant snow-capped mountains glistened, illuminated by the sunrise. *I love springtime.*

Beth approached the Heenehan Telecom Company corporate headquarters building, a four-story maze of soaring atriums, interconnected passageways, and catwalks between building sectors. From a fourth-floor window, ceiling lights emitted an icy white glow. *A janitor must have left them on.* Shadows moved across closed window blinds.

Beth lurched forward and stumbled a few steps, clutching her black shoulder bag. Pain jabbed her left ankle. *Damn cracked sidewalk!* A strong hand caught her elbow. She leaned on the steady hand, attempting to remain upright.

"Hey, are you all right?" Jim Dennis gripped her arm.

"I'm fine."

He released his hold.

Beth willed herself to walk with a dignified bearing on her tender ankle. She smoothed her hair with her free hand. "I tripped on that crack like a goofball. Ouch."

"Accountants tend not to be highly coordinated. You may want your doctor to take a look at your ankle if it keeps swelling. I reported that crack to Brad last week. He told me to step over it."

"Next time I'll do that."

Jim pointed upward. "Odd that lights are on in the fourth-floor conference room."

"No one is normally in that room at this hour."

"If Tom came in early, he'd be working on the garden level. He's finishing our appeal of the city's tax assessment. It should lower our tax to around 85 percent of the amount we paid last year. Brad should be happy with the results of Tom's hard work."

"Tom nailed this one. We're lucky he's on our team."

"Did you work this weekend?" Jim asked.

"Well, yeah, from home." At Principal, Beth often worked seven days a week during the busy periods, then took comp time during a slower period. If she got behind due to pressing assignments, she worked on weekends to catch up. At Heenehan, there was no catching up. At least forty hours of work lay ahead of her to meet tax return deadlines. Audits, projects, and other assignments would take more time. Researching issues to maximize tax savings remained on the back burner.

"I worked online for a few hours," Jim said. His fine-featured face had a gray tinge. His intelligent, blue eyes were hollow, his shoulders slumped. "At least you can see the light at the end of the tunnel. You'll be relaxing on a sandy beach, sipping a tropical drink with a tiny umbrella."

"I'm counting the days. Hey, you look tired. Are you okay?"

"I guess so."

They held their badges to the card reader that beeped approval. Jim pushed the heavy glass door and held it open for Beth. Frigid air hit her face. *I'll pull on the blue wool cardigan in my cubicle closet.* The receptionist hadn't yet arrived at her workstation in the spacious lobby.

"What's that?" Beth gaped at a new hanging metal wall sculpture opposite the reception desk. A whimsical grid of vertical metal bars spread across the beige wall.

"A masterful image of the state penitentiary?"

"I can imagine faces of prisoners peering through it."

After they descended the stairs, Jim flipped on the light switch. Harsh ceiling lights illuminated faded beige walls, scuffed baseboards, and worn gray carpeting. Off-white horizontal blinds covered small windows fortified by iron bars. They walked down a hall between high gunmetal-gray cubicle walls. Employees' colorful desk lamps injected cozy charm into somber cubicles.

"I can't get over how massive this building is," Beth said.

"Several hundred employees on our floor," Jim said. "More on the upper levels."

In the corner of the garden level, they walked to the end of a narrow aisle between two rows of tax department cubicles. The tax staff had not yet arrived.

Jim stared at Tom Shuler's empty cubicle. Beth gasped. The vacant desk gleamed. No office plants, family photos, or racks of colorful manila folders. Their long-time colleague was gone.

The color drained from Jim's face. "This stinking company!" Jim shouted. "Tom has a family to support! Who's going to take over his work?"

"Shh! Keep your voice down! We need our jobs."

"Andy in the IT group is going to be furious. The three of us were updating the tax software."

At Jim's desk, he dialed his cell phone and put it on speaker. Tom's wife, Sherry, answered.

"Beth and I would like to talk to Tom."

"Tom isn't taking any calls right now," Sherry said in a tight voice.

Beth said, "I'm so sorry, Sherry. This is hard for your family, and it's terribly unfair. We want to meet up with Tom and talk."

"Please ask him to call Beth or me anytime," Jim said.

"I'll tell him," Sherry said. "I appreciate your concern. Thanks for calling. Goodbye."

Beth said, "Strange that Tom is keeping to himself."

"It's not like Tom to hide from his friends when things go wrong," Jim said.

Jim sat at his desk, unfocused. *Tom's gone. Heenehan's outdated technology can't handle the Principal acquisition. A cascading workload is falling on Beth and me.* Unlocking his bottom desk drawer, he removed a spiral notebook with a red cover. He filled a page, scratching out words, editing lines.

My office looks the same to me
But I sense it's a poisonous place to be.

11

THE TELECOM TAKEOVER

The halls are filled with ghosts from the past
Who trusted their colleagues, then got the ax.

We don't speak of their fates, we don't mention their names.
If they never existed, it would be just the same.

I remember their faces, the words they said,
Their laughter, their families. Now they are "dead."

I'm good enough now, but I can't pretend
It can't happen to me if it happened to them.

If I foolishly say something I shouldn't have said
Will I suddenly find myself terminated?

If I work every evening and most weekends
Will I keep my position and lose all my friends?

If I can't cover two jobs or three jobs or four
Will they hire youngsters half my age to do more?

If I appease the office gods who I meet
Will they still end up tossing me out on the street?

If my coworkers find my empty cabinet and desk
Will they be told I've left to pursue other interests?

Should I start over now at a new company
At a fraction of my current salary?

I used to be driving, I used to aspire.
Now I hope to retire before I expire.

Ha! Someday I'll recycle this old journal of bad poetry. Jim slid the notebook into the drawer, and locked it.

His cell phone vibrated, displaying an incoming call from Seb Medina in the sales group. Jim spoke evenly. "Yes, I'm going to the meeting at Ryan Ford's house. You'll like Ryan. He's a kind soul. I'm doing okay. See you there."

Chapter 2: Tuesday, May 2

Beth stared at her workspace in dismay. Emails filled her inbox. The message light on her desk phone blinked red. Her to-do list was three pages longer than it was last week. Dozens of hanging files in assorted colors waited for her attention. First things first. One minute at a time.

An email message required Beth to be present at a 9 a.m. staff meeting in a second-floor conference room. *I don't want to hear any spin about Tom's departure.* She clicked Accept.

Two minutes before 9, an email came up in her inbox.

> these return is picking up a fairly straight forward i will set some calendar appointment. u know this stuff we suppose to help each other!!!!!

Beth would try to decipher Amber's message later. Taking her notepad, she met Jim in the hallway.

Brad Mitchell, the tax manager, sat at the head of the conference table, arms folded. He greeted Judy Stump, the tax supervisor. Kessie Hinkle, the tax administrator, followed behind Judy. Brad acknowledged each tax accountant as they filed into the room — Sue Gatling, Cody Atkins, Amber Wolfe, Jim Dennis, and Beth Madison. They took their seats around the conference table.

"Let me start by saying thank you for your time today. The first order of business is Human Resources' request that we all update our passwords. HR expects that to be done before noon."

Brad removed a stack of papers from a folder on the table before him. "Our year-end bonuses will be calculated differently. These worksheets show how the amounts will be determined." Brad handed the papers to Cody, who took five stapled sheets and passed the stack to the person next to him.

"What's the main difference?" Sue asked. "I heard our bonuses gonna be smaller than last year."

"In that regard, the numbers we present externally to Wall Street vary from the way the numbers are aligned internally. It's complicated. Just read the sheets. You can figure it out."

Brad said, "I have good news. Your jobs are safe. I convinced our director, Scott Campbell, that we can cut costs by being more efficient. Sue, Cody, and Amber, you're going to continue preparing the Heenehan tax returns as you normally do. Jim and Beth, you are responsible for Principal Processing Company and the state audit of Heenehan. You both have three weeks to respond to the state auditors' preliminary workpapers."

Beth said, "Heenehan's state audit? Plus all of Tom's work? When do you expect us to get it done?" *I don't believe this.*

"Sandra Young, our corporate finance manager, graciously agreed to allow us to use her staff member, Hwan Cho, to help us when he's not working on finance matters. Hwan is very smart. He will prepare the simpler Principal returns. Hwan will sit in Tom's old cubicle."

Sue said in a honeyed voice, "If I was a manager, I'd make everybody do Heenehan's returns."

Beth regarded her with amusement. *Sly fox, trying to dump her work again.*

Judy gave Sue a warm smile.

Cody sat in silence, a twenty-year-old likeness of middle-aged Brad.

Amber said, "I'm gonna get a whole lot of work done today. I got it all figured out."

Brad said, "Good! Let's get the ball rolling. Kessie, please re-run this month's tax calendar with our new tax return assignments."

Kessie looked up. "Huh?"

"I said, please re-run this month's tax calendar with our new assignments. It won't take much time."

"It don't make me no nevermind," Kessie said with a dismissive wave. "I can get them new calendars out today." Burying her fingertips into her hair, she scratched her scalp vigorously.

"Each of you needs to plan your schedule accordingly. After this meeting, I'll be on vacation the rest of the week. Any questions?"

"Does that mean we'll work evenings and weekends on a regular basis?" Beth asked. "Jim and I are already overloaded with Principal returns, our own and the ones we took on from our downsized coworkers. We need a few vacation days to be with our families."

Muffled snickers. Cody half-smiled, gazing at the brown vinyl floor.

Lowering his voice, Brad spoke in a fatherly tone. "Beth, you work the hours you need to complete your assignments. Hundreds of people in this city would love to have your job. I'm sure you're eager to prove yourself. It's your privilege to work with the Heenehan family."

"Brad, our plates are full!" Beth said.

Brad rose an inch before settling in his seat. "Wouldn't you rather be busy than bored? Don't you agree too much work is better than not enough? You'd be amazed at the amount of work you can accomplish when you have to. Our IT people from India work twelve to fifteen hours a day. You don't hear them complaining about long hours. If you can afford to take vacation time, take it. We care about you and your family."

Beth eyed the window. *A quick shove into the bushes below might knock some sense into him.*

Jim said, "If we're required to work substantially more hours, our salaries should be adjusted accordingly."

Brad shifted in his chair. "I'm not going to set any precedents for employee pay, if that's what you have in mind." He looked around at the group. "Here at Heenehan we're fairly compensated, aren't we?"

The group sat silent.

"I'll speak with you later," Jim said to Brad.

"We will not backfill vacant positions. Our stretch goals take us beyond our targets, increasing our skills and building our resumes. Hwan will be a big help. He hasn't done accounting or tax work, but hey, training a new person is like training a new dog."

Brad peered at Jim. "When I did business with your father's law firm, his pro bono work and civic activities greatly benefitted our community. Let me ask you this, if Arthur was alive today, what would he think of you?" Brad pointed his index finger. "You need to decide how important this job is to you."

Beth spoke up. "Every time we print, we have to unjam our high-speed printer. It's been repaired eight times. You said —"

"Yes, I'm going to requisition a replacement printer." Brad turned to Judy. "I have the pleasure of announcing that Judy Stump won Heenehan's Employee of the Month Award. She created a database that works with our software to generate our tax returns. You can drill down to create a report. It's a home run for the tax team! You can begin using it today. Judy will be happy to provide any support you need."

Judy said, "The database will do almost all the work for you. I will continue to update it. You may expect occasional requests from me."

Leaning back, Brad clasped his hands behind his head. "Heenehan has contracted with a group of multi-state auditors called the Tech Team. Amber will coordinate their work with our department. Their job is to save us money on our tax payments."

"Great idea," Cody said.

"Also, within the next few months, we will have two important changes. High-walled cubicles are relics of the past. You will sit at long tables. Our open office layout will give us a more collaborative atmosphere. Managers and above will retain their personal offices."

Beth said, "The noise in open workspaces is distracting." *Shoulder to shoulder, bombarded with interruptions all day. Hell on earth.*

"Duly noted."

Cody said, "Open offices save the company money. Heenehan's growing. We need to fit more people in less space."

"Right, Cody. You hit the nail on the head."

Brad sat straight. "Over the next few months, all employees will be 'chipped' one department at a time. A microchip will be injected into one of your hands between your thumb and index finger. The implant will take the place of your security badge card to open the door to the building or to use the printer. It's voluntary, but I expect full cooperation in this important security measure."

Beth rubbed her forehead. I must have misheard. Did Brad really say that?

"Can the chips track an employee's location after work hours?" Jim asked.

"People implant things in their bodies all the time—earrings, nose rings," Brad said. "It doesn't hurt. A little swelling and bruising for a few days."

"I'm concerned about privacy."

"Interesting point. The executive team discussed it at length. There's no privacy issue unless you're hiding something. IT has always monitored your email messages. It will improve our security. Some departments are planning chip parties!" Brad surveyed the group. "Thank you for all your hard work. Each of you has a wonderful, long-term future. With our dedicated employees, Heenehan will continue to provide first-class voice, internet, data, and fiber optic services. By the way, if you haven't yet signed your annual Code of Conduct form, please do so and take it to HR. Keep in mind that our dress code requires everyone to maintain a professional appearance. Also, please complete the annual employee satisfaction survey on the internal company website today."

Jim raised his hand. "Brad, we need direction on how Heenehan's state audit has been handled in the past."

Ready to spring out the door, Brad said, "We'll circle back to the audit later." He grabbed his notebook and headed toward the stairs.

The staff shuffled back to the tax area, past rows of cubicles enclosing heads-down employees tapping on keyboards.

Amber hummed, "Another One Bites the Dust."

"Why is Brad even here?" Sue asked.

"Dunno," Kessie said. "At least this time he told us he was gonna be gone. He usually sneaks out and leaves his office door open, so everybody thinks he's still around."

Sue laughed. "It figures. Hey, Beth, what's your sign?"

"What do you mean?"

"Your zodiac sign. What month were you born?"

"August."

"Oh, you're a Leo. Leos aren't detail-oriented. People in your sign always pick the wrong jobs. You shouldn't be here."

"Leos are leaders who show pride in their work."

"Get your birth chart done. Find out the position of your planets."

"I'll think about it." *When pigs fly around the office.*

They passed a glass-walled room along a corridor. A group of men sat in rows of chairs facing a TV screen showing a man making a presentation. The group hooted with laughter, throwing crumpled sheets of paper at the screen.

"They're having way more fun than us," Amber said.

Jim kicked a hard object lying on the carpet. He picked up the black cell phone and put it in his pants pocket. Marching past him, Judy snapped, "Why are you so careless with your phone?" She lumbered on, hunched over her swinging arms.

As they descended the stairway to the garden level, Beth caught a glimpse of a workman of slight build and average height with medium-brown straight hair. He carried a storage box down a dim corridor and disappeared out the exit door. The man bore a striking resemblance to Tom Shuler. *It couldn't possibly be Tom. He never dressed in rugged workwear. Human Resources would have taken his badge card.*

"I'm not going to update my login password," Jim said to Beth. "The email isn't from HR's address. The letters after dot-com are suspicious."

"You're right. I won't respond to that email either."

"Did you complete your employee satisfaction survey?"

"Sure did," Beth said. "I gave every question the highest rating. Those anonymous surveys aren't so anonymous."

"Those rowdy guys in the conference room, what was that about?"

"The engineering group was reacting to the CEO's presentation on the screen."

"They were steamed up about something."

Sue whispered, "The coast is clear!"

Amber raced down the aisle and executed two powerful cartwheels. Landing on both feet, she extended her arms in a "ta-da" pose. Sue and Kessie clapped and cheered.

They giggled and darted around their cubicles, then showed each other funny videos and pictures of celebrities on their phones.

Beth peered around her cubicle wall. *How am I supposed to focus on my job with this circus going on around me?* She watched Jim insert wireless earbuds into his ears and begin typing. Taking earplugs from her purse, she pushed them into her ears.

Cody popped his head outside his cubicle. "Quit horsing around!" He gestured toward cubicles in neat rows beyond the tax area. "You're disturbing other groups and embarrassing our department! I'm not going to help you hit your deadlines if you're going to play around all day!" He returned to his desk.

"Oh, darn, I missed an opportunity to hit Cody in the butt," Sue said in a low voice.

Amber whispered, "Don't bother Brad Junior. He might decide to have a word with our fearless leader."

Amber said, "Where's my new cell phone? I can only find my old one. My friend from overseas fixed them, so I get my calls and texts on both phones. Them phones keep me from going nuts in this dumb job."

Kessie snickered. "I'd rather be digging ditches, if you want the truth. I reckon we should make the best of it. Brad says we're gonna keep our jobs. You need to fix your attitude, lady, 'cause it ain't gonna get you nowhere."

"Keep our jobs. Well, hats and horns, sunshine girl."

"Oh, horse feathers." Kessie took a quick, hard look at Sue. "I can't believe you got six grandkids. I want to invite my three over more. It ain't easy working and helping 'em out when your husband don't care."

"Jack's working odd jobs, isn't he?" Sue asked.

"He ain't working at all. Just sits in front of the TV drinking beer. The weeds around our trailer grow half as tall as me. Our son said he'd take care of our yard this summer. Jack told him to mind his own damn business."

Sue pulled her long, blonde hair into a high ponytail. Thick bangs covered her eyebrows. "Jack would make me edgy."

"Yep, glad he don't own a gun," Kessie said. "You know how he is."

"This downturn's bad on everybody," Sue said. "Dusty had a good job. Now he's not working. He tinkers with his cars most days. Yesterday we were fightin' over money again. He'd love to take off and ramble."

"Dusty's a good husband. You should thank your lucky stars."

"He's talking about opening up a store outside the city," Sue said.

"What kind of store?" Kessie asked.

"Dusty wants to sell food, gas, garden stuff, clothes, you name it. He wants to hire me 'cause I get antsy sitting at a desk all day long."

"You don't say."

"I told him he's nuts. He needs to get a real job."

Peering at her screen, Amber threw her hands in the air. "What the hell! My entire accounts payable file is missing! Over two hundred invoices. Here yesterday and poof! Gone today. I'm like, huh? So bogus. I'm ready to go home!"

"No big deal, ask the AP tech to resend the file," Sue said. "I want to buy a cheap plot out in the middle of nowhere. Live in a cabin. That's what my folks did. They didn't talk to another human for weeks."

22

"I want to open up a massage therapy business in the Caribbean," Amber said. "How sweet would that be?"

"Well, cut me in on that," Kessie said.

Their noisy chatter penetrated the soundproofing material on Beth's cubicle walls. She adjusted her earplugs. *I can't hear myself think.*

Cody held out a stack of papers to Kessie. "I need six copies of these."

Kessie stiffened. "Copy 'em yourself, junior."

"That's your job." Cody gave Kessie a black look and sauntered toward the copy machine, followed by sniggers.

Amber climbed on top of her desk and peeked into Beth's cubicle.

"Hi, neighbor! Whatcha doing?"

Beth glanced up. "Get a periscope."

Amber stepped down, laughing through her nose.

Beth stopped typing. *At Principal, that little rumpus would last less than a minute. Amber gets the other two riled up and hostile. And Judy let her get away with it. Why?* Beth removed her earplugs and walked to the front cubicle. She observed Judy, hunched over her computer, ignoring the commotion behind her. A stainless steel spoon stuck out of a carton of vanilla ice cream on her desk. Grasping the handle, Judy shoveled a scoop of ice cream into her mouth.

I need a quick walk around the building. She walked down the corridor, head high, studying a row of magenta tile chips along the top of the far wall. The shapes fit together perfectly. A tiny work of art in a Spartan office. A staff person or someone on the cleaning crew must have created it from leftover tile.

Beth returned from her walk, passing Sue and Kessie standing inside the lobby door. She went down the stairs to the garden level. Along the empty hall leading to the tax area, Amber ran toward her. Beth moved to the right to let her pass as Amber called out, "Step aside, Granny." She rammed into Beth, throwing her against the wall. "Whoops! My bad!" Amber scurried down the hall and up the stairs.

Hand against the wall for support, Beth stepped gingerly to Judy's cubicle.

Judy slouched over her computer, her matted, gray hair gathered into a rubber band like a small whisk broom protruding from the back of her head. White ice cream, melting through the bottom of a carton, pooled across her desk.

"Judy, Amber deliberately bumped me into the wall while I was walking in the hall."

Judy kept her eyes on her screen. "It was an accident. I don't have time to talk to you right now."

"I nearly fell."

"Can't you see I'm busy?" Judy continued typing.

"I'll speak to you at another time when you can give me your full attention."

Back at her cubicle, Beth moved her back, arms, and hips, massaging the sore spots. *Why won't Judy confront Amber?*

At 6:30, Jim's cell phone buzzed. *Time to leave for my group meeting.* Out of the corner of his eye, he saw the cursor drifting across his computer screen, clicking on a few icons. *IT must be working on the system.* He shut down his computer and left the office.

Jim inhaled an aroma of fresh, dark coffee as he descended narrow stairs to Ryan Ford's finished basement, followed by Seb Medina. Group members chatted in the kitchenette as they poured coffee or hot water for tea. Each took a brown folding chair from a cart and took their seats in a circle.

After greeting the members, Ryan asked, "Who wants to share?"

"I'll start. Jim, psychiatric survivor."

"Hi, Jim."

Sharing is awkward as hell. "I did better last week at cutting back on the Adderall, Prozac, and vodka. It's tough because the medications help me cope with my mother and my job situation and take the edge off. I don't want any of those drugs in my life. My new primary care doctor is weaning me off psychotropics, so I don't have to invent fibs to get the prescriptions I still need. Decreasing the Prozac and the nightly vodka are manageable. The Adderall's the hardest drug to drop. It snaps my brain to attention, gets me in focus. I put up with side effects you're familiar with."

"You're doing great!"

"Keep up the good work!"

"Thanks! Now that Dad is gone, I take care of Mom the best I can. I don't have the affection for my mother that a son should have. She never was a loving or kind parent, but I'm doing the right thing. When Dad's language and tone of voice play in the back of my mind, I'm better at tuning them out. I have lots of unlearning to do. It takes effort, but it's worth it. I don't want to end up a bitter old man. I'm making good progress. That's it for me." *Whew!*

The group gave Jim a round of applause.

"I'll go next. My name is Seb. I'm a psychiatric survivor. This is my first meeting."

"Welcome, Seb!" group members said.

"Thank you." He took a deep breath. "I grew up an angry kid with parents who were always ready for some pointless fight with each other. They hauled me to a smart-mouthed old shrink. In our sessions, he sat with his back toward me, making phone calls. At the end of our scheduled time, he took out his prescription pad, wrote down the latest drug, and sent me on my way. When I turned eighteen, I dumped him. I was lucky to survive him. I still take one of those drugs. Long story short, my wife helped me turn my life around. I love my kids. I'm not where I need to be, but I was getting there, until my recent job change."

His eyes clouded. "A couple months ago, I was transferred from Principal to Heenehan, like Jim. I was loaded with energy. I thought I could handle anything." His voice quavered. "Recently, my manager told us that one person in each of the sales groups would be cut." He sipped coffee. "He moved me into a cubicle outside our department. I'm trying to figure out Heenehan's sales methods and systems by myself. Nobody in my work group will even talk to me. I was set up to fail. I'm an outcast." A tear ran down his cheek.

A man sitting next to Seb gently patted his back.

Seb wiped his eyes with his sleeve. "That manager made my whole group believe I can't do the work. It's embarrassing. Last year I finally earned my degree, the first in my family. My sales stats were above average at Principal. I'm the breadwinner, and job stress is poisoning my family life. I don't want to lose the people who matter to me most. A guy from my past would love to make my black-hearted boss pay. I'm not going there."

"I'm so sorry about your ruthless manager," a woman said. "He wouldn't survive in a healthy company."

Seb spoke in a soft monotone. "I'll be going out with a termination on my record. I don't want to be another middle-aged statistic, but honestly, I've had enough. I've struggled too hard to end up a miserable loser. Company insurance will provide for my family. They'd be better off without me. Thanks for letting me share the fiasco that's my life."

Jim said, "I'm usually in my cubicle. We can talk anytime you want." *I'll check on Seb every day.*

Other group members spoke to Seb.

"Cutting someone off from their group and devaluing their work are political maneuvers. Those tactics have nothing to do with you, Seb. Your manager needs to reduce staff. You're his chosen victim. He's trying to make you quit. Your coworkers want to keep their jobs."

"You're too good for Heenehan. You'll never reach your potential there."

"The damage isn't permanent. There are ways to handle a termination when you talk to your next hiring manager."

"It will be good for you to stay away from Heenehan."

"Take time for yourself before you jump back into the fray. Sometimes the sidelines are your friend."

"Heenehan isn't a hill worth dying on. Imagine your family trying to find the strength to keep marching forward with broken hearts after their world ended."

"You're not crazy or alone. We're here for you, day and night. You have our member list. Call or email or text any of us, any time, day or night."

They each rose and gave Seb a hug.

Wearing pink pajamas, Beth fluffed the pillows and closed her eyes. *This day is finally over. I love my warm, comfy bed.* A ring burst from her phone on the nightstand. "Hello?"

"This is your neighbor, Carol."

"Is everything all right?"

"Everything's fine. I apologize for calling so late in the day. I'm coordinating our annual art fair at the Downtown Gallery. The style of your artwork would complement the pieces we've selected for the exhibition. Would you consider showing several of your paintings?"

"No, Carol. I did those paintings years ago. The others in the show are highly skilled artists. My work would come off as amateurish next to theirs." *Will you please call it a night and leave me alone?*

"Doesn't matter. I love your work. You don't need to do a thing. If you want to sell them, I'll suggest fair prices. I can come over in ten minutes to pick them up. What do you say?"

Beth rubbed her eyes. *I'm too tired to make Carol stop twisting my arm.* "Oh, all right. I'll pull out a few for you."

"Thanks, Beth! I'll be there in a jiffy."

Chapter 3: Wednesday, May 3

Hwan Cho shuffled over to Beth's cubicle for an overview of Tom's tax returns. A tiny, fortyish man wearing professional attire, he walked with out-turned feet.

Sitting before her computer screen, Beth motioned to her side chair. "Please take a seat, Hwan. Thank you for helping us. You'll be working in the cubicle behind Jim's, the one that used to be Tom's." She turned to him. "Our accounting system reports the sales tax we collected from our customers. We pay that tax over to the government. Also, we buy items for our business. If our invoice doesn't show sales tax, we pay use tax."

"What you want me to do?"

"You generate a report from the accounting system to prepare the tax returns. Judy reviews your work. After she approves it, you file the return and pay the tax due. Here are the steps I wrote out." Beth handed him a printed sheet.

Hwan looked over the procedures. "This is a friggin' nightmare."

Is that how he talks to Sandra? "It's simple. Let's prepare a return."

Beth pointed to each step on the sheet as she opened the state's website, filled out the tax return form, saved it, and closed the website.

"Now you prepare the next return. Here's an easy one." She opened another state's website.

Seizing the mouse, Hwan clicked wildly all over the screen.

"Slow down! Look at your procedures. Take it step by step."

He gazed at the procedures. "I like go fast fast fast."

Beth pointed to the screen. "Click here. No, Hwan, NO!" He closed the website. "I asked you to click a different cell."

"It not matter."

"It does matter. Accuracy comes before speed." *What on earth is wrong with him?* Beth reopened the state's website. She pointed to the cells to enter the data. Hwan entered numbers unrelated to the report. Before he could click the Send button, Beth took hold of the mouse, deleted the incorrect numbers, and told him to reenter them.

Beth read aloud each number, making him stop, delete, and reenter numbers he mistyped. She asked him to enter today's date on the tax calendar. He mistyped the date. She had him correct it.

"We will pay the tax after Judy has reviewed this return."

Hwan squinted at Beth. "How can you stand this?"

"You have to like sales tax."

He erupted in high-pitched, forced laughter. "You so funny!" With a bitter cackle, he stuck his finger in his mouth in a gag gesture.

Unbelievable!

Hwan stood and ambled toward the finance group, talking to himself in a whiny monotone.

Beth waited outside Jim's organized cubicle, behind hers. After he finished filing his return, she signaled with a quick wave. He removed his earbuds.

Their coworkers were bickering over the best lunch place. Beth tried to talk over them. Finally, Judy boomed out, "THAT'S ENOUGH!" The office became quiet.

In a low voice, Beth described her session with Hwan.

Jim said, "Let's both try training him here in my cubicle. I'll call him over."

When Jim did so, Hwan pushed past Beth and sat on the side chair next to Jim. Beth set the tax procedures sheet next to the computer.

"Hwan, here are the steps you reviewed with Beth. I want you to prepare a tax return for one state. Let's begin with an easy one. Beth's sheet describes how to do each step."

Hwan glanced at the sheet and snapped, "I don't remember a thing!"

"Take each step in order. If you run into problems, I'm right here."

Hwan began babbling in a high-pitched voice, making rolling gestures with his arms. "Hold on, hold on, hold on! I hear words you say. That not mean I know what's going on. If you want to show me how to do tax, you can. I don't get it. So why you want me to do this?" He pushed out his thin lips, making a sour face.

Jim spoke in a gentle voice. "Hwan, let's try again another day."

With a sickly grin, Hwan pressed his index fingers into his cheeks, tilting his head back and forth.

Jim and Beth stepped out into the aisle, leaving Hwan alone in Jim's cubicle to collect himself. After a few moments, Hwan bolted out the cubicle door and flew down the corridor.

"A chip in his brain is missing," Beth said.

"The poor man's lost it," Jim said. "Let's see if Katie can tell us anything about Hwan."

Katie Stanton, Sandra Young's administrative assistant, answered from the admin desk in the finance group. Their longtime confidante from Principal, absorbed into

Heenehan after the acquisition, agreed to meet them in a windowless small conference room, called a huddle room, with a glass door.

Katie took a seat at the oak table, her short, curly brown hair complementing a floral print blouse.

"How's it going, Katie? Staying out of trouble?" Beth asked. *Nice to see a friendly face.*

"Just barely. Sorry I'm late! I got held up with the delivery guys. Last week our group moved across the hall. In three hours, I packed, moved my stuff, unpacked, and helped a few others. Now I'm helping Sandra redecorate her new office. She settled on earth tones, with high-end contemporary furniture and accessories that express her personal style."

Beth raised her eyebrows. "Well, la-de-dah."

"What's happening?" Katie asked.

"We know you can't be away from your desk for long. Our training sessions with Hwan were difficult. What can you tell us about him?"

Katie talked fast. "Hwan's been in our group for about a month. He's a North Korean who escaped to China. China deports defectors back to North Korea, where they're abandoned in ugly prisons or publicly executed. When China's political situation became dangerous, he migrated here with his parents. He's out of his element in this company. I feel bad for him."

"Hwan has no background in accounting or tax," Beth protested. "He can't speak fluent English. I don't want him fired, but we're already struggling with Tom's workload, added to our own. Hwan's going to add another layer of work onto us. We'll have to do most of his work and correct everything he does."

"You guys don't deserve him. Sandra wants to keep him as far away from the finance group as she can. Her staff threatened to quit if they had to work with him. Hwan interrupts their work every few minutes, asking questions he has asked before. They explain simple concepts to him six or eight times. He stares back with a blank expression. I suspect depression or early dementia."

"And Sandra still keeps him around?" Beth pulled her blue cardigan around her neck as an overhead vent blasted out cold air.

"Why she doesn't terminate him, I don't know. Sandra had to password-protect her group's spreadsheets, so IT doesn't need to restore them every day after Hwan wrecks them or deletes them. Yesterday Hwan called IT nine times saying his computer wasn't working right. Andy's people are ready to kill him."

"I feel sorry for Andy," Jim said.

"Hwan rattles on using big words. It's all nonsense. Your director, Scott, thinks Hwan's an industrious egghead."

Jim rested his elbow on the table, his chin in his hand. "Oh, man, this is not the professional support we need."

"Where did Hwan work before?" Beth asked. *My stomach's unsettled.*

"Another group in the company, for two weeks. Sandra's preferred candidate was a tall, pretty blonde named Vanessa who'd been a director at another company. Sandra would've hired her at manager level. But her references disclosed horrible performance reviews and a tangle of lawsuits."

Jim said, "You're describing my ex-wife, Vanessa. I'm sure those performance reviews and lawsuits were well-deserved. When we were married, she yelled and cursed when she didn't get her way. Said I didn't know what I was talking about. Never told me about her plans, but demanded I tell her everything I was doing. Monitored my emails and gave me hell about them. Vanessa would do the same things or worse in the finance group."

"I'm sorry, Jim," Katie said. "Don't ever take her back! Hwan was on the verge of being dismissed from Heenehan. Sandra had him transferred to her group at entry level."

"A better choice than Vanessa," Jim said. "I'm going to hazard a guess that Sandra's covering for Hwan."

"According to the employee handbook, the procedure for reporting problems is to speak to Judy and Sandra. Then you're in the clear if he doesn't work out."

Jim winced. "Judy's mean as a snake, and Sandra wants Hwan out of her hair. I guess we can try."

"Judy and Sandra need to know you're aware of Hwan's incompetence." Katie lowered her voice. "Steer clear of Judy whenever you can. She's after Brad's job."

"I suspected as much," Beth said.

"Brad's a typical jerk. But Judy and Scott take it to a whole new level. You're lucky if Judy just tears your face off. She's boogity-wacko."

"Thanks for warning us. We'll be careful."

Katie checked the door, scanning for passersby. "Someone's going to see me through the glass door and tell HR. I need to find another job, like now. My husband gave me an ultimatum because I work most weekends. Last Saturday after I put in eight hours, I ran into Sherry Shuler, Tom's wife, at the grocery store. Sherry said Tom was devastated after he lost his job. But he's doing better now."

"I'm glad he's okay," Jim said.

"We're worried about Tom," Beth said. "He wasn't talking to anyone. We'll try calling him again."

Katie brightened. "I have good news. Elly Burke is launching a telecom start-up."

Beth sat up straight. "What! If anyone can get a business off the ground, our director from Principal can. When will it be up and running?"

"It may be a while. She's still working on funding, a business model, and a million other things."

"Is she hiring?" Jim asked.

"A few part-time positions so far. I'll keep you in the loop."

"Maybe Elly can find a place for us." Beth said. "I sure miss her."

"I do, too."

"I wish you were sitting closer to us, Katie. You're a dear."

"Thanks for a glimmer of hope," Jim said. "Catch you later."

"Gotta run!" Katie gave a quick wave, opened the door a crack, looked both ways, and disappeared into the hallway.

Pulling the conference table phone toward him, Jim dialed Judy's number. She agreed to a short meeting. "We're throwing gasoline on a fire."

Beth caught a glimpse of a man passing by, his face turned away from the glass door, dressed in workman's clothes, carrying a storage box. It had to be Tom.

A short, stocky figure in a loose-fitting, gray pantsuit swung open the glass door. Judy plopped down on a chair at the table. Her bloodshot eyes bulged under wiry gray eyebrows.

Jim said, "Judy, you need to be informed. Hwan is a ... challenge. Lacking skills, untrainable, making messes we don't have time to clean up. Tax work is not his cup of t—"

"SHUT UP!" Judy bellowed. "You waltz into this company and tell me our employees aren't good enough. Don't waste my time. Hwan has the basic knowledge. Teach him the job." She heaved herself up, flung the door open, gave a snort, and marched down the hall.

Jim and Beth sat in silence for a moment.

Beth said in a hollow voice, "That woman drains me down to my skeleton."

"Yeah, she sucks the breath right out of me."

"Speaking of breath, Judy must be using some strong mouthwash."

"I don't think it's mouthwash," Jim said.

"Let's talk to Sandra."

In the hallway, they passed their director, Scott, a steel-haired man with a slight paunch.

Jim greeted him, "Hey, Scott!" Scott gazed off into the distance, hurrying past them as if they were molecules in the air. Jim turned to Beth. "Am I invisible?"

"Nope. I see you. Scott's not going to waste his high-priced time on us. Just before Judy came into the room, did you notice a workman who looked like Tom Shuler passing by the glass door?"

"I saw a man. Tom's average-looking. It was someone else."

Jim and Beth stopped at the open office door, next to a brushed gold, plastic laminate sign that read "Corporate Finance Manager." Sandra Young smiled up at them from behind her retro chic modern desk. "Come in, sit down," she said with affected warmth and a hint of folksy cadence. A sapphire blue business suit with a dainty necklace and earrings complemented her straight shoulder-length black hair.

"Sandra, we need to talk with you about a problem that's affecting our work," Jim said. "We've found that Hwan doesn't have the skills for tax work. He —"

Sandra interrupted, "I stick my head in the sand. It works for me! I suggest you do the same. Rise above him."

The cell phone on her desk rang. Caller ID showed "South Korea" in large, black letters. She tapped the silent mode icon. "Hwan can do the work. Stand back and let him do it. Just casually ask him if he needs any help. He may need a little reminding."

"Sandra!" Beth said, "Hwan takes valuable time from our workday. We have to clean up everything he —"

"Pace yourself. Don't stress out about it. You know he doesn't read his email. Things are hard for him that aren't hard for us. We're not paying him very much."

"Sandra, you're not getting the picture. He's incompetent."

"Are you doing Hwan's work yourselves? Learn to say no. You're letting him take advantage of you. Communicate in a win-win way so you're all happy."

"Listen!" Jim said.

"Have a sense of humor when you work with Hwan. Don't take yourselves so seriously. You should get a dog! And wear black. It will make you look more professional."

Beth raised her voice. "Can I jump in here?"

"Think outside the box when you're training Hwan. Be nimble and flexible. Show Hwan how to contribute to the team. Make sure he's clear about his next steps. Then drop everything at five o'clock and go home."

Beth broke in. "Sandra, thank you for your time. We need to get back to our work. Big deadlines this week."

"Of course. Thank you for stopping by. You're very welcome to come by anytime."

Back in the huddle room, Beth and Jim sat in a stupefied daze.

Beth said, "What the heck just happened? Sandra spun us 180 degrees. It's not our fault Hwan isn't fit for his job. What's she hiding under that waterfall of words?"

"Sandra's shifting her problem onto us. It's not easy to outsmart a gaslighter. One employee from hell can pull down systems that took years to set up. Since Hwan's using Tom's old cubicle behind mine, I can disconnect his computer from the network. I'll create an offline spreadsheet and give Hwan a stack of old accounting reports to enter. That should keep him busy. Andy will be happy to be free of Hwan."

Beth leaned tender elbows on the conference table. "Do you get how senseless that is? We've taken a trip through the looking glass and dropped into an alternate universe."

"Unfortunately, Heenehan's culture isn't uncommon for a declining organization. People are unpredictable when their foundation is collapsing. Problems snowball, workers flee, the company folds."

Beth spoke in a faint, furious voice. "It's maddening. Whenever I act like the capable professional that I am, I get hit with gibberish or verbal brickbats. Communication equals gotchas and insults. There are no productive discussions here."

"'Productive' is not a word I connect with the Heenehan tax staff. You know a technical tax discussion is over their heads. Our coworkers don't want a good-faith dialog. They want us to say things they can attack. Bait us into battles that don't matter. Bury us under judgments and criticisms. It's about winning, not communication."

"We're on the front lines dealing with taxing jurisdictions. Our jobs require critical thinking and good judgement. How can I work with these people? Brad doesn't train them or hold them accountable. For the same salary, he expects us to do the work that's over their heads, check and recheck any work they find time to do, and clean up their messes. The work hours are endless."

"It's like running a marathon every day."

"I thought my new coworkers would ask about my tax background. Instead, Sue quizzed me about my astrological sign. She broadcast to the group her opinion of my capabilities based on the position of the planets. It's too much for me. I can't be good at this job. I've seen my best days. I'm finishing up my career as a failure."

"You're not a failure. Let's go to lunch."

The scent of savory hot peppers and sweet cinnamon filled the air a block before Beth and Jim arrived at the Mexican cafe. They stood in line along a wall painted with floral designs in terracotta and sunshine yellow. In front of them, a mother held a baby girl dressed in a pink onesie while her father placed their order. The baby watched the lights on the menu board above the servers working the line. Four laughing teenage boys in line behind them cracked jokes.

Beth scanned the menu board. *The spicy enchilada looks delicious, but my stomach can't handle it today.* "I'll have hot tea and a bowl of brown rice." Jim ordered ice tea and a large vegetarian burrito. They carried their lunches on trays to a booth in a far corner.

Jim bit into his burrito with gusto. "Good thing they turned off the Cumbia music. When everyone's talking over the maracas and trumpets, the noise level makes conversation impossible."

"I feel better just being here." Beth sipped the hot tea and nibbled the rice. "Earlier this week Amber collided with me in the hall. I lost my footing and grabbed hold of the wall. I tried to tell Judy about it. She said it was an accident and shut me out. I'm still sore."

"How did that happen?"

"When I passed Amber, she deliberately crashed into me."

"That's outright assault and it's illegal. She shouldn't get away with it."

"It would be Amber's word against mine. She's menacing me for no reason whatsoever."

"You can leave this company any time. Pay for a few months of health insurance yourself," Jim said, chewing. "This burrito with salsa roja is tasty."

"We should call Elly at Analytics."

"No doubt Elly's gotten an earful about Heenehan," Jim said. "She's going to be mobbed with Heenehan applicants."

"We should let her know we're interested."

"Who are you, Beth Madison? You've been busting your back for over forty years. I thought you were a sane person, planning to retire."

"I miss Elly. We'd get more advanced assignments. She makes it normal to think and act like a professional. We wouldn't worry about seven-day workweeks. She keeps all her teams on track. And she's fun to be around."

"Start-up businesses need people willing to work long hours," Jim said. "And in this city, competition among telecom companies is fierce. We have to be realistic."

A college-age woman wearing a purple polo shirt removed a large stack of trays from the recessed top of the trash bin and carried them past their table.

"I think I can do the job. In some ways, I'm sharper than ever. I know what works, what doesn't, what's more and less important, what to pay attention to. I can better evaluate people's opinions. I'm quicker to size up a situation. I'm more aware of the consequences of my own and others' actions. I've kept up with technology. I take pride in a job well done," Beth said, and took a sip of her tea.

"On the other hand, I tire out easily, and then I can kiss my memory goodbye. I get stumped trying to recall words

I rarely use. It takes willpower to push new concepts into my brain. I'm aware of my aging reflexes. If my attention is divided, I don't move quickly. I've had a few scary doctor appointments. It's quite a reckoning. Sometimes I get this Twilight Zone sense that nothing is familiar anymore. I'm older and it's just the nature of the beast." Beth shrugged. "I'm going off in a ditch here. Young people have an edge over me." *Aging sucks!*

"I disagree with you there. Young people act confused and forget stuff all the time. You're healthy. Heenehan burns out responsible employees. You've had more experiences, so your brain has to sort through more information. If management needed an important analysis, they'd want you doing it, not some twenty-year-old. It's just that Analytics' lead-in period could be brutal. And hey, nobody I know likes young people. Those hipsters with the man buns should be strung up from the nearest cell tower."

"You crack me up, Jim! I actually like young people. I'm just going through some sort of values shift. Earning more money and exceeding expectations no longer energize me."

"You need a change. How about part-time work?"

"Ten hours a week might work. I'll ask Elly." Beth gripped her cup with long, delicate fingers. *How am I so lucky to have these dear friends?* "Jason's going to pick me up on Saturday morning for my grandson's soccer game. Children's teams are a hoot. The weather should be warm and sunny."

"Sounds fun."

"They're a sports family. If it rolls or bounces, they're in."

Jim's phone buzzed. *What's going on with Mom now?* He took a gulp of iced tea and wiped his mouth with a napkin. "Excuse me, I need to answer this." He tapped his phone. "Hi, Doris. Oh, no. Good thing you got her turned around.

41

I'll give you a call this evening." He set his phone on the table. "Mom normally spends the day sitting in front of the TV. Her neighbor looks in on her and calls me if a problem arises. Doris caught Mom wandering around outside and walked her back into the house."

"Oh my gosh! Doris is a lifesaver. Rose needs full-time services."

"I'm weighing my options. The visiting nurse didn't work out. Mom belongs in memory care. The cost is astronomical. Doris and I are checking out the places Mom's doctor recommended. Dad donated most of his money to charity. The small amount he set aside for Mom's old age won't be enough, even if I contribute a big chunk of my salary." *I'll never be able to afford it.*

"I hope you find a way to work it out. My parents lived in a memory care facility before they passed. It was pricey, for sure. I miss them. I wish they were still here. How does Rose feel about moving into a rest home?"

"She's resistant, to put it mildly. I'm afraid I'd have to carry her kicking and screaming. I don't know how she'd do as a resident. Quite a temper. Never stops ordering me around. Complains her batty head off. I'm living in the basement, and she's fine with that. I do the housework, make sure she has prepared meals, grocery shop, pay the bills."

"You're doing a great job coping with all this. Getting Rose into memory care is going to be a difficult thing to do."

"I'll have to find something affordable that works for Mom. She can't drive or keep track of the day of the week anymore. She repeats herself on an endless loop. I force her to take a shower; otherwise, she'd go weeks without one. I make her get dressed on days when I'm not working. I'm her only child, and I'm determined to do right by her."

Jim tapped his phone. "Here's a photo of Rose in her early twenties." *The picture that breaks my heart.*

Beth gazed at the photo. "She's lovely."

"She was funny, articulate, and full of energy." Jim closed his phone's photo app.

"I met your Dad. He came across as a dynamic guy with a great sense of humor. Hollywood handsome, too."

"You saw his public image. I watched him put on his big show, getting people to think and act the way he wanted them to. When Mr. Congeniality stepped inside our front door, he threw off his mask. Arthur had a dark side, and that side was very dark." *Does Beth want to hear about this?*

Beth set her spoon on the table. "What!"

"I had no idea when the well-respected Dr. Jekyll would turn into the deranged Mr. Hyde. An innocent remark, or nothing at all, would set Dad off on a wild tirade, followed by a triumphant smile. I was an eggshell walker. Speaking back to him could've gotten Mom or me killed."

"Where was your mother? She should have protected you. She abandoned you."

"Mom was taught to rise above any unpleasantness and not make a fuss. Grandma made excuses for Dad, blamed Mom, or didn't believe her at all. Dad enjoyed reducing Mom to hysterical fits. She could have left or tried counseling or just focused on her own interests. She chose not to. Instead, she set her sights on controlling everything and everyone around her, including me. I've had a tougher time getting over Mom's behavior than I have with Dad's."

Beth touched Jim's hand. "Why would Arthur do that to his own wife and child?"

"He liked how it made him feel. Trying to make sense of his behavior is pointless."

"I'm sorry that Arthur was a different person behind closed doors. What an astonishing lack of empathy."

"Yes, he had an uncanny ability to pick up on our emotional states and target our self-worth with surgical precision. He homed in on our personalities and our looks. Told us we were worthless over a thousand times. He cornered me and shouted into my face with such fury that I was terrified he would murder me. I tried to float under his radar. The adults I confided in thought Dad had great people skills and that my unhappiness was a private family matter. I escaped at eighteen and made it through college on my own. I couldn't keep Mom out of harm's way."

"How sad. I can see why you're wary of imposters in plain sight."

"I still feel iffy about take-charge types. Getting away from someone doesn't mean it's over. Sometimes I hear his voice berating me, but I'm learning not to pay attention."

"Good for you. I understand Rose better now."

"My poor mother, what she put up with. Not a day of her married life was easy."

"I feel bad for her. How did you make it through those years at home?"

"I hung out with two neighborhood friends who also were stuck in messed-up homes. We weren't drug and alcohol types. We played around with musical instruments and formed a garage band. Even the cool crowd liked our band."

Beth picked up her spoon. "Who were the other two members of the band?" She ate another bite of rice.

"Andy Price and Tom Shuler. We go way back."

"Andy and Tom!"

"I learned the guitar, Andy was on keyboard, and Tom played the drums. None of us could sing, so we played our instruments with no vocals. We practiced in

Tom's garage because his folks were hardly ever home. Andy's dogs howled when we played at his house. And my house, well, Tom and Andy voted no. Actually, we're kicking around the idea of restarting our musical group. First I need to get control of my work hours and resolve Mom's situation."

"Let me know when your band starts playing again. I'll bring my friends."

"We'd love an audience. When we're good enough, that is."

A high school boy wiped the table next to them. He moved to the serving station near the entrance, where he stocked napkins and plastic utensils.

"How is your psych support group going?"

"Good. I'm making progress."

"Do you ever talk to Vanessa?"

"A hard no on that," Jim said. "Not since the divorce. She's working somewhere in the city. We cross paths occasionally. I just wave. She's in finance, with good earning power."

One of the teenage boys burped loudly and yelled, "Excuse me!" The boys resumed their noisy chatter.

"Vanessa didn't want me to talk to Mom or work on my music. Trying to keep her happy wore me out. I was losing my confidence, my enthusiasm, and my sanity. Tom and Andy wouldn't come over unless she was gone." *Never again. Snakebitten for the last time.*

"Vanessa's a controller, like Rose."

"Yes, she is. After Dad passed, Mom's health was declining, so I moved back home. I own the house now."

"You wouldn't know who Vanessa really was until she showed you."

"I'm fine without her. In all honesty, I like accounting. I'd rather investigate a complicated financial statement or tax return than climb the corporate ladder. The work I do is about as unsexy as it gets. Perks and awards don't interest me. My work speaks for itself."

"We do our jobs with competence and courtesy. It's easy to fail in a workplace where that's not possible."

"I agree. I hate being the center of attention. I wouldn't want the executive team to work me over. If I get a bad performance review, I read it once, then recycle it. I keep the good ones. I've outlasted a lot of my former colleagues."

"I've read your tax research," Beth said. "The issues are so complex, they make my head spin. You clarify and resolve every point."

"I just stick with it after others give up. You're an accomplished professional yourself."

"Thank you, Jim. We save our companies millions. You're one of the few businessmen I respect."

Beth raised an eyebrow, nodding in the direction of the window. Amber, Sue, and Kessie paraded by, chatting among themselves.

Jim popped the last bite of burrito into his mouth. "I've been having a little fun during work hours. I map musical tones to the data streaming through my computer. It's called sonification, the creation of music from data. First, I customize the software settings. For example, I make the pitch higher as the numbers become larger. I import my data and listen to it while it's importing. When I have time, I modify the rhythm, tone, dynamics, and mood. I also slow it down or speed it up. I've created jazz, electronic music, ambient music, even pop tunes. I expect future sonification apps will be more sophisticated and easier to use."

"I'm amazed you can do that."

"I'm experimenting, hoping to sell my songs on music platforms."

"I envy your musical talent."

"Accounting is fine for my day job," Jim said. "But music is my purpose in life. Unlike you, I can't retire for another sixteen years. Some days it takes all my willpower to nail myself to the office chair."

"Yeah, likewise."

"I don't mind the work itself. It's the other stuff that gets to me. Our wall clocks don't work because the company won't replace the batteries. We have to buy our own office supplies. Last week I worked ungodly hours for my modest salary. Last year Heenehan's CEO took home six million. The other officers aren't far behind him. That's beyond obscene. I've never seen the CEO. I can't recall his name. Our 1 percent cost-of-living raise doesn't cover the rate of inflation. We've been rolled. Our only choice is to suck it up." *If the Heenehan building burst into a giant fireball, I'd be okay with it.*

"I have to agree," Beth said. "The CEO is Mark Humphrey, Heenehan's third CEO in three years. We saw him making the presentation to the engineering group on the TV screen."

"It looked like the engineers weren't crazy about him. In this bear market, we're forced to play the hand we're dealt. We should devise a master plan."

"We can identify Heenehan's landmines and figure out how to sidestep them. Ride out the nonsense and keep it from swallowing us alive. How does that sound?"

"Good," Jim said. "We'll disengage until we can jump ship."

"So we have our master plan," Beth said. "Get through it and get out."

The teenage boys stood up from their table, emptied their trays into the trashcan, and moved to the exit door.

In the kitchen, a metal tray hit the floor. K-BAM! A young woman's voice shrieked, "Ay-yi-yi!" Heads turned toward the kitchen.

As the teenage boys pushed through the door, one of them yelled, "Ay, Caramba!" Everyone laughed, except for the baby, who burst into tears. The mother bounced the little girl in her arms, carrying her out the door. The father tossed their trash into the can and joined them outside.

Jim said to Beth, "You look better."

She consumed the last bit of rice. "I have more energy. I wish I had chosen a career that didn't require such extreme stamina. I simply can't work harder or smarter." *Pathetic, Beth, not a good look.*

"You've worked hard for decades, juggled so many roles, I can't imagine how you ever did it all. Can I help?"

"Thank you, but I need to figure out how to wrap up my career the right way."

"After you retire, you won't be confined to a small cubicle with odd stuff going on around you."

An elderly worker moved past them, sweeping between tables with a corn broom.

"I can already taste my freedom. My neighbor, Carol, talked me into showing my old artwork at the Downtown Gallery art fair. She knows I'm busy with work, so she's doing the setup herself. I'm going to display several semi-skilled paintings I did years ago. I stopped painting when work and parenting became too demanding. Over the years my creative spark faded away."

"I want to see your artwork. If you like, I can provide ambient background music."

"Jim, about the music. Please don't suggest we pipe in today's popular songs. They're alien to my ears and just dreadful. If I died and went to hell, it's the music I'd be subjected to for all eternity—agonized wailing, heavy thumping, robotic voices, and horrific lyrics. The youngsters remake the good old rock 'n roll classics and rip the soul out of them. I put in my earplugs when I go shopping. Blasting that in-store noise at customers is just wrong."

"Most trendy music comes out loud and aggressive. I can give you a retro sound."

"For this exhibition, we need instrumentals. No pulsating rhythms. Instead make it natural, gentle, and up-tempo."

"I like that style, too. Would you be willing to give a listen to one of my compositions?"

"Sure," Beth said. *This better be good.*

Jim tapped his phone's screen. A tune played.

"It has the right energy. I like it!"

"Would it work for the art fair?"

"It would. I'll talk to Carol. Thanks, friend."

"We'd better get back. I have hours of work to finish before I go home. And they're turning up the Cumbia."

"I need to make a stop at the ATM outside our building," Beth said.

"I should withdraw some cash. I'll go with you."

Jim and Beth stood in line behind a fortyish man at the free-standing ATM machine next to the Heenehan parking lot. Others lined up behind them. A woman finished a transaction, took her receipt, and stepped away. As the man moved toward the ATM, the lights surrounding the money slot blinked neon green. Amber Wolfe ran to the ATM, cut in front of the man, and stood before the machine. She held open a large pouch below the slot. Numerous bills dropped into it. She pushed the cash into the pouch, zipped it, and ran off.

"What in the world did Amber do?" Beth asked.

Turning around, the man in front of them said, "I saw it happen before. That woman doesn't use a credit or debit card. She usually stands in front of the machine and waits a minute or two before the money falls into her bag. No receipt spits out."

"And she does this in broad daylight," Jim said.

"Once when she didn't show, the lucky people who happened to be at the ATM swept up all the bills."

"Well, that's bizarre," Jim said.

"I'm with you on that." The man stepped to the machine to make his transaction.

Beth squinted. "How is Amber making all that money?"

"She must've landed a well-paid side gig," Jim said.

Chapter 4: Thursday, May 4

Amber shrieked, "Aargh! Oh, no! I don't believe it! Why? Why? Why?"

Kessie hurried to Amber's cubicle, followed by Sue.

Amber sat with her neck stretched out, staring at her screen. "Dear Lord! This pisses me off!"

Kessie waved her hands birdlike, stepping around papers. "Hey, hey, what's the problem?"

"This tax return's all effed up. Ain't nothing coming together right. I'm gonna grab me a sledgehammer and smash this machine." *Wow, I deserve a damn Oscar.*

"Stress much?" Sue examined Amber's return. "You're going at it the wrong way. You imported last month's data. You're using last year's tax return forms. The first four lines on the return should agree. It's all gummed up and goofy."

"I can't find my calculator. I added the numbers in my head twice. Both times the total came up exactly the same." *Well, close enough.*

"You don't need a calculator. If you're doing it right, the software calculates the numbers automatically. You shouldn't have to hassle with it."

"I'm new to this software. I ain't in the mood for jacked up tax returns. I think IT won't let me connect 'cause I didn't fill out all my permission forms. I do too many boring-ass returns and Judy wants me to cross-train on Principal's. She says I need more work. As if." *C'mon, bite.*

Sue said, "Too. Much. Work. I sweet-talked Judy into assigning forty of my returns to Jim and Beth. Send me the reports for that return and any more you run into trouble with. I'll prepare them for you. You have to file and pay them online by yourself, so Judy doesn't figure out I'm helping my friend, Amber. Be sure to pay the bottom line amount."

"Thanks." *Score!*

"Poor Amber," Kessie said. "You're gonna wear yourself out. You're still new! Judy dumped such a big, heavy workload on you. That ain't fair."

"I totally agree." Amber twisted a strand of green hair.

Kessie's eyes glowed. "I'll fill out your IT permission forms for you. Holler if you need anything else."

Well played, girl. "You guys are the best. I owe you big time. I promise to help you with your work when I figure it all out. One more small thing, I need the passwords to our bank accounts for that project Judy gave me. Sue, you used to work in the treasury department. Do you still have the passwords? Can you send them to me?"

"Not the current passwords," Sue said. "Shontae goes by treasury's rules and won't give them out."

"Send me the email address of the bank person you worked with. I'll ask her for the passwords."

"Sure thing. Myra at Ledger Bank's a sweetheart. She'll give you anything you need. I'll tell her to expect your email."

"I can't thank you enough." *Great teamwork, suckers.* "I'm leaving early. I'll make up the time on Saturday." *Like, Saturday in 2050.*

"I'm gonna take a two-hour lunch, do a little shopping," Sue said. "It's nice outside, perfect for errands. Maybe I'll get a quick cup of coffee."

"I'll go with you next time. We'll take off the whole afternoon. Judy won't miss us." Amber put on a jacket over her black wrap dress.

"Rats! That reminds me," Kessie said, chewing on her lower lip. "Jack was supposed to pay the water bill. They shut us off last night. I have to go over to the water department and pay our bill in cash." She made a sly smile. "I hid some money away from Jack so I don't have to go borrow from my kids."

Amber moved toward the hall.

"Hey, our meeting starts in a few minutes," Kessie said. "It won't last long."

"Oh yeah, I forgot." Amber took off her jacket. *If it's another snoozefest, I'm gonna check my phone, look all shook up, and run the hell out the door.*

Sunlight streamed through security bars on the garden-level windows, forming grid patterns on the colorless walls. Beth and Jim sat in front of Jim's computer.

"We need more time to do a thorough analysis of Heenehan's state audit," Beth said. *I'm feeling washed out.*

"Is everything in order?" Jim asked.

"Yes, except for files that weren't scanned. I'll look for the paper files in the storage boxes. The haphazard filing system is frustrating. Boxes missing from our file room. Other departments' boxes on our shelves." *I feel like I accidentally overdosed on sleeping pills.*

"Since no current list of computers exists, the auditors will do a physical count. They'll estimate the cost of the computers Heenehan purchased during the audit period. The seller didn't collect sales tax, and Sue didn't pay use tax. So the auditors will assess tax, penalties, and interest. We'll ask them to waive the interest."

Beth took a sip of strong, hot tea. "We could offer to pay the interest in exchange for reducing the cost estimate by 10 percent. Heenehan bought the cheapest computers on the market, so we have room for negotiation."

"Good thinking," Jim said. "Pam Taylor and Ron Shields are reasonable auditors."

"Pam belongs to my women accountants' group. I've seen pictures of Ron. He's been with the state for years." *I feel awful.*

"I talked to him on the phone when I worked at Principal," Jim said.

"This morning I promised to answer tax questions from the accounts payable group," Beth said. *Oh no, I'm going to throw up.*

"You don't look well."

Beth made her way to the door. "I'll be back in a few minutes," she whispered.

"Take your time." Jim gazed at a poster hung on the back wall of the aisle. Bright red letters on a black background screamed, "Lean and Mean! Challenge Yourself at Heenehan!" Jim removed the poster, folded it into a small rectangle, and stuffed it into his wastebasket.

Beth returned to her chair. "Sorry. I worked at home last night. I'm cruising on four hours' sleep. I feel like I've lost several pints of blood. I get queasy when I'm this tired." *Fatigue is kicking my butt. I never got this worn out working for Elly.*

"Your health concerns me."

"My desktop thermostat says it's 62 degrees down here. In this heavy sweater, I'm still shivering."

"This building is a walk-in freezer."

"I'm about done," Beth said. "When I'm finished at accounts payable, I'll try to make a dent in the research."

"I plan to work on research, too," Jim said.

"A few dozen of our returns are waiting for Judy's approval."

"She'll get around to them the day before the due date, so we'll have to work late."

Tax staff walked to their cubicles, carrying notepads. Heavy footsteps approached Jim's cubicle entrance.

Eyes hard, Judy barked, "I TOLD you there would be a mandatory meeting at nine o'clock! Amber sent an invitation to each person in the tax group. Where were you?"

Beth found her voice. "We never received an invitation. You could have walked over here and said something to us."

"You haven't convinced me that you belong here." Judy wheeled around and clumped down the corridor.

Amber appeared at Jim's cubicle door. "Snooze equals lose! So why haven't you changed your login passwords?"

"How would you know if we did or didn't change our login passwords?" Jim asked.

Amber whispered, "Judy ain't puttin' up with you rat bastards much longer."

"Are you on a mission to get rid of us?" Beth asked. "Is that why you're here? Who ARE you?"

Amber raised her chin.

"Get out of my cubicle," Jim said.

"Leave us alone," Beth said.

"So bite me," Amber said, baring white canines.

Fingers on the keyboard, Jim looked up when Judy stepped into his cubicle. "Report to the large second-floor conference room immediately. Both of you." She turned and left.

Jim said, "What is she going to throw at us now?"

Beth stood, with a quick assist from Jim. *I'm really wobbly on my feet.*

They took seats at the large oak table. Across from them, Judy sat stiffly. Next to her sat Corabell, a joyless dowager from Human Resources in a loose-fitting black dress. Corabell pulled her buxom torso ramrod straight and made a facial expression as if a bad smell had wafted into the room.

"Heenehan has a strong culture committed to excellence," Judy began. "Our evidence indicates that you have fallen short of expectations."

"What evidence?" Jim asked.

Corabell glared. "You're not as productive as you should be. You're struggling with your work. You lack self-confidence. Instead of being proactive, you wait to be told what to do. You haven't maintained a sense of urgency. You don't handle pressure appropriately. Your coworkers won't help you because you can't get along with them. No one wants to deal with your unpleasantness."

"Your complaints are mighty vague," Beth said. *I'm so drained, I can't think straight.*

"Amber harasses us every day," Jim said.

"Don't waste our time with your petty squabbles!" Corabell said. "You're not being harassed because of your age or sex or race or anything else. Why are you provoking altercations in a professional office environment? I'm waiting for an answer."

"We don't provoke altercations. Amber never stops harassing us," Jim said.

Judy craned her neck forward, boring into him with piercing eyes. "You're interpreting Amber's way of speaking as negative. It's not. Reach out to her, help her engage in her work, empower her. Make her a success. Try to be kind even when it's hard. She says you never come to her cubicle to talk to her, she always has to go talk to you. Tell Amber if she sounds offensive. If any incident occurs with anyone, come and tell me."

Judy addressed Beth. "Yesterday I asked you for the tax calendar so I could send a copy to the treasury department. You told me you corrected Kessie's mistakes. Treasury found it full of errors."

"I worked under extreme pressure through my lunch hour to correct the calendar for you. You sent Kessie's old version to treasury, before my corrections. Shontae called me and I sent her the corrected calendar."

Checking her notes, Judy moved on. "Help me understand why you missed two large tax payments last month to Georgia and North Carolina. That's a big stumble."

Beth said, "I received confirmation from Georgia. We filed and paid all our returns accurately and on time. Not a fraction of a second late."

"I have confirmation of the North Carolina payment," Jim stated. "We haven't received a single delinquency notice on any of our returns."

Beth forced a strong voice. "As far as productivity, last week I analyzed six pages of audit work papers. I filed four refund claims for tax overcharged on our invoices. I talked to the vendors who will correct our tax in the future. I filed fuel tax returns for Sue, who usually files them late. I provided reports to the property tax group. All that in addition to preparing, filing, and paying my returns."

They concocted those phony allegations before we stepped into the room. It's a turkey shoot.

Jim spoke with confidence. "Last week the accounts payable supervisor asked me to research five questions. I copied you on my response. I filed our unclaimed property reports. They were never done right. I fixed them. I reviewed a delinquency notice from the IRS saying we owe $5 million. Sue made a mistake on the federal excise tax returns. I'm amending those returns. I also prepared, filed, and paid my returns."

Corabell sat expressionless. "Judy and I developed your performance plans to level-set our expectations. We will schedule another meeting in a month. If you have not met the stated measurable goals, you both will be terminated. This is all communicated in your plan documents." She pushed one packet of papers to Jim, another packet to Beth.

"We report to Brad Mitchell," Beth asserted. "We don't report to you, Judy."

"Brad authorized me to handle this in the way I see fit," Judy said. "Any comments you make will be entered into your permanent records. Whether or not you choose to sign off on your plan is inconsequential." She rapped jagged fingernails on the table in front of each of the packets. "Look at your papers."

Jim and Beth scanned two pages of ambiguous demands and threats.

Jim pointed to a paragraph. "It says here that within two weeks all of Amber's and Sue's tax returns will be transferred to us. What are Amber and Sue going to do?"

"They will be responsible for special projects," Judy said.

"What special projects?" Jim asked.

"You're on a need-to-know basis, and you don't need to know," Corabell said.

"So we're expected to prepare Sue's and Amber's returns by next month's due dates and all of Principal's returns?" Beth asked. "Plus, you want us to take on Heenehan's state audit? We're so new that we're barely familiar with Heenehan's business." *Defending ourselves against those two hellcats is a waste of time.*

Jim spoke in a steady voice. "You're accusing us of incompetence for not performing our work the way you want before discussing it with us. Did you expect time traveling?"

Beth asked, "How can we not make missteps? Heenehan's methods and systems are different from Principal's. It wouldn't take long to learn this job if basic written procedures were in place. Why didn't Sue write out the steps she uses to prepare her returns?"

"Then you'd have a real cushy job, wouldn't you?" Judy snapped. "Sue doesn't have time in her busy day to write out any steps. Work smarter. Stretch your skills. Show us that you belong here. I've assigned Amber to cross-train on the Principal returns. Amber is a tax expert with a master's degree. Sue will answer your questions about the Heenehan returns. She's a pleasant person with years of experience. Ask her for the purple file with the vendor list. That will help you. And, of course, Hwan is already assisting you."

"Amber will have trouble with Principal's taxes," Beth said. "The returns are complex. Every one of them is different."

"All of Principal's tax work is easy," Judy said. "It would take less than a month to train a new hire to do your work."

"That's false," Jim replied. "And this company has serious problems you need to be aware of."

Corabell pointed a stubby index finger at Jim. "You have no voice in this company. None. If you don't like it here, leave. Don't sit there like a block of wood. Look at me. Do you understand?"

Jim stared past them.

Beth answered with a small nod. *What can I say to that?*

"Sign your papers."

They wrote their signatures at the bottom of the last page and handed the papers to Corabell.

"We have another major issue." From her briefcase, Corabell removed a half sheet of crimson paper, then a book with a plain gray cover. She laid them on the table. Holding up the paper, she scrutinized Beth. "Explain this flyer advertising your pole dancing classes that we found in your cubicle."

"What!"

Corabell studied Jim. "Tell us about this gay sex manual that was on your desk."

An astounded grin flashed across Jim's face. "Amber's trying to—heh—discredit us. She ..." Jim dissolved into laughter.

Beth coughed, held her breath, giggled, and then burst out laughing. "It's not an easy job to teach my women's accounting group to pole dance!"

Jim's face crinkled. He turned to Beth. "How many times have I told you to behave yourself?"

"What's with that silly manual, when you're straighter than the pole I dance on?"

Judy pounded her fist on the table. "This is not a laughing matter!"

Corabell folded her arms across her belly.

Jim snorted, regaining control.

Beth made an effort to bring her expression back to neutral. *Why are they buying into Amber's wild nonsense?*

Corabell's response was flat. "Your relationship with Heenehan Telecom is uncertain. We will follow up next month. If you have not achieved your goals as stated in your plans, you will be terminated. At that time, we will review with you the details of your package. You can find Heenehan's severance policy on the internal company website. If you have no further questions, go back to your desks."

In the hallway, Jim said, "I think that trashed our chances for Employee of the Month. Let's take a quick walk."

Blue-violet irises bloomed along the concrete walkway circling the building.

"They're going to accuse us of who knows what, despite anything we say or do," Beth said, walking slowly. "I can't believe what people do to each other."

You'd believe it if you spent time around my dad. "I assume your experiences with HR departments were similar to mine."

"How can Human Resources people like Corabell live with themselves? They turn a blind eye to power imbalances and retaliation schemes. They ruin careers. The old personnel departments were kinder and savvier about political dramas going on in their companies. It wasn't unusual for them to advocate for employees—imagine that!"

Chilled by a light breeze, Jim walked faster. "The ethics hotline isn't an option. It would peg us as troublemakers."

"It's so unfair. We should sue this company."

"We wouldn't stand a chance. We'd bankrupt ourselves with legal expenses. Blow ourselves up for nothing."

"You're right. We'd end up unemployable," Beth said. "I should have known Judy would get HR on us. It won't be the last time. That repulsive woman."

"So much for making ourselves indispensable." *Common sense fails me. We're roadkill.*

"They can't do permanent damage to me since I'm going to retire."

They stopped as two gray-brown cottontail rabbits darted across the sidewalk in front of them and into the bushes, as if being chased by an unseen predator.

Jim rubbed his chin. "Wait a minute. If they were going to fire us, they would've already done it, right? Disappeared us overnight, like Tom. I suspect Scott's planning to cut staff again. Either the company's in trouble, or Scott wants a bigger bonus."

"Last quarter's financials looked good."

"Company risks might not be fully disclosed in the footnotes. Corabell's a hired gun who only hears Judy's and Scott's lies. There's got to be a reason they're trying to terrorize us into working multiple jobs. Just speculating, but next month, we could still be here and our coworkers out on the street."

"Of course," Beth said. "We keep our jobs and everyone else's. They could hire a productive staff. Or, outsource the whole tax function. But no, it's cheaper to make the two of us do everything. They'll sack our coworkers, move their work onto us, then hassle the living hell out of us to get it all done. You're right. If the company's in trouble, we may be the last ones turning out the lights."

"Andy's converting Principal's state-of-the-art technology to Heenehan's outdated, patchwork systems. Not a good sign."

"Judy's been interrupting me with questions about the Principal returns for her database. She still doesn't grasp the concepts behind Principal's work."

Two plump, gray mourning doves sat together on a budding branch high in a tree above them, making sorrowful coos.

"I checked out Judy's database," Jim said. "The one that won her Employee of the Month. A few tables contain information from a company downtown. It isn't test data. Judy evidently got hold of a copy of their database and tweaked it. There were problems with fields, tables, even the spelling. I corrected her mistakes, so it works the way it should. The way Judy had the database set up, we'd produce crazy returns."

"Good work! One of Judy's contacts must have given her their company's database on a flash drive."

"Makes you wonder about other information they're passing back and forth. Cody's more tech savvy than Judy. He wouldn't leave errors in the database. Judy should assign more work to Cody. He has half our workload and spends hours playing esports."

"Judy's not going to interfere with Cody, Brad's alter ego," Beth said. "And she has to be perfectly aware of Amber's incompetence. Judy would've handed Amber a pink slip by now, if it weren't for Scott and Brad. She'll dispose of Sue and Kessie when it's to her advantage."

"Judy the puppet, lit up with her taste of power. Scott believes everything is running smoothly. Poor, sad little Judy."

"Said no one ever. Right now, she's too subservient to Scott to speak plainly. She's pushing for that promotion. The fallout from being in Judy's orbit is coming our way."

"Hiring the right people would save more than their salaries," Jim said. "Eliminating positions isn't the answer. What is Scott thinking?"

"It's not nuclear physics. It's his year-end bonus."

"I'd like to punch him in the eye."

"Bad idea."

"I could make it look like an accident."

"Okay, moving on. Imagine cross-training Amber. She'll challenge every word we say. Blast through the work. Screw it all up. If we don't fix Principal's returns before she sends them out, we'll have to amend them. We better not take any days off, so she never gets her hands on them."

"Last week a state's rep called me to inquire if Amber is still with the company," Jim said. "She said she'd left several messages on Amber's voicemail. One of Amber's returns was deficient by more than $12,000. I told the woman I'd ask Amber to contact her. I sent an email to Amber and copied Judy. Amber was shopping on the internet, ignoring her calls."

"If we return Amber's work to her for correction, she'll insist it's fine. We can't access her files and passwords because she keeps them on her personal drive instead of the network drive. We won't have a clue about her past work, unless we open every state's website, which we can't do without her passwords." Beth's voice was shaky. "Heenehan's code of conduct requires us to maintain accurate books and records. How in the world are we supposed to do that?"

"We need to keep a daily diary of how we spent our time in fifteen-minute increments," Jim said. "Include descriptions of work done, problems with workflow, our own money spent on office supplies, harassment and insults from coworkers, and impossible deadlines. We should save every one of our emails." *And work longer days and weekends to offset our lost time documenting.*

Beth frowned, clamping her lips together. "A monster of a time waster. But the law says if we didn't write it down, it didn't happen. We've got to protect ourselves."

"We should make note of each policy from the Employee Handbook that applies to our situation," Jim said.

"After Elly hires us, we won't be jerked around like this anymore."

An aluminum bench with intricate designs came into view. "Let's sit and relax a minute."

A pair of Canada geese beside the pond flew off together into the clear air.

Chapter 5: Friday, May 5

From Kessie's cubicle came whooping and hollering. "I'm the twelfth caller! I won two tickets to a country music festival! Hot diggity!"

"Wow! Congrats!" Sue exclaimed.

Judy stomped over to Kessie's cubicle. "Is that radio station's phone number on your speed dial?"

"Huh?"

"I said, do you have that station's phone number on speed dial?"

"I hit redial."

"Your productivity will be discussed in your next performance review." Judy returned to her cubicle.

"Hey, Beth! Don't you love country songs?" Kessie shouted.

Beth walked over to Kessie's cubicle and sat on her side chair. "I like a few classic country artists." *Modern country music makes me stuff my fingers in my ears.* "Hey, your office supplies are the same burgundy color as Jim's."

"I like his, so I bought me some. My grandkids play with them, too." Kessie eyed Beth. "How come you ain't married?"

"Well, that's a pretty personal question, don't you think?"

"Don't mean to stick my nose in your business. I bet you ain't never been to a tractor pull or a monster truck rally."

"No, I haven't. I can't drive a truck or heavy equipment."

"Well, me and Jack can drive all kinds of machines," Kessie said. "You're good at book learning and nothing else, ain't you?"

"That's a cheap dig." *This poor woman has the manners of a buffalo.*

"You and Jim throw your highfalutin talk at us folks who built up this company from scratch. You think you're better than us."

"You don't respect us."

"I take care of my family. You're a CAREER woman."

"Don't talk to me that way," Beth said. "I worked hard for my education. Nobody gave it to me. I earned it. For over forty years, I've been using that book learning. You can't fathom the struggles of a responsible single parent. If you think I had it easy, think again."

"Sorry if I hurt your feelings. I try to be nice. Everybody here talks smart-alecky, even the bigwigs."

"I appreciate your apology. Okay, let's move on. If you want to advance to the next pay grade, I can show you how to prepare simple returns."

"No thanks. I know my job. I don't need to learn somebody else's. My mom says the more you learn, the dumber you be. Don't get above your raisin', she says. After I got my degree off the internet, Mom wouldn't talk to me for a month."

"Suit yourself." A ball of lilac-colored yarn sat on the corner of Kessie's desk. "What are you making?"

"I'm knitting a sweater for my granddaughter, Starla. Mom taught me. I do different kinds of needlework and make lots of crafts."

Beth stroked the work in progress. "Soft, and a lovely shade of lavender. You added a sweet floral design to the front."

"It looks complicated, but it's easy for me. I can make one for your granddaughter if you want."

"Claire would love it. She's about the same size as Starla. I'll pay for your expenses and hours."

"Okay."

"I need to get back to work."

"See you later."

Kessie and I will never be buddies, but I think we can work on the same team.

Midafternoon, Beth called out from Jim's cubicle, "Amber, would you please come over here?"

Amber strolled to his cubicle door. "Whaddya want?"

"You do not have our permission to speak to us in a rude tone." *I can't even imagine her conversations with taxing authorities.*

Amber regarded them with half-closed eyes. She pushed out her glossy lips, pouting like a sultry film star. "You're soooo sensitive," she said, her voice a smoky croak. "Relax. Don't be so serious. Whassup?"

"Amber, why are my office supplies disappearing?" Jim asked. "I've had to buy new supplies several times."

"You couldn't pay me to swipe your supplies. Burgundy ain't my color. You been leaving your stuff around."

"Judy asked us to cross-train you on the Principal tax returns," Beth said. "What time tomorrow morning do you want to meet?"

Amber flicked away strands of green hair hanging over her face. "Don't bother to train me. Your buggin' returns are, like, so simple. I can figure 'em out after you're gone. I got enough to do. I don't even know where to start with my own work. So, no."

"Get a grip," Beth said. "They're tax returns. You said you have a master's degree. We'll need your help if we're out of the office or busy with an urgent priority." *She's way out of her depth. What college would let her in? Why is she here?*

Amber sighed like a tire going flat. "Oh, what the hell. I'll come over to your cube on Monday at nine. I'm bored of being here. Everybody else left early. I'm going home 'cause I can. Bye!" She swept her arm across the top of Jim's cabinet. Pens, a stapler, scissors, and a tape dispenser flew across the floor. Glancing over her shoulder, she sashayed down the corridor, jingling her keys.

Jim and Beth retrieved the items, placing them back on the top of the cabinet.

Beth took her seat on Jim's side chair. "Training Amber to prepare Principal's tax returns is insane. Jeez, she's worse than Hwan."

"Too bad we can't stick her in Tom's cubicle with Hwan," Jim said.

Beth nudged Jim, pointing to the moving cursor on his screen.

"The last time this cursor issue happened, I assumed IT was working on the system," Jim said. "I'll ask Andy who's making mischief with my mouse pointer."

"It hasn't happened to my computer. The techs always give us a heads-up when they'll be doing systems work." *Whoever is messing with Jim's computer isn't from IT.*

"It's been doing that since Hwan sat at my computer. Could he have done something to my computer while we stood outside in the corridor, waiting for him to compose himself after his training meltdown?"

A workman walked briskly along the hall in front of the tax area, looking straight ahead.

"Jim, that man looks like Tom. Grab those storage boxes."

They stacked empty cardboard boxes as a wedge behind the file room door, keeping it open. They ran back to the tax area and ducked low in Jim's cubicle. Hearing footsteps, they peered over the cubicle wall. The workman kicked the boxes into the file room, entered, and closed the door.

Jim and Beth sprinted down the corridor and burst into the file room. Beth locked the door.

The man jumped, eyes wide.

Jim muffled a shout, "Tom! What are you doing here? You can't be inside this building after being let go."

Beth cried, "I knew it was you! You can't fool me wearing those coveralls." *He looks thinner.* "We miss you!" She gave him a hug.

Tom pulled a footstool from the corner of the file room and sat on it. Jim and Beth sat in front of him on file boxes.

Tom's voice dropped low. "I'm working part time for Analytics Telco, until they raise enough money to hire me full-time. Elly Burke, our tax director from Principal, hired me. Her friend, Mike Shore, is the CEO. They're building the company from scratch. I conceived this project and I volunteered for it. It's significantly increased our revenue. Elly doesn't exactly go along with it 100 percent. If I get caught, I'm on my own. I thought it best not to keep you in the loop. It's a little dicey."

"What's the project?" Beth asked.

"Heenehan's customers are trying to sever their contracts so they can get over to Analytics. I'm here to check the file rooms around the building for boxes containing certain documents. I'll load the boxes into my van and drop them off at Analytics."

"Hmm." *So illegal.*

"Did you find the documents you need?" Jim asked.

"I found dozens of contracts in boxes stamped 'shred.' Heenehan doesn't practice the correct procedure when converting paper documents to digital images. So they can't prove the authenticity of their digitized contracts. If

I find a customer's paper contract, I keep it and we initiate service right away."

"Are you looking for other records?" Jim asked.

"Customer lists are useful for marketing. In the 'shred' boxes, I've found legal documents that should never be shredded, or the retention period is not yet completed. I keep some of them. I watch for unusual papers. Analytics' part-time IT person is looking for evidence of a security breach at Heenehan."

"How do you identify which boxes to carry off?" Beth asked.

"I'm interested in the legal, sales, and accounting departments' boxes. I scan the useful documents at Analytics, then return the boxes to one of Heenehan's file rooms. I don't always remember where I found them."

"We noticed that," Jim said.

"Sorry. I do my best. From boxes marked 'shred,' I take contracts and other papers I need. Heenehan doesn't like to pay for offsite storage, so most of their file boxes are on their way to the shredder."

"Wouldn't it be easier to hack into Heenehan's network?" Jim asked. "I'm not suggesting you should."

"Oh, we wouldn't do that. Anyway, we don't have the manpower or expertise."

Beth winced. "Those are confidential and proprietary documents. The code of conduct requires safeguarding them. I'm not okay with this, Tom. It's criminal theft. If you were caught, you could be fined or sentenced to prison time. How would that impact your family? Is it worth the risk?" *What's come over you, Tom?*

"When Corabell fired me, she told me I should have known my performance was unsatisfactory," Tom said. "Unsatisfactory. That's what she said. I'm going to help this whole damn company get everything they deserve. I've always kept to the straight and narrow. Now all bets are off."

"Think hard about this, Tom," Beth said. "Corabell just carries out orders. She has no concern about facts. She knows nothing about you. Shake it off." *Tom's always been sensible. He's not himself.*

"We can't condone your activities here," Jim said.

"Fair enough," Tom said. "I know the work I'm doing is technically illegal. But in the scheme of things, it's not so bad. Most companies use legal or illegal strategies to spy on their competitors. Analytics hired me as a tax accountant. For this project, I'm acting as a competitive intelligence analyst. Whoever is responsible for tracking Heenehan's storage boxes probably figures someone took the boxes marked 'shred' to the shredder."

"You're rationalizing your unethical conduct."

Heavy footsteps in the hall came closer. The locked doorknob turned back and forth. The footsteps continued down the hall, gradually becoming inaudible.

"How did you get in here?" Beth whispered.

Tom tapped a card attached to a lanyard around his neck. "My master security badge gives me access to this building and any room in it. Andy requisitioned it for me when we worked on the software project. I turned in my regular employee badge. HR didn't ask for my master badge. They must not have a record of it. No one paid attention to me when I worked here, so they're not going to recognize me wearing workman's clothes and a plain ball cap. It's a natural disguise."

"Tom, we're just glad you're all right," Jim said. "We're worried about you. We think about you and your family every day. How is Sherry doing?"

"Sherry's fine. So are the kids. Analytics has great health insurance. I'm happy over there. Who's the Asian guy asleep in my old cubicle?"

"Hwan Cho," Beth answered. "Sandra Young from the finance group sent him over to help us prepare your tax returns."

"Don't wake him up," Jim said. "Hwan's more valuable to the company asleep than awake."

"He sure doesn't have much hustle. I've seen him wandering around on the fourth floor. By the way, I found an odd document in one of the boxes. I was going to leave it on your desk after hours." Tom checked his pockets, located a folded paper, and handed it to Jim. "It's a contract between Amber Wolfe and someone named Li Chang. Amber must've filed it in a storage box with her tax reports by mistake. She's making serious money working for Chang's Tech Team. No doubt that's the group I see her with in the big fourth-floor conference room."

Jim and Beth studied the contract.

"It says Amber agrees to carry out her duties through completion of the project. But there are no other details. You're right. Her compensation is shocking. I don't know what to make of this." Jim folded the contract and stuffed it into his pocket.

"I don't, either. How are the two of you doing? You must be swamped."

"We're way behind schedule," Beth said. "We've been doing our work and your work. Now they're pushing Sue's and Amber's work on us. If we did the bare minimum, working 24-7, we still couldn't complete it all." *I'm feeling queasy again.*

"Are you paid for your overtime?" Tom asked.

Jim said, "Overtime? What are you talking about? Exempt, salaried employees don't get overtime pay. No extra compensation either. We do what we have to do. We need our jobs."

"Shame on Heenehan," Tom said. "It's straight-up wage theft. I can help you with the Principal returns before Elly hires me full time. Pay me out of pocket at a reasonable rate. Email me the reports. I'll remote into your company computers and get the returns done."

"No, Tom," Beth said. *I'm not going to spend my golden years behind bars.*

"Absolutely not," Jim said.

"Keep my offer in mind," Tom said. "I need to get going. It's great seeing you. I'll be around here for a while." He unlocked the door and left.

"Jim, this project is completely out of character for Tom. I can't believe Elly approved it."

"We should report his activities to someone at Heenehan," Jim said.

"Who would bother to listen to us?" Beth said.

Before leaving work, Jim texted Seb Medina. "See you at the meeting at Ryan's."

Chapter 6: Monday, May 8

Beth woke to the creaking of a loose board on her front porch. She crept toward the front door, checked that the deadbolt was locked, looked out the peephole, and froze. A shadowy figure of a young woman wandered around, then sat on the front porch steps. The woman wrapped her scarf over her head and around her neck. After several minutes she stood, turned the doorknob back and forth, and then walked away. Beth continued peering through the peephole for several minutes. She returned to bed and curled into a ball. *Is this stranger going to come back and break into my home?*

Through half-closed eyes, Jim made out the silhouette of his cat crouched on the windowsill, ears flat against her head, making low, guttural growls.

"What is it, Hannah?" He sat up, removing a tangle of sheets and blankets. He reached for the lamp, then decided not to turn it on. Parting the curtains slightly, he discerned a woman reaching under the twisted window well cover. She stood, picked up a crowbar from the ground, and walked off. Alarmed, Jim shut the open window, locked it, and pulled the curtains closed. He picked up Hannah, set her on his bed, and laid next to her. Hannah licked his neck with her rough tongue.

Beth sipped her morning tea, her disposable cup resting on her cubicle desk to keep her hands steady. "Jim, I'm on edge this morning. Noises outside woke me up last night. I looked through my front door peephole and saw a woman walking around, checking out my house. She scared me out of my wits. I'm still jittery." *She could be inside my home this very minute, stealing my stuff.*

"You too? Hannah woke me up, growling at something outside. When I opened the curtains, a woman was reaching under the window well cover, then she picked up her crowbar and was gone."

"Oh my gosh. She targeted us the same night."

"In mild weather, I leave my basement window open a crack," Jim said. "The window well has a plastic cover. A pin unlocks it from inside. She tried to pry the cover off, and managed to bend and break it. At least that old cover kept her from climbing in my window. I'm going to get a sturdier model."

"Good idea," Beth said. "My doorbell camera didn't catch more than a shadow. This morning I forwarded the video to the police department anyway."

"On my way home, I'm going to file a report at the police station," Jim said. "Her lurking around outside my home is trespassing. She caused property damage to my window well cover. That's vandalism. Lock your doors and windows tonight."

"I certainly will." *I'm a sitting duck.*

"I can't be certain, but I thought she resembled Amber."

"She did."

"Amber agreed to meet this morning to cross-train on Principal's returns," Beth said to Jim. "Our scheduled nine o'clock meeting time has come and gone. Amber normally doesn't show up on Monday or Friday, and this is Monday. Maybe she'll roll in for a few hours this afternoon. What a great gig for a full-time, salaried employee. Let's see if

Sue is available to explain how she prepares Heenehan's tax returns."

Sue was sitting at her desk, chatting with Kessie, who exclaimed, "Hide your cash! Somebody's stealing money around the office. Betcha it's the accounting department's new college intern, that little Miss Whosey-Whatsis."

"I'll be careful to lock my desk," Beth said. "I haven't seen any strangers in the office." *A college intern in the tax department would be more conspicuous than a unicorn.*

Kessie scurried to her cubicle.

"Sue, would you please give us an overview of your methods?" Beth asked. "Judy wants us to prepare the Heenehan returns for your states."

"Huh? Tell it again?"

"I said, we need training. Today."

"I'm leaving early to buy feed for my chickens," Sue replied. "One's gonna be dinner tonight. Training's out of my wheelhouse. Just try different things until the system does what you want."

"Sue! We have statutory deadlines. You've been here for years. We need direction. What systems did you use? What steps did you take? How did you handle complications? One simple mistake can trigger a fine or an audit. We're asking for a few hours of your time."

"Figure it out for yourselves."

"We need the purple file folder with the list of vendor contracts," Jim said. "Judy told us you have it."

Sue fiddled with her phone. "What were we talking about?"

"You heard me."

"Your problem, not mine. Follow what I did. My files are on the network drive. I lost that purple folder. You need to recreate it," Sue said, texting.

"Sue, I'm speaking to you," Jim said. "Would you please set your phone aside and talk to me?"

"How come you don't get a smartphone? Are you Amish?"

"Amish people use smartphones," Jim said. "We're asking you to make time for us."

"Just click the anchor icon on your screen."

"You're way too light on the details," Jim said.

"No anchor icon appears on any screen," Beth said.

"Judy told us not to unpack the process for you. She wants you to sink or swim."

"Well, that's just delightful," Beth said.

"Thanks for the helping hand, Sue," Jim said.

Sue tossed her ponytail. "I'm hungry!" She escaped into the kitchen.

In Jim's cubicle, Beth said, "Trying to find help is a losing battle. Where do we even begin?" *Run away and never come back?*

"Let's list the steps we think Sue takes," Jim said. "I'll sketch out her procedures as we go along." He opened a new file, naming it Sue's Methods. "We should save our files on our own personal drives. Amber will be tempted to sabotage them if they're on the shared drive."

"I'm impressed with the way you set up methods, Jim. I see how logical you are and how you work so quickly. Your user-friendly tax calendar and color-coded reports make it difficult to make a mistake."

"Thanks! Most people don't appreciate the brainwork I put into them. This morning I searched for Sue's passwords all over the network. I found most of them and entered them in one file."

"Great! We can open the states' websites to figure out how she prepared her prior months' returns." Beth squeezed her eyes shut. "We'll still stumble over unfamiliar complications."

"I'm documenting everything we're dealing with. The workload is crushing." Jim brought a hand to his forehead. "We'll never get it all done."

"Let's give Tom a call," Beth said. "He offered to help us out. We need to take him up on it." *At this point, it's the right solution.*

Even if Tom finishes the returns we can't complete, we'll barely make the deadline."

They called Tom on Jim's phone from a huddle room.

"I'm happy to help," Tom said. "Preparing Heenehan's returns when I'm not an employee may not be, strictly speaking, legal, but I need the work. I'll look for your email this evening."

"What a relief," Beth said. "You're an angel, Tom."

"I won't disillusion you. We'll be working together at Analytics before long."

"It can't be soon enough. Talk to you later." Jim rubbed his temples. "We might as well call the ethics hotline and report ourselves. We're paying an employee of a rival company to access our systems and prepare our company's tax returns. Stress has strange effects on people. We're all behaving out of character."

Beth said, "In reality, we're taking the moral high ground. We're justified. We're protecting ourselves and the company. Tom will do a good job with our returns. It's our only option." *And no one will suspect a thing.*

At 2 p.m., Amber wobbled to her cubicle and turned on her computer. Her matted, green hair stuck out in different directions over a rumpled gray sweat suit. She answered her ringing desk phone. "Yes, this is Amber. I know your return is important. I'll call you later."

Beth called out, "Amber, you're late. Come on over to my cubicle."

Amber shouted, "I gotta go pee!" She stumbled toward the restroom, leaving a sweaty, smoky smell behind.

She returned and sat before her computer.

Beth sat on the side chair next to her. *Good grief. Black and blue marks under her left ear and alcohol on her breath.* "Amber, you said you would meet with us this morning at nine o'clock to cross-train on the Principal Processing returns. Why are you so late and scruffy?"

Amber slumped into her chair, leaned her elbows on her desk, and held her head in her hands. She stared blankly at her desk with swollen, red eyes.

"Where did you work before Heenehan? Why are you here? Who are you?"

"Did I answer the phone with some other name? I'm so tired." Amber rubbed her palms together. "It's cold in here. I cut the fingers out of my gloves, so I can type. I'm a freeze baby. If I was a guy, I'd be a one-incher."

"Put on a jacket, or pour yourself a hot coffee."

"Nah."

"Then let's start our training."

"I woke up this morning coughing my ass off." Amber coughed into her elbow. "I stopped at a bar last night at about eleven, had three or four drinks. I didn't go looking for trouble, it found me."

"Why are you telling me this?"

"A girl started a fight with me. When the bartender wasn't watching, she kept hitting me with a stick and saying, 'You're not moving fast enough, you're not moving fast enough.' I dunno who she was or where she come from. I would've killed her. Like, oh my God! I hit her back, and she took off."

"You're making this up, right?" *Actually, I find Amber's story disturbingly believable.*

"Uh-uh. After she left, a man at the bar came over and sat on the stool next to me. He said he knows all my friends. He ordered me a beer. I said I didn't want it. I ran out the door and he followed me. I jumped in my car and locked the doors and drove. I mean, he stayed right behind me. I called the cops. They told me to pull into a parking lot. They caught him. Now he's in jail. I ain't never going into a bar again without a man. Didn't set my alarm last night. Slept in." Grimy hair hung in her face. She hiccupped and broke down crying.

Beth flashed Amber a dark look. "I'm sorry you're not well. It's your responsibility to show up on time, rested, and ready to go. We need your help. It's important. We can't prepare Heenehan's returns unless you take some of Principal's. We can't do all the work ourselves."

"Okay, fine. I'll be at your desk in a minute."

Beth returned to her cubicle. After several minutes, Amber sauntered over wearing a black leather jacket and sat in the chair next to Beth.

"All right," Beth said. "After you generate an accounting report, there are a few more steps. Click the icon —" Beth pointed at the screen and glanced over at Amber, whose head bobbed, eyes closed. Beth nudged Amber with her elbow. "Wake up! If you're drowsy, go get coffee or a soda. I'm trying to conduct a training session here." *Brad was wrong. Training Amber is harder than training a new dog.*

"Huh? That kitchen coffee tastes nasty. A Slurpee with vodka would be good."

Jim walked into Beth's cubicle. "Hey Amber, why were you poking around our homes last night?"

"Meaning what?"

"You went out drinking, running wild, and pulling pranks, and you woke up with a monster hangover. Looks like you crossed a big bruiser."

"I don't want to talk about it."

"Who are you mixed up with?" Beth asked. "Are you planning a heist on my condo?"

Amber froze, then shook with fury. She sprang from her chair. "Don't get judgey, Saint Jim and Miss Prudey Pants!" she shouted. "Why the hell are you still here?" Wild-eyed, she picked up a pressboard file folder and hurled it at Jim, who moved aside. The folder nicked the top of his wrist, drawing blood.

"I ain't doing no Principal returns! That's your flippin' job!" Amber stumbled to her cubicle. "I can't take this no more." She shut down her computer and left.

Beth peered at Jim's bleeding wrist. "Are you all right?" She handed Jim a tissue from the box on her desk.

"Just a superficial cut. Could've been worse, she was so worked up."

Beth pressed her palms to the sides of her face. "I'm losing it. Who's supposed to be doing what? What project's due when? How can we resolve audit and technical issues?"

Jim dabbed his wrist. "I'll book a conference room for nine tomorrow morning and notify the group. An hour will give us an opportunity to ask some of our questions."

"Thanks. Here's a Band-Aid."

When Jim arrived home, he called out, "Mom!" He found his mother asleep in her bed. *Where is Hannah? She isn't waiting for me in her usual spot by the door.* He descended the stairs to his basement bedroom. Searching the room, he spotted his cat lying on her side, curled in a ball in a far corner.

"Oh, sweetheart." He hurried over to her and petted her furry back. She tried to move and collapsed. He found vomit on the floor. *I need help.* He gently picked her up and put her in her carrier. He drove at high speed to the emergency vet clinic.

Chapter 7: Tuesday, May 9

Two gray mourning doves perched on a maple tree watched Beth as she entered the Heenehan building shortly after sunrise. She logged onto her computer, then stopped at Jim's cubicle to review their questions for the tax group meeting. Jim was sitting at his desk, his face buried in his hands.

"What's wrong?"

"My little Hannah came down sick last night and almost died."

"Oh, no! What happened?"

"When I got home, her breathing was rapid and shallow. She was vomiting and shaking. She tried to hide from me."

"Cats will do that when they need our help the most. Did you take her to the vet?"

"I did, and he thinks she's going to make it. She'll stay in the animal hospital again tonight."

"Did he determine the cause?"

"I found an odd substance along my basement bedroom window where the woman reached inside my window well cover. I'm going to have a toxicologist test it."

"Good idea. Poor kitty."

"She's only eight years old. I love her more than anyone in the world." Jim rested his head on his hand.

Beth touched Jim's arm. "She's a wonderful cat. I'm glad the vet says she'll recover. Let me know how she does. How are you doing?"

"It's tough. I hate knowing my little buddy is suffering. I need some space."

"I'll help you through our meeting. Just do what you can today."

Cody, Sue, and Kessie sat at the conference table, eating brightly colored candies from a big bowl.

Jim and Beth entered the room carrying spiral notebooks. Sue sized up Jim. "You look like crap. What's the matter with you?"

"Jim's cat was sick last night," Beth replied.

Sue sniffed. "Put it out of its misery. It's not hard to put a cat down. The sooner the better."

Beth glared at Sue. "She's going to recover."

"Cats are spooky, not friendly like dogs," Sue said. "There's dog people, and there's cat people. No wonder you have a cat."

"We can do without your sniping," Beth said.

"There's lots of strays around our place you could take if she dies," Kessie said.

Beth scribbled a note to Jim: "Ignore them."

Beth and Jim sat at the table and focused on their notebooks, turning to their list of questions.

Judy entered the room. She called Hwan from the conference phone on the table top. He quickly arrived, taking a seat at the far end of the table.

Beth began, "Jim and I scheduled this morning's meeting to ask for your help—"

Judy bulldozed over her. "Amber called in sick. She will be in later today. I asked Hwan to be present since he assists us. The first issue is our new database. Someone entered wrong amounts over the uploaded data."

Kessie sputtered, "I ain't entering wrong numbers!"

Hwan's mouth curved downward. "Don't look at me! I not do that. I not do anything."

Judy gave Jim a side-eye. "Is Hwan up and running on our new database?"

"Yes, he is," Jim said.

"Dammit, who took my pen? I set it right here!" Judy slapped the table in front of her, causing the staff to jump. Five index fingers pointed to a pen rolling toward the edge of the table. She stuck out a pudgy hand and caught it.

Judy scrutinized Jim, then Beth. "I'm not a mind reader. You said you had questions for us."

"Would you please provide a list of queries you use in your database?" Jim asked. "It would help us to learn the methodology."

"You're not proficient with our database. You don't need to worry about how it works."

"All right," Beth said. "Did you finish your process in the system so we can start preparing our returns?"

Judy hunched forward, focusing red eyes on Beth. "I guess you weren't listening yesterday when I informed the group that the process is complete."

"Can we generate the reports?"

"Of course you can."

"On some returns, the amounts don't carry forward to page one," Jim said. "And the numbers don't add up to the total at the bottom."

Judy crossed her arms, a gesture Sue, Kessie, and Cody imitated. "Stop and think. Page one computes from the numbers you enter. Verify that your formulas are working. I know for a fact those formulas were correct at one time."

"I've got this," Beth said to Jim. She turned to Judy. "We did not do anything to the formulas."

Judy pinched her lips tightly. "I'll review it later. I have other work to get out today."

"Andy Price and I discussed the tax software," Jim said. "We came up with some great ideas, and I copied you on our last email. Tell us what you think."

Judy stiffened. "Absolutely not. I've said it before, and I'll say it again. Please inform me prior to contacting IT. I liaise with every department in this company. I don't like it when somebody brings up something about tax work that I don't know about."

Beth made strong eye contact with Judy. "One of the returns didn't generate a confirmation."

With an indignant grimace, Judy straightened her shoulders. "So it was YOUR file that didn't complete. You held up all other returns behind it. You should have told me when it happened. Run it again."

"After I re-ran it, I called the state, and they got it."

"Then I don't need to know about that."

Jim said, "You asked for the number of prior months to report in the current month's return. I emailed you a list of each state's rules."

Judy threw up her hands. "Never mind, I'll extrapolate the data I need from your list. I can tell by the look on your face you didn't comprehend a word I said." She eyed each person around the table. "Who's humming? Who's humming?" she demanded.

Beth glanced at Jim, who was humming one of his songs. She said, "It must have been me. Sometimes I hum when I'm thinking."

"Stop doing that," Judy said. "And you don't need to write in your notebooks. Stop all of your documenting. If you can't remember how to do your jobs, you don't belong here. Here, give me your sheets from this meeting."

Beth said, "Our notes belong to us. You can't take them."

"Give them to me this minute!" Judy shouted.

Jim and Beth pulled the pages from their notebooks. Judy grabbed the sheets, tore them to pieces, and hurled the fragments into the wastebasket.

Beth and Jim stared at the wastebasket. The others looked down at the table.

Jim spoke in a monotone. "This morning I tried to amend the return I asked you about. The state still hasn't received my authorization."

Judy huffed. "We discussed this last week, remember? You can send your return after Andy fixes the problem."

"Andy said IT fixed it yesterday, so I was trying to—"

"You don't know what you're talking about. For future reference, please use the proper terminology. If you amend a return in that state, it's called a corrected file. Got it?"

"Why does Heenehan file zero use tax returns in most of the states?" Beth asked. "The company makes large purchases for which use tax needs to be paid."

Judy exploded. "Can't you see we're busy? We file zero returns every month, and the states don't bother us! We get them caught up once a year. IF we have time."

Scott Campbell opened the conference room door. Judy adjusted her facial expression. Scott called out, "Judy, I need you to come to my office for a few minutes."

Judy pulled herself up and strutted toward the door.

"How did your team do last night?" Scott asked Judy.

"Beat the crap out of 'em. It was fun to watch."

Scott appraised Jim and Beth. "Well, if it isn't our castoffs from Principal Processing. Buckle down and make your time productive." He winked at Sue.

Beth glanced at Jim, who sat motionless.

"Hwan, actually you don't need to be here; you can leave," Judy said.

Hwan rose and walked out.

"Carry on without me." Judy and Scott left the room.

Jim asked, "Sue, when you prepare your state returns, in what sequence do you enter each type of purchase?"

"OMG! How long have you been here?" Sue exclaimed, moving her eyes around in a circle.

"I noticed you rolled your eyes," Beth said. "Are you offended about something?"

Kessie frowned, wrinkled her nose, and turned to Sue. "What in tarnation is he talkin' about?"

Cody said, "It depends on the return. I'll send you the rules. You ought to find a simpler job."

"Thanks a bunch, Cody," Jim said.

Cody took his cell phone from his pocket. He began tapping the screen with his thumbs.

"We used to do fun stuff together," Kessie said. "We was a family before you Principal folks came along. Wasn't we, Sue?"

"Yep."

"Everybody stop by my desk and sign up for the lottery," Kessie said. "I'm buying a dozen Powerball tickets. If I don't win, my kids hafta support me when I'm old 'cause Momma ain't got no retirement."

Jim and Beth wrote in their notebooks, recreating the pages Judy ripped up. Cody sat with head lowered, playing video games on his phone.

"I bought a spiffy new dress for our family wingding last weekend," Kessie said. "I tucked in the tag and wore it to the park. Yesterday I brung it back to the store. It's where my sister works. They don't care. Customers do that all the time."

"You evil genius. Dusty and me camped out by the creek last weekend. It was fun. We went four-wheeling, and the dumdum crashed on his back. It knocked the breath out of him but he's okay. We're having the grandkids over for a barbecue on Saturday." She turned to Cody. "How about you? Doing anything fun this weekend?"

Cody looked up from his phone. He rubbed the top of his head, his buzz-cut sandpapering his palm. "I'm practicing my video game skills for a competition next month."

"In your own apartment?"

"Yes, I practice in my own apartment."

"You're anti-social," Sue said.

"I play with my buddies across the country. We compete against other teams in our league. Our games are complicated. We make hard choices about how to resolve problems."

Amber slipped into the conference room, wearing a deep V-neck black top, gray snakeskin skirt, and platform heels. Glitzy jewelry ornamented her ears, wrists, fingers, and neck. "I'm here!" she proclaimed. "How do you like my outfit?"

"Cutest thing ever!" said Sue.

"There she is, Miss Heenehan!" exclaimed Kessie.

Beth glanced at Amber and returned to her notebook. *Show pony.*

Kessie held out her fingers. "Hey, Amber, I got my nails painted!"

"Hot pink and super long! Love 'em!" Amber said.

Beth marveled at the extended nails. *Kessie could swoop over the pond and catch a fish.*

Amber took a seat at the table. She nudged Sue and Kessie and leaned toward them, whispering behind her hand. The three of them stared intently at Beth.

Sue warbled, "You're an artsy-fartsy. Artsy-fartsy, artsy-fartsy!"

Beth pointed an index finger in their direction. "Don't mess with me!"

Amber whispered to Sue and Kessie again. They directed withering looks at Jim.

"Music freak. Sooo cool," Sue taunted.

"Ladies, get a life," Jim said.

Sue cocked her head to the side. "Not making money out of it, but they're tryin'."

"Excuse me?" Beth said. "You have good jobs here. Be grateful for women trailblazers like me who came before you. We made your jobs possible. If we hadn't opened doors, you'd be in the typing pool or doing data entry. Did you ever think of that?"

Amber scrolled through her phone screens. "Blah, blah, blaze trailers, blah, blah, blah."

"Amber, you need to learn respect. And accounting."

"Suck it up, buttercup. Anybody can do accounting."

"Thank you for sharing that."

"Meaning what?"

"You think you know more than you do."

"You are literally so stupid. You might wanna watch yourself. Just sayin'."

Kessie muttered, "It's about time somebody knocked 'em down a peg."

Judy returned to the room, taking her seat at the head of the conference table. Cody put his phone in his pocket.

"One more item," Jim said to Judy. "I've seen many tax calendars in my career. I use a simple one that provides better data faster. The group could test it out, if you want to give it a try."

Judy studied Jim. "Just so you know, our tax calendar has worked for us for decades. It has minor problems, and we decided not to fix them. You are not going to undermine our process." She locked eyes with Jim, giving him a short, sharp nod of her head.

She straightened. "I was asked to inform you that a consulting group will audit our computer systems to help us streamline our tax processes. Ludmila Kozlova and Spartak Volkov are former state auditors who will provide us with valuable advice. Their manager, Li Chang, will be here as well. They will ask for input on your daily work. Please answer their questions as carefully and thoroughly as you can. Amber will facilitate their visits."

Beth glanced at Jim. *The Tech Team is moving in.*

"For today's potluck, volunteers will set up the tables by 11. Please bring your dishes over between 11:30 and 11:45. Lunch is at noon. I appreciate everyone taking valuable time out of their day to help train our new employees."

From his desk drawer, Jim withdrew his notebook and wrote.

Scott strides down the hall with a slight air of money.
He's smart, he's funny, he's smoother than honey.

He's on the best team, he loves to compete.
He crushes his rivals, enjoys their defeat.

Cool under pressure, he wins much respect,
But his answers to questions are never correct.

With verbal finesse, he dominates all.
Whoppers are misunderstood or just small.

When it's found he did something that's flat underhanded
He fibs and insists he's totally candid.

He's a leader but can't form a broad coalition
Winning his game is his only ambition.

What makes him high-powered is the tricks he will do
Without giving a thought to staff welfare or you.

He's a winner, a player, a rock star at work
And sure as hell everyone knows he's a jerk.

Jim laughed and locked the notebook in his desk.

Next to the kitchen, employees pushed long folding tables together and set out their dishes for the company potluck. Jim took a stack of disposable white paper plates from the kitchen cabinet and placed them on the first table. On the last table, Beth set out paper napkins and plastic utensils she brought from home. "We can always use those," she said.

Dozens of cold cuts, meat casseroles, potato chips, and desserts dotted the tables.

"It smells delicious," a woman said.

Beth surveyed the food arranged buffet-style on the tables. *Meat dishes that sat on people's desks all morning? Oh well.*

A man bit into a strip of beef jerky. "Extra tough. Like the cowboys ate it."

Amber pointed to an acrid-smelling dish. "I brung pickled cauliflower and grapes from the gourmet deli."

"That sounds like an acquired taste," Jim said.

Beth said. "On the plus side, it's the only vegetable and fruit on the table."

"Wrong! Kessie made deep-fried pickles."

First in line, Sue filled her plate with chips, meat, and chocolate pie. "I don't wanna be too healthy!" People behind her piled their plates with food.

Standing in line, Beth watched employees grab sodas from the kitchen and carry their lunches to their cubicles. They ate at their desks, surfing the internet or playing with their cell phones. *Why didn't the volunteers reserve a conference room, so groups could sit and talk to each other?*

Chatting with a burly man, Judy giggled and popped cocktail meatballs into her mouth. A woman in line told them they were blocking the flow of people. They moved a few feet from the table.

From her cubicle, Kessie shouted into her phone. "I'll be over there, once I get off work! Is Scooter potty-broke yet?"

In Jim's cubicle, Jim and Beth set their plates on his desk.

Beth tapped Jim's arm. "I'm sorry this group is so mean. How are you holding up?"

"I'm okay."

"Have you heard from the vet about Hannah?"

"The vet hasn't contacted me, which is probably a good thing. I'll check with him in a while."

Beth eyed her plate. "I don't find this food appetizing."

They ate a few bites, took their plates to the kitchen, tossed them in the trashcan, and returned to Jim's cubicle.

Kessie yelled, "You caught Starla smoking and you gave her a lecture? You know what I'd do? Make her smoke a whole carton! I never smoked!"

Beth said, "That meeting was an hour we'll never get back."

"We'd get better guidance from a Magic 8 Ball. It's a relief to be out of that conference room."

"Judy can't answer even basic questions. Are the two Tech Team auditors scheduled to examine your computer?" Beth asked.

"No. Andy says IT hasn't been told anything about this computer audit. He's going to monitor what the Tech Team is doing in the company's network."

"Last Friday, I had a mostly pleasant chat with Kessie. Her fancy needlework is impressive. She could have a handmade crafts business of her own. We actually had some camaraderie going. But this morning the Heenehan tribe pulled her right back in. I'm done trying to build bridges. I was foolish to imagine I could make an ally of Kessie."

"Amber's turned Sue and Kessie against us," Jim said.

"Sue's mind isn't on her work, and she doesn't give a hoot. That doesn't bother Brad. He's on the same wavelength."

Jim took a sheet of paper out of his desk. "This morning, smoke was coming out of the printer again. When I checked it, this spreadsheet was sitting on top. It's a list of salaries of the tax department staff."

Beth looked it over. "Our salaries are about right. It shows Amber makes more money than we do. No surprise there. She might have doctored her salary and left the sheet on the printer for us to find, so we'd make a fuss about it."

"I'll recycle it. Brad will be in for a short time this afternoon. If we can catch him, maybe he'll give us some insight into the state audit."

Amber stepped into Jim's cubicle, carrying a paper plate of pickled cauliflower and grapes, the pungent smell permeating the air.

Beth said, "Amber, after the potluck please make me a copy of the system auditors' contract."

"Contract?"

"The official contract lays out the responsibilities for Mr. Chang's auditors. I need a copy for the state."

"I threw it away. The auditors told me all the stuff they wanted. Here, take a taste of my potluck dish."

"What's that white powder sprinkled across the top?" Jim asked.

"Well, duh! Can't you see it's onion powder? It brings out the taste and makes it more flavorful. Try it."

Beth squinted. "Your onion powder looks like kitchen cleanser."

Amber glared. "You got a problem with it? You got a problem, huh?" She flipped the plate over and threw it down. Red grapes and chunks of white cauliflower bounced across Jim's cubicle floor. "I didn't think so." She strutted out.

Beth rubbed her forehead. "One more Amber clean-up job."

Jim and Beth kneeled, turned the plate right-side up, picked up each grape and piece of cauliflower from the floor, and set them on the plate. They took the reeking plate to the kitchen and dumped it in the trashcan.

"I'm sorry about your floor, Jim. The cleaning crew will vacuum up the Ajax, or whatever it is."

After the staff lunch had been cleared, Amber escorted three people to the tax area. They stood with rigid postures. She called out, "Hey! Everybody!" Sue, Kessie, Cody, Jim, and Beth gathered in the aisle between their cubicles.

Beth stared at them. *So that's the Tech Team.*

Amber gestured toward a slim, well-dressed Asian man. "This is Mr. Li Chang who's gonna make our jobs easier and save us some money." She gazed at him with shining eyes.

Beth extended her hand to Chang. The others followed.

"Meet Ludmila and Spartak," Amber said. "These auditors gonna go through our computers." They shook hands. Spartak was trim, with a gray countenance and a glum, efficient manner. Ludmila's brittle henna hair fell to the shoulders of a multi-colored dress draped over her skeletal figure. In a friendly, deferential manner she said, "pree-vyet."

Chang lifted his chin. "With our years of experience, we will make many recommendations to improve your daily work. Ludmila and Spartak will obtain data from your computers. Expect us to interrupt your work several times a day to ask for information and reports." He crossed his arms. "We will take as much time as we need to review your current practices. Brad will share our conclusions with you as he sees fit."

Beth said, "We don't foresee any problems with Principal's taxes." *Cocky little conman.*

Chang glanced at his smartwatch. "I have a meeting." He turned and left.

"Mr. Chang knows his stuff," Amber said. "The two auditors gonna start with Jim's computer."

Returning to their cubicles, Kessie said to Sue, "We don't need foreigners futzing around our office."

Sue said, "If I can't make out some outsider's babble, I talk slow and clear. I don't exactly make 'em welcome, so they go back to where they come from."

Kessie giggled, revealing rabbit-like front teeth. "That's a good way."

In Jim's cubicle, Ludmila and Spartak pulled up both chairs, assuming control of his computer. Jim and Beth stood, watching. They viewed Heenehan's billing and accounting systems, speaking to each other in a Slavic-sounding language. After a half hour, they stood, bowed slightly, and said, "Spa-see-ba, pahka." They met Amber at her cubicle door. She accompanied them down the stairs.

"The Tech Team in action," Beth said to Jim. "Li Chang's the guy Amber is working for, according to that contract Tom found in a box. Did you see how Amber acts around Chang? She's smitten with him."

"I noticed," Jim said. "That Chang has the ego of a rock star.

"I assume Amber's under Chang's thumb, reporting to Chang before she reports to Brad."

"Looks that way. Brad must've convinced Humphrey to sign Chang's consulting contract. Brad filed it in the purple folder and hid it in Scott's drawer."

"So Brad agreed to a contract with consultants who can't speak a word of English?" Beth asked.

"Amber sweet-talked him into it."

"Foreigners poking around the building should raise eyebrows. Maybe my imagination is working overtime, but the Tech Team might be a spy ring, stripping this company of everything they can get their hands on."

Jim ran a hand through his hair. "Would we be better off somewhere else? For all we know, Tech Teams are springing up in other companies as we speak."

"That's a scary thought. If that's true, and we left Heenehan to work at some other company, Amber's counterparts would pick up where she left off, trying to undermine us and send us packing."

"We need to update our master plan," Jim said. "It's not enough to disengage from our coworkers. The situation is too serious. It's time to think about self-preservation. We have to save ourselves, while we still can."

"Saving ourselves is our new master plan," Beth said. "I'll report the Tech Team to the FBI Internet Crime Complaint Center. I'll file my report online at home tonight. It will clear us in the long term."

"Good. Let's see if Amber will spit out some details that you can include in your report."

They came to an abrupt stop at Amber's cubicle entrance. Tax files lay everywhere—scattered across her desktop and shelves, piled high in her open coat closet, and spread across the floor under her feet. A few flies clung to fast-food wrappers on her desk and floor. Profanity-laced songs played from a portable music desktop player.

"Sup?"

Beth said, "You're supposed to remove a few files at a time from the file room and return each one when you're finished with it. Now I know why I can't find files. They're in your cubicle. And dirty lyrics aren't music."

Amber stiffened. "I didn't invite you to blow in. Take any file you want. Knock yourselves out. Then get your butts outta my cubicle. Bingo about street music. It's nasty."

Beth looked through a stack of jumbled file folders on the side chair, and removed one. A credit card fell out onto the floor. Amber grabbed the card and stuck it in her desk drawer.

"I been searching for that card since last week."

"What's the big box in the corner?" Beth asked.

"Can't you see it's a balloon kit? Great for celebrating birthdays and other stuff."

"You're breeding flies," Jim said. "It reeks in here. Is a rotting corpse lying behind your desk? I wish I could un-see and un-smell your cubicle."

"Smells fine to me."

"If you leave food remnants around, we're going to have a rodent problem."

"Brad don't care."

"What's that black spray can on your desk?"

"Air spray cleaner for keyboards. Brad gave me it."

"It's bug spray."

Amber examined the can. "So whaddya want, dorks?"

"Amber, who are those auditors?" Beth asked.

"Ludmila and Spartak look at computers and make sure people do their taxes right. Before, they was temps that the state hired 'cause they're smart and got their degrees in Russia. Nobody here wrote down steps to do returns, so ain't nothing to show them how we work. I'm too new and nobody else here can explain their job very good. We need 'em to help us."

"They can't speak English well enough to communicate with us," Jim said.

"Get over it. They figure out what you're saying. Me, I think if people can't talk right, they should stay in their own country. I'm all for people coming here to make a better life, but they shouldn't mangle up their words."

"Is Li Chang Chinese?" Beth asked.

"He's Oriental. Chinese, Japanese, I dunno. He's a hottie."

Beth said to Jim, "I'm going to call Pam Taylor at the state about those auditors."

After a few minutes, she stopped at Jim's cubicle. "Pam said none of the three foreign auditors ever worked for the state. She's never heard their names."

Chapter 8: Wednesday, May 10

Hearing Brad's voice, Beth dashed to Jim's cubicle and waved. Jim removed his earbuds. "Hey, Brad's here!"

Cody was standing in front of Brad's desk, arguing the merits of various sports teams and whether home-field advantage matters. Jim and Beth waited. At last, Cody turned and ambled out the door, failing to notice that he had kicked over a stack of papers on the floor. Entering Brad's office, Jim and Beth stepped around papers and files, avoiding his guest chair piled precariously high.

"Brad, we need to speak to you about a few audit issues," Jim said.

"Audit? Amber's handling Mr. Chang's system audit."

"Not the system audit. The state tax audit. The audit with millions at stake."

"So what are those issues?" Brad gave Jim a middle-distanced, bleary gaze.

"Here's how I would break it down—"

"You studied accounting, you deal with audit issues. I expect you to handle the upcoming meeting, as well as all audit meetings on a go-forward basis."

Beth tightened her fists. "Brad! You're our manager! We need to know the company's past positions. We can't even find all the records. I sent you an email summarizing the main issues with our best responses. I printed out a hard copy and put it on your desk. Did you read it?"

"I haven't had a chance to read it yet. I want you to drop what you're doing and clean up the Accounts Receivable miscellaneous account. Sue didn't get it done. It has to be reconciled this month."

Jim said, "That account's been a mess for years. We don't come close to having the resources to reconcile it now. It's the audit we need to talk about. Should we bring a dead dog to the audit meeting? Are you even listening?"

"Also, I want you to write the account number on each of the property tax bills and circle the amount due. Be sure to make a copy of each bill for yourself. It'll take you five minutes. Multitask—make all your assignments your number one priority. "

"Brad!" Beth shouted. "Accounts Payable has the account number, so we don't need to write it on the bills. I attached the transmittal form with the amount to pay, so I don't need to circle it. I'd have to work after midnight to write the account number and circle the amount due on each of the bills. That's a waste of time."

Brad yawned. "Sorry. Go on."

"We need help," Beth said.

"Hwan asked me if he can do some technical writing. I agreed. Tell him to analyze Heenehan's positions and write a report for the auditors."

"What are you talking about?" Jim asked. "The job description requires five to six years of relevant tax experience and good written and verbal skills. Hwan doesn't know the first thing about tax. He doesn't have full command of English. Why the hell was he hired?"

"Sandra Young said Hwan's more than qualified for his job. Oh, and by the way, I authorized Judy to put you both on performance plans. So far, I've given you a pass because you're new to the company. Challenge yourselves. You can handle it."

They glared at Brad.

"Those performance plans are horse manure, and you know it," Jim said.

"Yes, we do handle almost all of the tax group's work, and you're welcome," Beth said.

Brad folded his arms. "Are you going to just take the weekend off? You don't have children at home. What else do you have to do? People who need jobs are beating down our doors. They'd be delighted with your salaries and wouldn't mind working a little overtime without pay."

"No surprise that Heenehan has a high turnover rate," Jim said.

Brad held out a piece of paper. "Send out a group email with a link to this flyer for next week's mandatory anti-harassment training."

Jim turned and left.

Beth took the sheet and moved toward the door.

Brad slung his left arm over the back of his chair. He flicked his eyes from her head to her feet, and winked at her with a boyish grin. "You're a smart girl. Some of us are going over to the sports bar at the strip mall after work. Would you care to join us?"

"No thanks. I'd be a fish out of water in that bar."

"Then some other time."

"No, Brad."

"When are you going to find yourself a man? You'd look nicer if you learned to smile."

"You're beyond offensive."

"I'm paying you a compliment."

Beth spotted a printout of her email summarizing the audit issues lying on the floor. She laid it on his desk in front of him. When she turned to leave, Amber walked up to the doorway.

"I called you because we have business to discuss," Brad said.

Beth closed the door to Brad's office.

Jim was waiting for her. Behind the door, they listened in on the conversation, inaudible except for Brad's words, "Private equity" and "Do you get it?"

Walking to their cubicles, Beth said, "Never leave me alone with that hound dog. He makes my skin crawl."

"Don't worry, I won't. I've heard he can be overly familiar. I stayed right outside his door." *The creep saw me watching him.*

"Anyway, we're more prepared for this audit than he'll ever be. We can handle the meeting."

"I agree, but it's Brad's job to keep us out of the ditch with the auditors," Jim said.

"And this man is still a manager?"

"Katie told me Brad knows more about telecom taxes than anyone in the company," Jim said. "A few years ago he was a rising star, a front runner for the senior director of tax position."

"Hard to believe."

"Brad and his wife were front and center at lavish company events. Then Scott turned on Brad. Publicly contradicted everything he said. Bigfooted him out of the way in important company deals. They were like two cats in a bag."

"Office politics is such a hornet's nest," Beth said.

"Scott finagled around with the higher-ups and persuaded them to demote Brad. Now Brad reports to Scott. A perfect takedown job. Despite his thick skin, at some point Brad gave up. Anyone who supports Brad risks the Scott buzzsaw treatment. And our hard work is making those two banty roosters rich."

"So Brad's on the back nine of his career at Heenehan. I suppose he'll be leaving, taking his decades of experience with him."

"Scott's the director of strategic planning," Jim said. "He knows next to nothing about tax. He's growing his own empire, bumping managers, and taking over departments. Scott's a power player. Breaks people and destroys their reputations. He has no sense of the common good."

"Brad signs off on anything that anyone puts in front of him. He's let some doozies slip through. If he left the company, it would be weeks before anyone realized he was gone for good and not on vacation."

"After the dirty politics Scott played on Brad, the tax group couldn't care less. They're just going through the motions, despite Judy's bullying."

They passed a printer making a grunting, pig-like noise.

Beth said, "Scott has a rock-bottom opinion of Principal Processing. So Brad hired us from Principal. And he hired Amber, the rotten apple. Scott's going to inherit all three of us."

"Brad probably knows nothing about Amber's double life. Maybe he suspected the Tech Team was up to no good and deliberately sicced them on Scott with that consulting contract. Scott obviously likes Amber. Brad's going to get the last laugh. Our careers don't figure into their gamesmanship. Hey, you look beat."

"I'm completely exhausted in every possible way. All day yesterday I fought an overwhelming sensation of warm water washing over me, despite the ice-cold office. I couldn't keep my eyes focused, like someone sprayed my cubicle with chloroform. I bought an energy drink and forced myself to keep going. Driving home last night, I pulled out in front of a car. Almost caused a wreck. Even with Tom's help, I'll have to work every weekend to meet my deadlines."

Jim swatted at a fly. "I hear you. Last month, the IRS mailed me a standard twenty-day notice. I was so busy, I didn't realize the letter had arrived until after the twenty-day deadline passed. Technically, that makes Heenehan responsible for the entire amount assessed, about eight times the amount we actually owe."

"Good grief."

"It's unlikely the IRS will enforce the assessment, but it's embarrassing," Jim said. "Clearing it up will be time-consuming." His phone vibrated. "It's a message about Mom. She fell, but Doris helped her up and she's okay. I need to call Doris."

Neat stacks of papers sat on a long conference table. Two laptop-toting auditors entered the room. Beth introduced Jim to Pam Taylor and Ron Shields.

"We're going to miss you at the women's accounting group," Pam said to Beth. "Thanks. It's always an honor to speak to the group."

They sat at the table, Jim and Beth facing the two auditors.

"I expect we won't be here long today," Ron said.

Beth said, "In each of the stacks are copies of documents for the sample period. You may take them with you. A copy of your letter is on top of each stack. I highlighted on the letters the type of document in that stack."

Jim pointed to a dozen sheets clipped together. "We provided our written procedures to explain how the tax amounts are calculated. Your temporary password will allow you to view the electronic files. You may save those files to your laptops."

Beth said, "Unfortunately, some of Heenehan's documents weren't retained. We included all the records we found that are similar to the information you requested. We believe they will be sufficient." *I've never been so unprepared for an important audit.*

"Many thanks," Pam said. "So well-organized. Ought to speed the process considerably. We'll stick around here for a couple hours and try to make some progress before heading out."

Ron took the first stack. "We'll send you a preliminary deficiency list next week. You'll have two weeks to review the worksheets. We'll schedule a meeting to discuss our assessment. For any disputed items, please have your backup documentation ready."

Jim said, "We can set up a time for you to review the accounting and billing systems if needed. Call or email us if any issues arise."

Walking back to their cubicles, Beth said to Jim, "I'm not confident about those documents."

"We needed more time to do a thorough review of Heenehan's records," Jim said. "Let's hope the auditors find what we gave them acceptable."

Jim rose from his desk, walked to Beth's cubicle door, and said, "I want to show you something. Stop by when you have a—whoa! Did you make that?"

Beth was pinning a large rectangular mosaic to her cubicle wall. "I couldn't sleep last night. My mind was running through my to-do list, prioritizing tasks and working out steps to get each assignment done. I finally got up. I cut a few sheets of colored construction paper into pieces, and this arrangement took shape. The blue-gray tones are muted enough for a professional office. The light yellow and peach give it energy." She stood back to examine it. "What do you think?"

"Impressive. Lines are intersecting with squares and circles, and everything is so precise."

"Thanks! I want to make more designs in different media." *This mosaic would be interesting in shades of blue with rugged textures.*

"You could create a series and display it as a collection of related works of art."

"I'd love to do that. You wanted to show me something?"

In Jim's cubicle, Beth moved the guest chair next to him.

Swatting at a fly buzzing in front of his computer screen, Jim pointed to cells on a spreadsheet. "Last month's tax payments in the accounting system are significantly larger than the tax I paid."

He called to Brad, walking down the hallway. Brad ambled over to Jim's cubicle.

"We're trying to understand the gap between the tax I paid and the tax that was paid according to the accounting system —"

"Yep, yep, yep. Quantify it."

"I already quantified it."

"I want you to reconcile the last two years' tax accounts to the general ledger and email it to me in an hour."

"You know that project will take a week."

Moving toward the hall, Brad fixed them with a dead expression. "You two are putting out more work than anybody else in this group, as I expected from Principal employees. You can handle it. Tell me if the workload is too much." He left Jim's cubicle.

Beth glanced at Jim, then did a double take. "Are you okay?"

Jim sat with his head bent forward.

"Hey, what's going on?"

"I'm dizzy. Electric shocks going through my head. Like pop rocks."

"Take deep breaths." *I don't know what's happening to Jim or how to help.*

Jim closed his eyes, forcing breath in and out. After a few moments, he opened his eyes. "I get what's called brain zaps."

"Brain zaps?"

"It's a small seizure, like lightning or a strobe light flashing. It happens every time I reduce my medication. It's worse when I'm stressed. I'm slowly tapering off the Prozac and Adderall, so the zaps aren't so severe. I'll put up with them however long it takes."

"What does your support group say about those brain zaps?"

"They describe their own unpleasant experiences that resemble mine. They tell me to keep decreasing my doses little by little." Jim took another slow, deep breath. "I'm normal now."

"That seems like good advice. You should find a quiet, private place when your symptoms are coming on. Legally, you're allowed reasonable accommodations for recovery from a substance use disorder."

"That wouldn't go over well at Heenehan."

"I have to agree with you. I'm sorry."

"The energy drink I gulped down on my way to work hit me like rocket fuel. Along with taking the Adderall, my anxiety level went into the stratosphere. Last night I told Mom about the police report we filed on the woman. She came uncorked and shouted, 'Leave the police out of our business!'"

"Rose is not well."

"Mom wants to buy a gun for protection."

"A gun!" Beth lowered her voice. "You need to find 24-hour care for Rose NOW."

"I need to be on solid ground financially before I consider memory care. Something will open up for me at Analytics."

"You could quit this job and file for unemployment benefits until Elly hires you."

"And risk months of unemployment in this economy? I wouldn't be able to support Mom at home, let alone at an expensive facility."

"I see your dilemma."

"A new office might be worse than Heenehan. You wouldn't be there. I'd have to navigate it on my own. Every workplace is political, cliquey, and complicated. There are social hierarchies and shifting rival factions. It's easy to get lost in the corporate corn maze. I'm not going to water down my commitment to Mom just because my job is uncomfortable."

"Our jobs are beyond uncomfortable," Beth said. "We're drowning in deep water."

"Did you report the Tech Team to the FBI Internet Crime Complaint Center?"

"I included every detail. An automated response said my complaint is under review and that it will be forwarded to the appropriate law enforcement agency."

"Thanks. You made them aware of the Tech Team's subterfuge. We've done everything we can."

"Jim, we can't pretend Heenehan isn't affecting us. We fixate on our work like robots, walling off the craziness coming at us from every direction, so we can survive day-to-day. We're disengaging from our surroundings, cutting ourselves off from our natural range of emotions. We're becoming different people. Know what I mean?"

"I used to imagine a two-inch thick plastic coating all over my body. A trick of mind to keep Dad's brutality bouncing off me. If he detected any reaction, it made his day. I'm imagining that plastic casing around me again. Old reflexes clicking in. It's not healthy, no two ways about it."

"I don't want to turn into a shell of a person, closed off and shut down. We're becoming unwell here, priding ourselves on our thick skin."

"You're free to walk, Beth. You can live off savings and pay for health insurance until your Social Security and Medicare kick in."

"I'm here as long as you are. I'm not going anywhere."

"Then be careful, for God's sake. The situation here is serious."

"I will. You don't have to tell me."

"Another thing. This morning the test results from the toxicologist came back. The substance on my window was antifreeze. Amber poisoned Hannah."

"I knew it! That ruthless savage! Thank goodness little Hannah recovered. Keep her safe." *I wish I could grab that green hair and hurl Amber into outer space.*

"I'm keeping my basement window closed and locked," Jim said. "The officer at the station added the toxicologist's information to my report. Calls reporting vandalism and suspicious people prowling around a property aren't their top priority. They'll investigate it when officers are available."

"Now I lock my doors and windows, even when I'm home on nice days," Beth said. "I never go out after dark. I keep my window shades closed, so I'm not being watched from the outside. Noises startle me. I imagine Amber breaking in, creeping around inside my house. It's hard to sleep."

Jim said, "Yesterday evening a woman who resembled Amber passed by my house. I almost jumped out of my skin! It was my neighbor, out for a walk."

On his way home from work, Jim stopped at an electronics store and browsed through various surveillance monitors. He evaluated their quality, field of view, storage space, and other features. For his home, he selected an outdoor security camera. For his work cubicle, he chose a small, black desk clock with a wireless camera, motion detector, and a built-in night vision device.

When he arrived home, he downloaded the clock's camera app onto his phone. He made a trip back to the office, set up the clock, and tested it.

After returning home, he checked on his mother and retreated to his basement bedroom. He connected his laptop to his work computer. He downloaded reports to his laptop and emailed them to Tom, who replied that the returns will be ready in the morning. He continued working remotely from his laptop on his work computer screen.

Wanting to play, Hannah jumped on Jim's desk. She rolled on her back, then tapped his hand with her paw. Jim ignored her sharp claws poking his skin. Jim's fingers moved briskly over the keyboard.

After a few minutes, Hannah yawned, lay on her side, extended her hind legs, and closed her green eyes. Jim ran his right hand over her fur and continued typing. Late into the night, he worked to the rhythm, cadence, and tempo of the data flowing through his wireless speakers.

The tip of Hannah's tail twitched. Dissonant noise replaced musical elements. Toolbars containing unfamiliar icons appeared on the screen. Jim deleted the alien toolbars. They reappeared. Task manager showed odd programs executing in the background. *This is bizarre.* Jim deleted the toolbars again, restarted his computer, and reconnected to the network. The toolbars came up on the screen.

The mouse pointer on his screen came alive, moving between folders, making selections. The accounting system opened. Each tax payable amount increased by 3 percent. Ledger Bank's website opened. The total amount of the increase transferred from Ledger Bank to an international bank. The cursor continued to open files and close them. *Who is doing this to me?*

Jim checked his anti-malware, firewall, and antivirus software. All disabled. *Did intruders seize my work computer, not expecting me to be online at this late hour?* Jim shut down his computer for the night. *It's too late to phone Andy. I'll contact him tomorrow.* He slept restlessly. Hannah crouched on her paws next to him, tail close to her body.

Chapter 9: Thursday, May 11

"You don't look fully charged this morning," Beth said.

"I'm tired to the bone." Jim pointed to the new toolbars on his computer screen and described the money transfer.

"No one here could have gained entry to your computer. Your screen locks automatically when it's idle for ten minutes. You always shut down your computer when you go home. You memorized your network password. That's baffling."

Alarm crept into Jim's voice. "I want to find out if the virus has hit every computer. And who's on the other end."

"My computer screen is normal. I haven't heard anyone else complain about those issues."

"So it's only my computer that's affected. Ledger Bank would probably deny money was stolen because it would bring their reputation into question. Someone in the treasury department will see my new toolbars and the money transfer, and blame me."

"You'd be in big trouble," Beth said. "Bank fraud is a federal crime with serious consequences."

"I figured something was bound to happen, so I went shopping." He touched his clock.

"Your new clock complements your desk accessories. Nice."

"It has a motion-detector camera. Last night it recorded videos to my phone." Jim pushed a button on his phone. A shadowy image of Kessie came into view. She rifled around Jim's desk, shoved a five-dollar bill and a burgundy pen into her purse, and ducked out of his cubicle. "I suspected

Kessie was making her rounds searching for cash. I marked that five with a red circle."

"It should turn up in one of Kessie's stashes of bills. With her money troubles, I can't say I'm surprised. Her grandkids like the pens."

"The next video is time-stamped about an hour after Kessie left." The screen showed Hwan logging into Jim's computer, then tapping at the keyboard. After a half hour, he logged out and left. "How did Hwan get my password? I'm going to enlarge the text on the camera's screen so I can watch what he did."

"Where is Security? Anyone could be roaming around this building at night. I'm surprised Kessie and Hwan didn't bump into each other." She swatted at a fly. "Are you keeping a pet fly in your cubicle?"

"That fly's been pestering me for a few days, following me everywhere I go. I've been slapping it at home. It must be from that otherworldly mess in Amber's cubicle."

Beth back-handed the fly circling her face. "It looks peculiar." She unscrewed the top of a glass jar containing paper clips and emptied them onto Jim's desk. Jumping up, she caught the fly in the jar in midair, covered the jar with her palm, and screwed the lid on.

They examined the fly.

"It moves like a house fly, about the same size," Beth said. "It's weird, like a miniature helicopter. It doesn't have wings, it has spinning rotors."

"What the—oh lord, a drone! With a mounted video camera."

Beth turned the jar for a better look. "How would a drone get here?"

"Good question. China and North Korea have been using fly drones for surveillance for years. If it lands on you and attaches to your skin or clothes, you'll take it home with you. Which apparently I did." *Damn fly has been transmitting everything I said and did for who knows how long.* Jim put the jar containing the fly into a paper sack, put the sack in his desk drawer, and locked the drawer. "I'll give this one to Andy to disable. He can help us figure it all out."

Judy was waiting for Jim and Beth when they arrived at the conference room. As they took their seats, Judy blew out an alcohol-tinged breath. She tilted her head back, peering at them with lowered eyebrows.

"Judy, we believe there is a serious breach in company security," Jim said. "My computer has new toolbars—"

"IT regularly updates our computers. Do NOT bother IT with your petty issues. They are very busy." Judy pulled herself up from the chair.

"IT isn't moving my cursor," Jim said.

"Of course they are! IT overrides the mouse. I thought you wanted to meet with me about something important." She slammed the door shut.

"I'm done with General Stump," Jim said.

Jim and Beth waited for Scott Campbell outside his half-open office door that was next to a silver nameplate on the wall engraved "Director of Strategic Planning."

Behind his cherry wood desk, Scott leaned back in his black leather chair, chatting with George Weston, director of treasury, who sat across from him. Scott was playing with his pen when the cap came off and the spring shot into the air. "Reminds me of my last golf game." They erupted in loud guffaws.

George said, "I'm working with HR for a stricter policy on vacation time for managers and below. I don't know how Brad's going to take it. He likes his vacations."

"Don't worry about Brad. He's off the playing field. Tighten up your department's vacation time, and lay off one of your staff people."

"We need more staff people, not fewer."

"You've got dead wood over there," Scott said. "I told Corabell we didn't need all three slackers from Principal. She picked one and canned his ass. Tom something. I snagged a nice bonus for the cost saving. I'm going to do the same with my other groups."

Beth backed away from the door. *We struggle to keep our heads above water, so Scott can collect another bonus for eliminating Tom. That monster! I'd pay money to see Corabell lay off Scott the way she did to Tom.*

Jim slid Scott's nameplate out of its wall mount. Breaking it into four unequal pieces, he placed each piece back into the holder, like a jigsaw puzzle.

Scott and George analyzed sports teams. "Spring practice games went great," Scott said. "If our defense can blitz the quarterbacks, the passers can throw bombs like they did last year, and we can blow away any opponent."

George said, "We're prepared for mortal combat."

They reviewed the office women. "I like girly girls," George said. "That sweet Sue's a cutie."

"I prefer exotic types," Scott said. "Like steamy Amber and brown sugar Shontae."

"It's a good thing we're gentlemen."

Beth gazed at the hall ceiling. *Paragons of gender equality and diversity.*

Scott checked his smartwatch. "I have a meeting in five minutes. Good talking with you." George left, and Scott dashed out his office door.

Jim called out, "Scott! We need to talk to you!"

"No time."

"It's urgent!" Beth said.

Scott darted down the hallway.

Jim turned to Beth. "Now we know why Tom disappeared. I give up on Heenehan. I've had it."

"I'm with you. If Scott even pretended to listen, he'd blame us. With no functional HR department, we'd be the ones in hot water. They've got us muzzled."

"Heenehan's like a broken-down old car. If someone sabotaged it, you'd never notice."

Beth pointed to a purple folder in a half-opened credenza drawer behind Scott's desk. "Is that the file Sue said she lost and told you to recreate?"

Jim pulled out the folder. "That's the one." He walked into the hall with it under his arm, opened it, and flipped through it. Beth followed him. "The vendor list is here. Two more documents are behind it."

"Are they important?" Beth asked.

Jim scanned the sheets. "A memo from IT recommends steps needed to prevent a cyberattack. The next one is a contract to review Heenehan's tax systems, signed by Mark Humphrey and Li Chang. It says Chang's an independent contractor."

"Someone deliberately hid those two documents behind the vendor list."

"I'm going to make copies. I'll ask Andy to take a look at them and our fly drone."

Jim copied the vendor list and the two documents. He put the copies in the purple folder. Returning to Scott's office, he placed the folder into its spot in the credenza drawer.

From his own desk drawer, Jim pulled out Amber's contract with Li Chang that Tom gave him in the file room.

He placed it on top of the IT memo and the contract to review the tax system. He slipped the three documents into a manila envelope. Taking the envelope and the sack containing the jar with the fly drone, he walked to Andy's desk in the IT department. "Would you check out these papers and disable the thing in this bag? Please don't tell anyone who gave them to you. And there's an issue with strange toolbars on my computer screen I want to run by you."

Andy was putting his personal possessions into a cardboard box sitting in the middle of his desk. He took the envelope and sack from Jim, setting them in the box.

"Why are you packing up? Did you get fired?" Jim asked.

"Nope! I resigned. You're looking at the new systems administrator for Analytics Telco. I've been working with Mike and Elly for a few weeks. I'm ready to hit the ground running."

"Wow! Congrats, Andy!"

"Thanks! When I'm back home from the park, I'll check out your items. I promised Sneakers and Max a trip to the park to play Frisbee. Our little celebration. I'll head over to my new office this afternoon. I'll call you then."

Amber trembled with fury. "Hwan, you yellow-skinned dummy! What's your only job? To write the code. It didn't happen 'cause Hwan freaking Cho didn't do it."

At the head of the conference table, Li Chang said, "Stop it. We do not use racist language on our team. Did you notice both Hwan and I are of Asian descent?"

"Yes, sir."

Hwan shouted at Amber, "You think I do nothing all day but sit on my ass! I am going to scream! I put on code so you can do anything in bank computers. Why I need finish this today? It not matter. I get everything done by three o'clock tomorrow."

"Write the code to connect Heenehan's system with Wong Tel's. How hard is that? You shape up, or you're a dead man."

"Right, right, right." Hwan made the sourest face possible, stuck out his tongue, and duck-walked out the door and down the hall.

Hearing their voices while on an errand, Katie Stanton stopped outside the door.

"Amber, do not threaten Hwan," Chang said. "The mistakes aren't all his fault. You don't belong in a corporate tax department any more than he does. Your behavior in the tax group has been excessively disruptive. I'm ordering you to dial it way down."

Amber spoke softly. "Li, I got the tax department under control. Once Hwan installs the code, we can haul ass." *Without Hwan ching chong Cho.*

"He must do his work correctly, so we can record our keystrokes and take our screenshots properly."

"Hwan's gonna do it right. It don't help that Boris and Natasha here have trouble with their English."

"You have trouble with your own English. I'm surprised Myra at Ledger Bank gave you the passwords. Your email to her was incomprehensible."

"I can talk better'n I can write. I got Sue and Kessie to take a bunch of my work. Now I can get more stuff done for our team. I better get my butt back down there." *Lighten up, slave-driver.*

Chang glowered at Amber. "If Hwan doesn't connect Heenehan's network to Wong Tel's, Ludmila and Spartak will have to do it. You will suffer the consequences if that happens. It's easier for Hwan than for them."

Amber threw the door open, unaware of Katie behind it, who caught it as it was swinging before it hit her. Following Amber to Hwan's tax department cubicle, Katie stopped in the corridor, pretending to read a document.

Amber hovered over Hwan, who was sitting before a computer in the cubicle behind Jim's. "You stupid little runt," Amber hissed. "What do you have to say for your sorry loser self?"

Hwan squinted his eyes and twisted his face. "So I make mistake. Easy fix. Take few minute. I do that after Jim leave tonight."

Katie returned to her desk in the finance group.

"Hey, Jim, it's Katie. Meet me on the far side of the pond and bring Beth. I overheard the fourth-floor gang talking crazy."

Fish created ripples in the surface of the pond, causing it to sparkle in the sun.

When Jim and Beth arrived, Beth shaded her eyes with her hand. *I wish I could work out here where it's warm.* "So Katie, you're saying the Tech Team can log into Ledger Bank's system? And Hwan is going to connect Heenehan's computer network with Wong Tel's?"

"Hwan said he would connect the two networks tonight. If Hwan doesn't get it done, Chang will tell Ludmila and Spartak to make the connection. You know how Hwan is."

Jim said, "No wonder my reports don't agree with accounting. Ludmila and Spartak are messing with Heenehan's bank accounts."

"I reported the Tech Team to the FBI Internet Crime Complaint Center," Beth said. "I thought an agent would have contacted me by now." *What are they waiting for?*

"I'm going to call Andy," Jim said. "I'll fill him in. Thanks for telling us about this, Katie."

"You're welcome. You'd think these spies would be more careful. They're behaving like they're in a cone of silence, talking out loud about their private business, assuming nobody hears them."

In a huddle room, Jim dialed his phone. "Hi, Andy. How's it going at Analytics?"

"Great so far. There's room for the future IT division right next to my office. But there's a major issue. Someone connected Heenehan's network to Analytics. I can monitor everything going on in Heenehan's system. In addition to Tom, two others are using your password, working at the same time. I've informed Elly."

"Weird toolbars are on my work computer and I can't delete them. The accounting system shows too much tax due. I paid the correct amount."

Andy said, "The hackers inflated the tax payable in the accounting system. You paid the right amount. They paid themselves the difference."

"I tried to tell Brad the account reconciliation is way off. Katie overheard some inside information. Myra at Ledger Bank provided Heenehan's passwords to Amber. She gave them to Hwan, who put a code in the bank's system. The Tech Team's inside the bank's network."

"Oh, Lord. Is anyone at Heenehan aware of any of this?"

"Oh come on, Andy, you're throwing softballs. It's Heenehan. Those transfers are small enough that no alarms go off. They appear to be normal transactions. Ledger Bank would be reluctant to admit to a breach. Amber is enabling the Tech Team hackers to do their work."

"The toolbars on your computer make it look like you're the enabler, Jim."

"I hope you don't believe that, Andy."

"Of course I don't. But some people at Heenehan would. You need to document all of it. You've got a lot of career left. If this goes to the state labor board, you'll need a good defense."

"Beth and I are documenting everything. Our written history should clear us in any legal proceeding."

"Good."

"I've been reviewing last year's financials in depth," Jim said. "The execs' pay packages are draining the company's revenue. Reserves are low. The asset values on the balance sheet are wildly overstated. Most of the technology and equipment are obsolete."

"Elly and Mike met with Mark Humphrey. He's exploring plans to sell Heenehan's assets to Analytics and close Heenehan. Merging the two companies' networks may or may not ever happen. At this point, their networks shouldn't be connected."

"Beth and I believe those three system auditors are foreign hackers connected to the Chinese and Russian governments. Beth reported the Tech Team to the FBI Internet Crime Complaint Center. Did you get the fly drone and the three documents I gave you?"

"Your drone can't spy anymore because I tore it down," Andy said. "Your documents are here with me. Humphrey declined to sign off on IT's plan to secure the network. We told him it was critical. He refused to increase staff size or authorize paid overtime because IT is over budget this year. His decision was the last straw that convinced me to resign from Heenehan and accept the job offer from Analytics."

"Why would Humphrey approve of hiring Chang's group?"

"Chang claimed the state requires a system review. He promised to find mistakes in past tax returns that would result in sizable refunds. Amber got Brad to persuade Humphrey to sign the standard contract."

"I've never seen Mark Humphrey in person. Once I saw him on a screen from a distance."

"I've been on one conference call with him. Hold on a minute. Something's happening to the network. I'll call you back."

Jim's cell phone rang several minutes later. "That was close. Someone connected Analytics' and Heenehan's networks to Wong Tel's in China. I caught it right away and broke the links. We were connected for a couple minutes, not long enough for any real harm. I reconfigured the systems so it'll be difficult for them to reconnect. I'm meeting with Elly in about five minutes."

"Andy, Katie told us Hwan was supposed to connect Heenehan's computer network with Wong Tel's. If Hwan didn't get it done, Chang said Ludmila and Spartak would do it. They must have connected the networks a few minutes ago. You broke the connection."

"Damn! I'm sure those two Russians did it. Wong Tel's in league with the Russian and Chinese governments. That company allows cybercriminals to use their networks. Wong Tel's trying to connect with established U.S. networks."

"The Tech Team's squatting on Heenehan's network through the toolbars on my computer," Jim said. "I secured it the best I could. I changed my password. If I unplugged my computer, they'd wait for me to sign in on another one or attack someone else's. They may be installing their malware on Ledger Bank's network, or scoping out the utilities— the electric, gas, and water systems—from Heenehan's network. They're nosing around in all the systems they can hack into."

"I strongly suggest you watch your back, Jim. The Tech Team is arranging the arrows to point to you."

Amber let herself into the fourth-floor conference room. "I got your text, Li. Do you—"

A sharp, open-handed smack stung her face. Ludmila and Spartak winced.

Amber regained her balance, rubbing her cheek. *I don't get it. Li turns totally mean, out of nowhere.* "What was that for? The team's in Ledger Bank's systems."

"Guess."

"Hwan didn't connect Heenehan's network to Wong Tel's. I'll make the lazy moron do it!"

"Too late. Ludmila and Spartak did it. Wong Tel started receiving Heenehan's data. A few seconds later it unlinked. Whoever broke the connection fixed Heenehan's network so it will be nearly impossible for Wong Tel to reconnect."

"I'm sorry, Li. I'll make Hwan do anything you need."

"Forget about Hwan. He isn't reliable. Cut him loose. Leave him alone."

"I got him on a short leash."

"I mean it, Amber."

"Yes, sir." *Like, in another life.*

"And stay away from Jim Dennis and Beth Madison. I asked you to eliminate them. You didn't make it happen. That's a black mark on your record."

"I won't bother them no more." *Yeah, right.*

"Hello, Beth. This is Pam Taylor. I'm sorry to tell you our audit has come to a temporary halt. The backup you gave Ron is deficient. We need more detail."

"Heenehan's staff filed those returns before Jim and I were hired. We did the best review we could in our limited time. Would you please give us more time to examine the records?"

"Of course. I was just a little surprised the work wasn't up to your standards."

"I'm disappointed, too, Pam. I take full responsibility. I'll get back to you as quickly as I can."

Despite the cold office air, Beth felt her face flush.

"Thanks, Beth."

Beth peered into Jim's cubicle. "Jim, Pam called. What are you doing?"

Bent over his desk drawer, Jim was working at it with a flathead screwdriver. "Amber glued my drawer shut again." The drawer popped open. He sat in his chair.

"Pam Taylor called me. The audit backup is deficient. Pulling an all-nighter is out of the question. Penalties could run into the millions."

"Our only option is to put Heenehan's state audit on the back burner."

"I agree, we simply don't have the resources," Beth said. "Katie Stanton called me. She resigned from Heenehan. She's happily working as Elly Burke's admin at Analytics Telco. Shontae's going over there, too." *I'd celebrate if I were going with them.*

"Good for them! We should call Elly."

"A second-floor huddle room is usually vacant."

They found the empty room along a hall, which was dimly lit due to cost-cutting measures.

Elly answered. "Hey, good to hear from you! How are you guys doing?"

"Could be better," Beth replied.

"We're okay, taking one day at a time," Jim said. "Heenehan has problems."

"Katie gave me the story. Andy's keeping me updated on the system's issues. He showed me the drone fly he disassembled. It's in pieces on his desk. The situation's bizarre."

"Beth and I believe Heenehan's network has been compromised. We tried to report it to our supervisor, manager, and director. We haven't had success in getting our voices heard."

"That's not what you need from management. The system's issues are affecting both our companies."

"We're staying in contact with Andy," Jim said.

"Good. Andy's working on countermeasures. The internet is never 100 percent secure."

"How are you doing?" Beth asked Elly.

"I'm fine. It's great having Katie here to help us figure it all out. Surprises every day. Lots of curveballs. We're building Analytics on Principal's foundation into a technologically advanced company. We've already had dozens of inquiries. We'll bring more of our Principal colleagues on board when we can. Our new sales and marketing manager's a busy man, Seb Medina."

"I know Seb!" Jim said. "How's he working out for you?"

"He's a dynamo and is already up to speed. Tom Shuler recommended him."

"Seb's a good guy. Beth and I ran into Tom here in the hall."

"Tom told me he talked with you. I admit this is an irregular situation. Heenehan won't miss the file boxes. We're using them here for setup. Heenehan's customers go through complicated requirements to terminate their service before they can move to Analytics. We're helping them with that."

"We're concerned about Tom's activities at Heenehan," Jim said. "We hope they're short-lived. When will you set up a tax department?"

"Before we can proceed with our plans, we need more robust financing. Mike and I used money from our personal savings, and we raised a few hundred thousand in seed money. Right now we're pursuing additional funding."

"It must be tough working on fundraising while you're in the middle of building the business." Beth said. *Speed it up, Elly!*

"We met with a representative from Chonko Capital Partners. Chonko offered to invest $2 million for 30 percent of the equity of Analytics."

"I've heard rumors about Chonko," Jim said.

"On the plus side, Chonko would give Analytics respectability, strong financial backing, and publicity. They'd provide us the funding in a matter of days. After three years, Chonko would sell their investment, expecting a high return. It's the best offer the market will deliver for a risky start-up," Elly said.

"They sound ideal," Beth said.

"But we don't like them," Elly said. "Chonko has a reputation for running the show. They demand board seats, veto critical decisions, and oust the start-ups' founders. They micromanage companies in ways that don't reflect those company's values."

Jim said, "You can do better."

"The execs are big-ego people who love to hear themselves talk. It could be a full-time job for Mike to manage Chonko. Their objective is to sell the company or take it public. High returns for their investors always triumph over any personal relationships."

"With Chonko in charge, Analytics' standards would suffer," Beth said. *If Elly and Mike decide on Chonko, I'll never work there. I know someone else who might help. I wish I could remember his name. Alan something.*

"Mike suspects Chonko would solicit a mature or declining company like Heenehan to buy Analytics. An old-line company would thwart Analytics' growth with their obsolete assets, advertising costs, and financial obligations."

"I agree," Jim said.

"At Analytics, we value innovation. We want to increase our market share of dark fiber, the network that's not yet being used. We share our videos to publicize our products and services online. With our minimal advertising budget, we reach millions of people globally. We can sell telecom services for a fraction of the cost of established telecom companies and still make a healthy profit."

"I'm a future customer," Jim said.

"So Mike's going to decline Chonko's offer. But we need more money to start hiring staff."

"Elly, do you remember Alan Pennington?" Beth asked. "An officer of Principal Processing who retired a few years ago. Alan owns his own company, and he's doing well. He might consider being an angel investor for Analytics."

"I hadn't considered Alan. Thanks for the tip! I'll give him a call. We do need tax people. I'll let you know right away when we're ready to hire."

"Thanks, Elly," Beth said. "Let us know when the new positions open."

"Keep in touch, guys. Talk to you soon."

"While we're here, let's call Katie." Jim dialed his phone. "Hey, Katie, this is Jim. Beth is here in the room with me. We talked to Elly. She's going to contact us when the tax positions open."

"That's great! I like it here. Everything's moving so fast, I can hardly keep up. I miss you. Hey, there's something I need to tell you. Before I left, I saw Hwan on the fourth floor past the security doors that take a smartcard for entry.

Tom can make you a master badge card. It'll give you access to Heenehan's building and all its rooms." Katie recited Tom's cell phone number.

"Thanks, Katie, we'll give Tom a call," Beth said. *I'm not going to ponder the ethics. It's a gray area.*

"You're welcome. Catch you later."

"Hi, Tom. It's Jim, and Beth is here. We can't thank you enough for helping out with our returns. You're a lifesaver."

"No problem."

"Our check's in the mail. I'll send you reports for another set of returns due this week. Okay with you?"

"Sure. Happy to help."

"Tom, Katie suggested we ask you for master security badge cards. Can you do that?"

"Of course. I'll print a couple of barcode ID cards. I can meet you at four on the block west of the Heenehan office park."

"We'll be there."

Chapter 10: Friday, May 12

Brad sat behind his desk, head down, eyes closed.

Jim said, "We need your input on the state audit."

Brad raised his head. "Make it quick. I have to jump on a call in a few minutes."

"Your opinion please. The state tax auditors are pummeling us with questions. We have options, maybe some negotiating room."

"We don't negotiate. Our strategy is to catch the flippin' auditors off balance. We go after their weaknesses, and we get everything we want."

Jim talked faster. "The backup we provided to the auditors for the last two years is deficient. The billing and accounting reports don't match the tax returns. The auditors can't reconcile them. We were working at Principal when Sue filed those returns."

"So what do you want me to do about it?"

Beth said, "You must have some insight as to what happened and how to proceed."

"No, I don't. You handle it. That's why you're paid the big bucks."

"Big bucks, right," Jim said. "Heenehan's inventory records are incomplete. The auditors will count the computers and estimate the tax. Beth and I plan to offer to pay the entire amount of interest in exchange for—"

"We never pay interest. Never."

"—in exchange for the auditors reducing the historical cost."

"I want you both to step away from the state audit."

"What?"

A sly look crossed Brad's face. "Amber will take over the state audit."

"Be serious," Jim said. "One misstep could cost the company millions."

"Tell Amber to notify the auditors there was a staff change. Give her all your documentation. Have her take it from there."

Jim and Beth walked out of Brad's cubicle.

"He's lost to reason," Beth said.

"Brad's sticking it to Scott every way he can," Jim said. "Amber's going to create a holy mess, leaving Scott to deal with it."

"Turning our work over to Amber won't reflect well on us. Brad's throwing us under the bus for his last-ditch revenge on Scott."

Scrolling through vacation websites on her computer, Amber made a slight jump when two figures appeared in her peripheral vision. Jim and Beth set stacks of papers on the side of her desk.

"Brad ordered us to turn the state audit over to you," Beth said. "Here are the documents. We provided copies to Pam Taylor and Ron Shields. Brad wants you to tell them you're now their official contact."

"I'll get right on it."

Beth stepped backward onto a soft lump and recoiled. "Amber! A dead mouse is lying on the floor next to your desk!"

Amber lifted the mouse by the tail and flung it into the corner wastebasket. "No big deal. Are you done?"

Jim edged toward the door. "I'll email you the file folder they reviewed."

"Do anything you want. I ain't workin' on no state audit. I'm busy with Mr. Chang."

Beth spoke from the doorway. "Amber, it's your audit! The last two years' reports don't match the tax returns. We weren't working at Heenehan during that time. Sue filed those returns. Talk to her. You need to explain them to the auditors."

"Oh, dang. You ain't smart enough to figure it out, and I don't have time." She studied a photo of a Caribbean beach on her computer screen.

Beth raised her voice. "Amber, pay attention! Serious money is at stake in this audit!"

"Fine. Good as done."

"And don't paste any of your personal photos into the auditors' documents," Jim said. "It's not professional."

"I'll just give them a pic with my big, happy smile."

As Jim and Beth were leaving at 6 p.m., Hwan turned down a hallway before the exit.

Jim whispered, "Let's follow him."

Keeping their distance, they moved silently beside walls, stopping under stairwells and behind turns in the halls. They trailed Hwan through the building's labyrinth of dusky passageways, across catwalks, up the stairs, and along corridors between clusters of cubicles.

At the end of a long hallway, Hwan took a plastic card out of his pocket and held it to a card reader. The door unlocked, and he entered. Jim and Beth waited behind a recessed wall. After several minutes, Hwan emerged from the room, and started down the hall. When he passed them, they flew at him, taking hold of his arms.

"Let me go!" Hwan struggled to break free. Jim and Beth held onto the diminutive man, moving him forward down three flights of stairs and out a door to a small plaza outside the building.

They escorted him along the walkway around the flower-lined pond. They dropped his arms, flanking him on either side, ready to restrain him if he tried to run.

The recently activated fountain in the center of the pond sprayed water high into the air. They sat on a cast iron garden bench by the pond, Hwan between Jim and Beth.

"Hwan, what are you doing?" Jim asked.

Hwan frowned. "Why you ask?"

Beth raised her voice above the fountain's falling water. "We're going to get to the bottom of your shenanigans. Who are you?"

"Maybe you help me?" Hwan talked fast. "My parents from North Korea, a bad country. They doctors. Have many patients. They flee to China. People's army make them low class. Drag out of home. Make them building cleaners and road sweepers. Whip with belts. We find out army will march to our town, burn it, send us back to North Korea. We escape."

"Slow down," Beth said. *His story is consistent with Katie's.* "How did you and your parents come to this country?"

"Friends take us at night to Bangkok. We take airplane and ferry to Hong Kong. Friends hide us on airplane to United States. They save us. Find us jobs. North Korean goon squads still follow us. My parents old, cannot fight gangs. Amber has friends in gang. I need help."

"How are you involved with Amber?"

"Horrible girl. Yah! She drive me nuts. I tell her leave us alone. She say if I not do everything she want, she tell North Korea army officer where I am. We move many time but she find us. Amber make trouble for this company. She work for that thug Chang. Call selfs Tech Team. Pfft!"

"What did Amber tell you to do?" Jim asked.

"Amber tell bank lady she need passwords to pay taxes. Amber give me passwords. She tell me put code in bank computer, so Tech Team gang can hack in. I tell Amber to code it by herself. She not know how. I made code so they cannot get past main screen. Those two Russian geeks fix it. Now they can do anything in bank."

"So the Russians gave the Tech Team access to Ledger Bank's entire network?" Jim said.

"Right. Amber make system show we pay more tax than we did pay. She send extra money to her bank overseas. Chang mad if he find out. He going to make her put it back. He mean to Amber."

Jim turned to Hwan. "The tax payable in the accounting system increased by 3 percent more than we paid. That increase was transferred to an international bank. You tell Amber to move that money back into Ledger Bank where it belongs!"

"I can tell her but she not do it."

"Did you connect Heenehan's computer network to the Wong Tel telecom company in China?" Jim asked. "There'd be terrible consequences. We won't defend you."

"I not put on bad malware like Amber told me. Instead, I connect Heenehan to Analytics Telco. I tell Amber I put on code. Amber not good with computers. She not check I did it right. Those two Russians found out. They put in code. It only link to Wong Tel for few minutes. Somebody cut it off, so code won't work. Russians going to try it again. Amber mad at me. I make her look bad."

"Can you turn off the Tech Team's access to Ledger Bank and to Analytics Telco's system?" Beth asked.

"Sure, I can. Amber will send her goons to kill me and my parents."

"We don't want that to happen, Hwan." *This mess is giving me the mother of all headaches.*

A Canada goose dove into the pond directly in front of their bench, splashed down, and raised his hindquarters above water.

Jim focused on Hwan with sharp eyes. "How are you able to write code in Heenehan's network? You can't prepare a simple tax return with the steps right in front of you."

"Do not talk to me about tax. I not have patience."

"You're in the wrong job, Hwan."

"I know that. Sandra help me get job here. You make me type numbers in computer all day. I hate you."

"I'm sorry you feel that way. What's with the drone fly?"

"Amber put fly on your desk. Tech Team launch it. Somebody else in China run it, use remote control."

"Great."

Across the pond, the office park maintenance crew turned on a noisy weed whacker.

Beth talked louder. "Why did the Tech Team pick Heenehan?"

"Heenehan easy to hack. Tech Team crooks belong here."

"Strange as they are, they do a good job of blending in," Jim said.

"They cannot do any tax. They watch how systems connect together. They figure out how everything work. Heenehan pay Tech Team to do it."

"Insane," Beth said. "Are the Chinese getting ready to blow up our systems?"

"No. North Koreans and Russians do that."

"So the Chinese are gathering intelligence."

"Chinese suck in lots of data. Drone fly took many pictures. I plant code in your computer so they can use you for a spy. You saw new toolbars? You already broadcast data to Chinese government and companies."

"So I unwittingly exposed who knows how many networks to foreign hackers," Jim said. "What does China do with the data?"

"Find trade secrets to use in their companies. Figure out how to knock out power, water, cellphones, roads, buildings, emergency systems. They can turn off everything. If war happen, they already won."

The electric trimmers buzzed more loudly as the maintenance workers moved closer.

"You're saying the Chinese are implanting code all over our country's computers to use against us?" Jim shouted. "And the Chinese plan to provide the North Koreans or the Russians a map of any system they want to strike?"

"Yeah. Tech Team do tests soon. They shut off services for short time to check their code. After Chang finish Heenehan, North Korea people come in."

Jim peered intensely at Hwan. "North Korean people are coming into Heenehan? What are they going to do?"

Hwan shrugged. "Make trouble. I cannot be here when they come. They will get me."

"How do you think we should go forward?" Jim asked Beth. "The Tech Team is a small part of a massive global organization. Heenehan's a powder keg. We may be risking our own lives."

"You're right. These people are dangerous," Beth said. "We can't stop their whole operation. Let's try a strategic maneuver, take a page from Amber, and throw them off their game." *What am I saying? I'm a tax accountant, not a CIA operative.*

Hwan crossed his arms. "You mess with Tech Team, they make life hell. I not care about any country's rulers. Tech Team make me a puppet. I do what they tell me. The government here promise me and my parents a home in different state. I want you help me stay alive until we out of here."

Jim gazed at the wispy clouds for a moment. "Hwan, this is what we will do. On my home computer, I'll write an official letter to Li Chang on Heenehan letterhead. It will say Heenehan canceled its contract with the consulting group, they must vacate the premises immediately, and if they're still here in the afternoon, they will be reported to the FBI. I'll scribble an unreadable signature at the bottom. Tonight at two-thirty, we'll meet you at my cubicle. We'll take the letter to the Tech Team's conference room on the fourth floor and put it on the table in front of Chang's chair."

"Okay. I think FBI already watching Tech Team."

"Good. Tonight before we do that, I want you to remove the toolbars you put on my computer screen. Delete the code connecting Heenehan to Analytics and any code related to Wong Tel. I won't let you or the Tech Team ruin Analytics' future. Also, delete the code that gives the Tech Team access to Ledger Bank. Can you do that?"

"Yes. Won't take long."

"Do you want to be in on this, Beth?"

"Of course. I'll be at your cubicle tonight at two-thirty." *At this point I can't tell them no.*

"How do you think this will work?"

"For a first pass, not bad," Beth said. *Unless we're fired. Or murdered.*

Hwan's expression clouded. "After we done here tonight, I want you drive me to a house. My friend help me and parents be safe until we can escape."

"We would be happy to drive you to your friend's house," Beth said.

Jim spoke to Hwan. "We'll see you tonight at two-thirty."

They stood up from the bench. Hwan dashed out of sight.

Beth looked at Jim. *What did I just agree to do?*

"We're in way over our heads," Jim said. "Heenehan is hosting a foreign power network we can't even imagine."

Behind the gritty rear entrance of the Heenehan building, Jim parked his Outback in the space on the left side of Beth's Civic. He emerged from his car and waved to Beth, who stepped out of her car. In his hand, Jim carried a manila envelope containing the letter for Li Chang. A streetlight illuminated the misty night air.

Jim's master security badge card opened the back door. Jim and Beth walked through dark corridors and down the stairway to the garden-level tax office.

Hwan was sitting at Jim's computer. "Toolbars gone."

"Let me see." Jim verified his desktop screen was back to normal. He sat on the side chair next to Hwan, who continued his work. Beth stood, observing.

"Heenehan not linked to Analytics." Hwan typed violently, moving from screen to screen. "Bank code gone." His fingers danced over the keys. "Wong Tel code gone. I remove backup, too."

"Congratulations, Hwan!" Beth clapped her hands soundlessly.

Jim gave a thumbs up. "I knew you could do it!"

"Hwan, did the Tech Team possibly save backup files that you don't know about?" Beth asked.

"Maybe."

"At least we threw a wrench into their schemes," Jim said, envelope in hand. "Let's carry the letter to the Tech Team's room upstairs."

Hwan led them through the dusky maze.

Beth walked through unfamiliar surroundings. *I have no idea where we are. Hwan knows this building better than I do.*

They ascended a stairway to the fourth floor. Upon reaching the landing, Hwan opened the door a crack. They peered out. Across the hall, a small woman with short, dark hair emerged from the conference room, holding the handle of a fluffy duster. Hwan quietly closed the door.

"In here!" Hwan whispered, pointing to a narrow door in the wall. They squeezed into the tiny broom closet.

They heard the woman walk toward the stairway, swing open the hall door, and briskly descend the flight of steps.

Beth whispered, "I can't breathe!"

When they no longer heard her footsteps, they emerged from the closet.

"Why do we need to hide from the cleaning lady?" Beth asked, gasping for air.

"She not a cleaner. She come from China, check Tech Team work. She here two, three time a week. I hide from Amber in that closet many time."

Hwan's card unlocked the Tech Team's conference room door. He pointed to the head of the table. Jim laid the envelope on the tabletop in front of Li Chang's chair. They left the room, the door locking behind them.

Leading them along the fourth-floor hall, Hwan said, "We use shortcut to back door. Watch your step!" They wended their way down a circular, narrow stairway to the ground floor. Hwan led them to a dark utility room, where he unlocked a door to the rear entrance of the building. Amber's black Mustang was parked to the left of Jim's Outback.

Beth ran to the passenger side of her Civic. "Use my car! Jim, you drive!"

Jim climbed into the driver's seat. Hwan slid into the backseat.

Amber burst through the back door, jumping into her car.

"Where's your friend's house, Hwan?" Jim shouted.

"Corner of Park and Maple."

"Fasten your seatbelts!" Jim sped around the Heenehan building toward the main exit. Speed bumps caused uncomfortable jolts. Amber raced the Mustang through the lot, passed the Civic, and blocked the exit.

Jim made a 180-degree turn with headlights off. He drove over the manicured lawn, down a curb, and onto the street.

"Go faster!" Hwan yelled.

The Civic accelerated and squealed around a corner. Jim dodged random cars, narrowly avoiding a lone runner wearing black. Traveling a chaotic route through alleys and residential neighborhoods, he ran stop signs and a stoplight. He handled Beth's light, agile Civic like a race car driver. The engine roared and belched gasoline into the air. Catching sight of Amber's car in pursuit, Jim made a violent turn. The Civic fishtailed, leaving the Mustang in a swirling cloud of dust and a smell of scorched tires. Swerving a hard left into a side street, he lost the demon Mustang.

Beth's screams were inaudible. "Slow down! We're all going to die!"

Accelerating down an affluent residential street, Jim blew through an intersection and swept over a hillcrest, tires hitting the pavement. He braked and pulled the Civic to the sidewalk in front of Hwan's friend's house.

Mist hung over the long, narrow lawn. A slender female figure with straight, shoulder-length hair opened the front door. An elderly couple stood behind a window, the woman's hands covering her mouth. Hwan flung open the car door and took off running for the house.

The Mustang pulled up behind the Civic. Amber jumped out and chased Hwan. She kicked the back of his knees, causing his leg to buckle. He fell and skidded across the grass, shrieking. Hwan shielded his head with his hands and arms as Amber kicked him.

Jim sprinted across the grass, leaped into the air, and unleashed a snap kick to Amber's backside. She hit the ground, picked up a rock, and jumped to her feet. She hurled the rock at Hwan, who was zigzagging across the grass toward the door. The rock missed his head by a few inches.

Amber turned and attempted a ferocious punch to Jim's gut. He dodged her fist and responded with a roundhouse kick that knocked her off balance. She scrambled to her feet and took off after Hwan. Jim rushed toward Amber, giving her a hard, open-handed shove. She fell face first on the damp grass, climbed to her feet, and stood unsteadily. Jim backed away.

Beth sprinted up behind Amber and yelled, "Hey!" Amber turned her head, and Beth delivered a hard swat across her cheek. Amber staggered sideways and hit the ground, shouting curses. Beth removed her left shoe and grasped the toe. With the heel, Beth whipped Amber all over her body. Amber pulled herself into a tight ball. Beth blasted Amber's ankle with a sharp kick and stomped on her foot. *I wish I'd brought my pepper spray.* Amber writhed on the ground, holding her ankle.

The woman opened the door wide and Hwan ran in. She closed the door and clicked the lock. Jim and Beth exchanged glances, having observed that Hwan's friend was Sandra Young.

Beth put on her shoe. Breathing hard, she and Jim walked to her car.

Chapter 11: Monday, May 15

After Beth arrived at work, she stopped at Jim's cubicle door. "Oh, no!" She pointed to a manila envelope on Jim's desk.

"It was sitting there when I came in this morning. The letter's inside. I assume Amber retrieved it before Chang saw it."

"Oh, dammit! Why wouldn't Amber just destroy the letter?"

"I'll tell you why. She wants us to know she's onto us. She's sticking up her middle finger at us."

"Are the toolbars back on your computer screen?" Beth asked.

"No, they're still gone."

"Well, that's good. How are you feeling?"

"Wired. And I don't feel right about roughing up Amber."

"Your self-defense techniques didn't hurt her. I'm shocked at the pent-up fury I let loose on her. We had to defend Hwan because we're decent human beings."

"Your shoe attack kept Amber under control. Where did that come from?" Jim asked.

"My sweet grandma suffered from rage bouts. She'd take off her shoe and go after anyone in her path, swatting and screaming. Back in her day, therapy and crisis hotlines weren't a thing."

"Witnessing your grandmother's attacks had to be traumatic."

"Mom was always there to protect me until Grandma wound down and the episode passed. Her shoe-swatting spells came back to me last night."

"How are you feeling?"

Beth massaged the back of her neck. "My neck's stiff. This morning I dropped off my car at the shop. It's unbalanced, like driving on a bumpy road. My mechanic's going to check it over."

"I'd be happy to drive you over there to pick it up," Jim said. "I'll help cover the repair cost. It may need a little work."

"Or a lot. Where did you learn to drive like that?" Beth asked.

"A long time ago Tom and Andy and I watched car racing videos. One night we decided to test out Andy's car. You don't want to know the rest. We were idiots."

"I'd love to hear the whole story sometime. Right now, I'm concerned about Hwan's safety. The North Koreans could easily have captured Hwan at Sandra Young's house. They must be aware he's living there."

"Sandra's house is covered with video cameras. Last night I saw small, red lights around the lenses. Kidnapping Hwan could trigger an official investigation. The North Koreans and the Tech Team want to avoid that. Sandra's untouchable."

"Makes sense," Beth said. "I don't think we should report last night's escapade. Amber's not going to inform Chang that Hwan reversed all his own work. She'll cover her bruises and scratches and brush off questions about her ankle."

"I agree. Reporting last night's incident to the authorities would open a can of worms."

Hwan sat in his assigned cubicle behind Jim's. With half-closed eyes, he entered numbers from a report onto the screen. Sue worked on a lottery pool. Kessie handed Sue a five-dollar bill with a red circle on it. Amber limped toward her cubicle, an elastic bandage taped in a figure eight around her ankle.

"Whatever happened to you?" Beth asked, returning from the file room.

Amber glared. "I missed a curb."

"Sorry if your ankle hurts like hell and swells up and turns black and blue." *You asked for it, sister.*

The phone system delivered a pre-recorded message about a transitory glitch in the network. A message from Brad Mitchell announced a staff meeting in five minutes.

Notebook in hand, Beth met Jim on the way to a second-floor conference room. They passed Sandra Young, who beckoned them with a quick hand motion. Stepping aside, they allowed the others to pass.

Sandra spoke in a low voice. "Hwan is fine. He'll be working here until the company closes, or possibly before."

"After last night, isn't it risky for Hwan to be here?" Jim asked.

"He's safe here. Security guards stay with his parents at all times. The authorities are monitoring the entire situation."

"What authorities?" Beth asked. "You mean the FBI?"

"He'll assume a new identity and relocate up north, Minnesota or North Dakota, when his sponsors are ready. I told him not to work as an accountant."

"Sandra, who's investigating this operation?" Jim asked. "Foreign powers are involved! We're in over our heads."

"I have a meeting." Sandra turned and power walked down the adjacent hall.

Brad slouched, face dusted with stubble, surveying staff members around the conference table. "I have impactful news. This morning our CEO informed us that senior management plans to sell Heenehan Telecom's assets to Analytics Telco.

Our customers will be absorbed by Analytics. Heenehan will close within a month or two."

Stricken faces gazed incredulously at him.

"You and your jobs will transfer to Analytics. Before the sale is finalized, Scott will be promoted to senior director of strategic planning. Judy and Cody will move up to tax manager. Amber and Sue will be promoted to senior tax accountant, and Kessie will be elevated to tax accountant."

Brad turned to Jim and Beth.

"Unfortunately, the former Principal Processing Company employees will be terminated at the time of the sale, in one to two months. I will write letters of recommendation for you to provide to your new employers."

"Thank you," Jim said.

Beth reflected Jim's flat tone. "We appreciate it." *What a knife in the back.*

Cody gazed at Brad with admiration. "This is a game changer."

Sitting alone at the end of the table, Hwan looked out at the maintenance crew mowing the lawn.

"At this juncture, Heenehan's core business has a low market price. After selling its assets to Analytics, Heenehan will pivot from telecom carrier to partnership with a future industry leader. What questions do you have?"

Silence.

"Our new network administrator, Gary Hudson, took over from Andy Price and will handle the systems aspects of the transition. I asked him to replace each of our standard-size computer monitors with two wide monitors. They'll give us a better view of our spreadsheets."

"We all need to cooperate fully with this important project," Judy said.

"Unfortunately, the new wide monitors aren't fully plug and play," Brad said. "The fonts will be hard to read, and the colors will have a reddish tint. To clear up the screens, IT will reformat our computers. You'll need to save all your files to the network servers to allow IT to complete their work. I understand the project will be time-consuming during the busiest time of the month, and there may be ongoing issues."

The staff members' faces sagged.

"Is this necessary?" Beth asked. "Our computers might be out of action for days. We're under tight deadlines. We don't want to incur delinquency notices and late penalties for Analytics to deal with later. Can't we keep our standard monitors?"

"No. I want all the monitors in this group to be uniform."

It won't be easy to get everything done from home. Brad is begging for a few solid whacks with my shoe.

"Corabell asked me to announce that HR will present half-day seminars in 'Wellness,' 'Good Habits to Achieve Your Goals,' and 'Change Management.' I encourage all of you to take this opportunity to advance your own personal and professional development."

"I signed up for all them classes," Amber said.

"Good for you! Today Corabell will distribute your personality tests. You will complete them and return them to her by tomorrow. Next week she will facilitate our mandatory session to discuss our profiles."

"So she can weed out the wrong people?" Sue asked.

"Of course not. You'll study the way you and the others make decisions, so you can work better as a team. It will be fun to find out your true personality type."

Judy said, "Keep in mind your profile will become a permanent document in your employee personnel file. You may choose not to share your test results with the group.

But if you do that, you are not a good fit for Heenehan's company culture."

Brad stiffened. "It is crucial that no employee makes any statement to the media. Don't talk to reporters or post comments about the company on social media. If you receive an inquiry from anyone, refer him or her to our company spokesperson who handles all information requests. Wear your company badge cards at all times. I expect every one of you to give 100 percent effort to make this a smooth transition."

In a third-floor huddle room, Jim drew crude pictures of Brad and Judy on the whiteboard. "So everyone's getting a raise and promotion, except us. They're gonna terminate us? Fine. We stop working. Fire us earlier! Why should we care? Let's quit worrying about our gazillion tax returns and audits and to-do lists and research issues and written procedures. No more pressure."

Beth leaned her elbows on the table and rested her chin in her hands. "I expect Elly will come through with jobs for us. Wouldn't she consider this a test of our professionalism? She'd expect us to stay engaged, not give up. Brad said Heenehan will be absorbed by Analytics, so we should make an effort to keep the taxes in order."

"We should call Elly."

They did, and Elly answered on the first ring. "Hey guys. Mike and I came to work this morning in the wee hours. We're slammed. Beth, thanks for the great tip! We're working out a deal with Alan Pennington to raise capital. I was just going out the door to meet my husband for lunch."

"Good luck with Alan!" Beth said.

"We had an interesting experience last night," Jim said, placing his cell phone on the conference table and lowering the volume. "Tomorrow we're going to lunch at the cafe with Andy to try to make sense of it. He'll fill you in."

"I'll touch base with Andy."

"At this morning's staff meeting, Brad told us Analytics will acquire Heenehan in about a month or two," Jim said.

Elly laughed. "Not quite. Heenehan wants us to make an offer. They're saying we need their fiber optic network for our business. At this juncture, we have no interest in acquiring Heenehan. I doubt the company could squeak through our due diligence process."

"Brad said everyone in Heenehan's tax group will be promoted. They will move over to Analytics Telco at their new level, except us," Beth said.

"Brad's misinformed. No one from Heenehan's tax department will ever set foot at Analytics Telco, I guarantee you. Mike and I are running on fumes, but we'll be here late. Can you come downtown after work for an interview at six? It won't be much longer before I can make you firm job offers."

Beth said, "We'll be there!"

"Thank you, Elly. We'll meet you at six," Jim said, ending the call.

"What are you saying, Beth? You're fried. You've got to take a breather."

"Don't be concerned about me. I'll deal with it." *Not your business, Jim.*

Jim gave her a sideways look.

"Okay, I hear you," Beth snapped. "When I see myself in the mirror, I know how I'm going to look when I'm eighty-five. Takes the guesswork right out of it."

"Setting up a tax department is not going to be a walk in the park," Jim said. "Frankly, I have a gut-punch reaction. We've been through too much here. We can't start a new job at Analytics dog-weary. We both need serious time off to rest and regain our equilibrium."

"Elly's offer sounds exciting, doesn't it? I'd love to be part of her team."

"Let's interview tonight and talk about it later."

Returning to their cubicles, Beth and Jim encountered Sandra Young in the hall. "Did you hear about the theft of the ATM next to our building last night?" she asked. "It's a lead story on the local news."

"That ATM has been there for years!" Beth exclaimed.

Jim said, "This morning I walked over to use it, and it was gone. I figured it was being replaced."

"Someone scooped up the ATM with a front-end loader and dumped it into a truck following behind it. Got a small amount of cash, about $1,000."

"Did they identify who took it?" Beth asked.

"The camera's pictures were grainy. Security can't make out the license plate numbers or tell if a man or a woman drove the vehicles. They found a bright pink fingernail on the ground."

Jim chuckled. "The thieves must be disappointed with their measly haul."

"Beth, are you planning to work until normal retirement age?" Sandra asked.

"Yes, I am."

"You should retire at age seventy. It will significantly improve your financial situation." She hurried away.

"Never expect a rational conversation with Sandra," Beth said.

"That's Sandra, deflecting our concerns. How weird about the ATM."

"I wonder if Kessie borrowed a front-end loader," Beth said. "She said she can drive all kinds of machines, and she has hot pink nails."

Jim said, "I bet Kessie and her husband loaded the ATM machine onto their truck, took it home, and removed the money. Then they covered the ATM and disposed of it at the dump. Just a guess. One thousand is big money to Kessie."

From the garden-level window, Jim and Beth saw a TV station's van parked outside the front door of the building. On Jim's phone, local media broadcasted sketchy information about the stolen ATM.

Jim logged into his computer and buried his face in his hands.

Beth frowned and pressed her lips together. "Oh, no! Don't tell me the toolbars are back."

"Afraid so." *A hot blowtorch would clear them out.*

"Hwan must've put them back on your screen after the meeting, when we called Elly. Or the Russians did it."

"And they likely reconnected Heenehan to Analytics. We're just shooting rubber bands at the Tech Team. Andy will have to show us where to go from here." *I'm at the end of my rope.*

"He'll give us direction," Beth said. "Personally, I can't wait for the day I clock out of technology forever. Well, as much as I can."

"You're not going to miss high tech?"

"I've had enough of clever little devices. Their strange ways baffle us average users. They hook us in and follow us around wherever we go."

Dusty Gatling hung his ball cap on the kitchen wall hook and gave his wife a peck on the cheek. "Mmm, the house smells spicy."

Holding a pair of tongs, Sue turned pieces of sizzling, seasoned fried chicken in a cast iron skillet. "Dinner's ready. I set the table. Would you pour us some milk?"

Dusty took the carton out of the refrigerator, set it on the table, and removed the lid. "I've been thinking about this Gary Hudson. So he's working for Heenehan and the Tech Team and the FBI?" He poured milk into two glasses.

Gripping the tongs, Sue lifted the fried chicken pieces and set them on a cloth inside a wire basket. She placed the basket on the table next to bowls of carrots and potatoes. She and Dusty sat down to eat.

Sue took a sip of milk. "Gary wants me to help him out for a few weeks. He talked Chang into hiring me. Gary's on the up and up. He already did my background check, and he done one on you, too. We can't tell anybody else."

Dusty bit into a drumstick. "This whole thing gives me the willies. What if you get mixed up with some worldwide gang that's way bigger than you ever imagined?"

"Gary's watching out for me. We need the money."

"The store will be up and running before long."

Sue chewed on a wing. "I'm not saying it won't. Right now, we're barely scraping by."

"I don't like the idea of Li Chang thinking you're a hot number."

"Chang's a creep. I can take care of myself."

Dusty paused. "Okay, but if anything goes haywire, you tell Gary and Chang and Brad that your husband told you to quit Heenehan and work at his store. Then do it."

"By all means. I ain't never gonna put myself in harm's way. I never liked working at Heenehan anyway. I had enough of their cow flop a long time ago."

"I finished cleaning the store, so you won't need to wash my coveralls after today. I started stocking shelves."

He peered out the kitchen window. "Did you feed the chickens?"

"I fed them an hour ago."

Dusty regarded his wife with worried eyes. "I love you, babe."

"I love you, too. You know those blueberries I canned last summer? I made a pie with them for dessert."

"Yum."

Chapter 12: Tuesday, May 16

Outside the building, Amber spoke to Li Chang on her phone. "Somebody stole our ATM."

"Our cameras show a skinny woman with frizzy hair lifting the ATM with a front-end loader onto a truck some guy was driving," Chang said.

"Damn Kessie! Sticky fingers, filching all the loose cash in the building. Now Ms. Front-End Looter takes our ATM. How am I supposed to get paid?"

"The same way the rest of us are paid. Have our bank move the money to your account. Amber, come up here."

"What the hell are you doing? I told you to leave Hwan and Jim and Beth alone. Harassment violates Control Team standards! And I told you not to withdraw tax money from Ledger Bank. Heenehan transfers plenty of money into the consulting group account."

"I'm sorry, Li." *Why is he picking on me? I'm only doing my job.*

"Correct the tax payable in the accounting system. Move the same amount of tax money back into the bank that you took out."

"I promise I'll do that today." *Maybe tomorrow.*

Chang's eyes hardened. "You deliberately flouted the team's methods. I will not allow you to harm our mission. From now on, someone who's around you every day will monitor your behavior. One false move and you're off the team. Got it?"

"Who's watchin' me?" *I'll straighten them out.*

"Get out of here." He pointed his finger at the door, glaring at Amber.

"Nothing's more important than the Tech Team."

"Out!"

Amber ran out of the room, shouting, "I'm gonna keep on working for the team no matter what, if you want me to or not!" Leaning on the wall, she sobbed, her face bright red. After a few minutes, she shuffled down the hall, sniffling, choking, and gasping. *How can he do this to me after everything I did for him?*

Moments later, there was a tap on the conference room door. Chang opened the door. "Hi, there!"

"Hi, sweetie. Are you ready to help us out?"

"I sure am," Sue Gatling replied.

Sue stood at Amber's cubicle door. "You didn't give me your report for accounting. It's due today."

"I'm not talking to you."

"Why?"

"You know why, you snake in the grass. Leave me alone."

"Give it to me, or I'll tell Judy."

"Okay, here it is." Amber picked up a sheet from her desk, folded it into a paper airplane, and flew it to Sue.

Jim and Beth met up with Tom and Andy at a cozy cafe. They sat at a round table with a red checkered tablecloth in the corner, next to a window, after ordering sandwiches and drinks.

They discussed the late-night incident with Hwan and Amber and their conversation with Sandra.

"Li Chang's group is spying on everything they can," Jim said. "We can't stop their global ambitions. But maybe we can try to prevent them from using Heenehan to spider out into more widespread networks. For starters, we can remove the damn toolbars on my computer screen." *I can't deal with them another day.*

Beth said, "The Tech Team seems to be shuffling the deck. Out of the blue, Amber's acting like Sue double-crossed her. I'm guessing Chang demoted Amber, or kicked her out, and hired Sue. Sue would be an easy recruit for Chang. Disengaged from her job and jealous of Amber's flashy style."

"I suspect our new network administrator, Gary Hudson, is a Tech Team operative," Jim said, talking faster. "He doesn't belong in the IT group. He hasn't introduced himself to us yet. He's rarely at his desk."

"Or, Gary is an undercover FBI agent," Beth said. "You're right, he definitely doesn't fit IT. What about our duty to report security breaches? We could be held liable."

Andy took a sip of soda. "You already did, Beth. You tried your best to communicate your concerns to Heenehan's management. You reported our suspicion of foreign cyberattacks to the FBI. Your warnings fell on deaf ears. At this point, responsibility for criminal activity taking place in their company falls on them."

They ate their sandwiches, surrounded by the heady scent of good coffee.

Beth took a bite of her Mediterranean veggie sandwich. "Amber couldn't get away with her stuff unless someone was looking the other way."

"You mean Brad?" Tom asked.

"Brad, Judy, Sandra, Scott. All of them."

"Brad told us Analytics will acquire Heenehan," Jim said. "He said he and his staff will be promoted before they move to Analytics, except us. Why would he say that?" *Barefaced liar.*

"Maybe Scott told Brad it's a done deal," Beth said. "I don't know who I can believe, who's doing what, who knows a little, who knows a lot."

"They have us right where they want us, confused and helpless," Andy said. "Let's focus on a game plan."

Jim handed Andy a black cell phone. "Here's the phone Amber dropped on the floor. I took out the battery so its location can't be tracked." *I'm not as careless as Judy thinks I am.*

"Amber's such a hammerhead. She's already forgotten about it. I'll put the battery back into the phone and turn off location tracking. After I test the phone, I'll let you know what I find."

Jim pulled a flash drive from his pocket and set it on the table next to Andy. "Here's Judy's database. I saved it for you to make it easier for Analytics to process returns. Judy copied it from some other company and adapted it, so you'll encounter random data."

"Thanks. I'll customize it for Analytics. The Tech Team is constantly trying to reconnect our system with Heenehan's. I fixed it so they'll never get access."

Tom banged his fist on the table. "Damn straight! Block every trace of those cyberpunks!"

"Tom, whenever the Tech Team leaves the conference room, go on in," Andy said. "Take photos of their computer screens and anything lying around. If you get caught, you're checking the electrical systems."

"Got it. I'll wear my khaki coveralls. They're in style, so I'm fashion-forward."

"What other measures can we take?" Jim asked.

Andy said, "I know you're all swamped, but we need to stay on top of the hackers. I'm on the lookout for phishing emails, computers that crashed, and data transfers to unusual destinations. Please watch for those."

"We'll do that," Jim said.

"After the Tech Team pulls out, I'll advise Heenehan's IT team leader about the hack, so the department can take routine steps to recover. They'll figure out the systems and machines affected, pull them offline, reinstall the programs, determine the weak links, set up firewalls, change passwords, and communicate the issues."

"My head's spinning," Beth said. "That's a big job for IT. What about the employees' Social Security Numbers and company bank account information?"

"We can only do what we can," Andy said. "Right now, the Tech Team isn't interested in Social Security Numbers or looting Heenehan's bank accounts. They're pecking around, checking out the network's strengths and weaknesses, and lifting business data. According to Hwan, they're leaving malware to control Heenehan's systems anytime they want. IT needs to remove it."

"The Tech Team is patient," Jim said. "A sudden shutdown of Heenehan's network would put agencies on red alert. Their mission is more far-reaching than greed or theft."

For a moment they sat in silence, finishing their lunches.

"Tom, thank you for sending me the Tech Team's diagram of Heenehan's systems and their description of the network layout," Andy said. "That's a good start for my analysis."

"I never sent you those," Tom replied.

"You didn't? Then who did? Hwan?"

"Not likely," Beth said. "Hwan wouldn't take that risk."

Andy frowned. "Weird. I need to go back to work."

As they walked to their offices, music from a mellow classical guitar filled the air, played with skill by a street musician. Jim rolled the chords around in his mind. *I'll blend that melody into one of my songs.* His buzzing phone grabbed his attention. "Okay, good. Thanks, Doris, I don't know what I'd do without you."

Beth pointed to a group at an outdoor cafe. Li Chang was holding an animated discussion with a round-faced, pudgy Asian man. Seated at the table with them was Amber Wolfe.

Midafternoon Beth answered her desk phone.

"This is Pam Taylor at the state. I haven't received the information you promised explaining the difference between the tax returns and the backup."

"I'm sorry, Pam. Our manager, Brad Mitchell, removed us from the state audit and assigned it to Amber Wolfe. She's a tax accountant in our group. Did she notify you or Ron?"

"No one notified us of a change in our contact person."

"I'll speak with Brad." *Who couldn't care less.*

"Yesterday the state's system had a serious breach," Pam said. "An unauthorized individual or group viewed and possibly copied hundreds of lines of confidential data. Our IT department told us all signs of the origin of the breach point to Heenehan. They patched it by the end of the day."

"That's bizarre. I'll notify Brad and our IT network administrator. We'll do what we can to get the audit on track." *We're toast.*

"Thanks, Beth. I'll talk to you soon."

Beth left Brad a voice message saying, "I received a call from Pam Taylor, one of the state auditors. Amber has not contacted either of the auditors. Pam mentioned a data breach at the state that originated in Heenehan. Please call her and talk to her yourself."

At Jim's cubicle, Beth said, "No doubt the Tech Team is behind the state's security breach," Beth said. "Amber and Brad are blowing off the state audit. Brad has probably already deleted my message."

"We can't do anything more about the audit," Jim said. "You made it clear to Pam it's out of our hands. Let's tell Gary Hudson about the breach now. He's so busy learning Andy's job, it's hard to catch him."

Unable to locate Gary at his desk in IT or anywhere in the area, they returned to their cubicles.

Jim said, "I'll send Gary an email with 'urgent' in the subject line."

Judy called Jim and Beth, demanding they immediately report to a second-floor conference room. They took their seats at the table where Judy and Corabell sat waiting. The airless room reeked of the acrid smell of alcohol breath.

Corabell turned a frigid gaze on Jim, then on Beth. "You met the requirements of your performance plans by the narrowest of margins. You will remain on the plan. We're not afraid to cut the deadwood. One strike and you're out. Let that sink in."

Judy said, "Since the projects are not getting done, you will assume half of Sue Gatling's projects and half of Amber Wolfe's projects. You must prove you can step out of your comfort zone into a fast-paced environment."

Jim and Beth sat in silence, drawing minimal breath.

Judy spoke in a loud voice, permeating the room with a sour alcohol vapor. "If those projects are not completed within the next two weeks, you will be terminated. Be aware you are at-will employees. You signed a statement acknowledging your status at the time of hire. That means the company can terminate your employment at any time for any reason, or no reason. Just like that. It will not be based on your age. Do you understand?"

"Yes." They stood.

Judy pointed an index finger, commanding them to sit. "Since we had to transfer the state audit to Amber, you can expect low ratings on your performance reviews. Just so you know."

Beth forced a firm voice. "Brad told us Heenehan will be sold in a month or two. Both of us will be terminated. So we won't be here."

Corabell snorted. "Think about it. You have two weeks to get your projects caught up. Less than a month. Your personnel files from Heenehan will follow you when you apply for jobs. Do you want letters of recommendation to provide to your new employers?"

"Yes," they said.

Jim and Beth met in a third-floor huddle room.

Jim said, "We're being held hostage in exchange for our letters of recommendation."

"No sensible supervisor would fire us because we can't do multiple people's jobs."

"Judy's brain is permanently pickled."

Beth waved a hand in front of her face. "I wish she would guzzle her firewater after work."

"Or switch to vodka. Her breath could kill a horse."

With his cell phone on speaker, Jim called Tom. "Judy dumped half of Sue's and Amber's projects on us. If we never slept, we couldn't finish all this work. Can you take a few more returns? We can agree to a fair rate of pay."

"It's a temporary situation," Beth said. "Something is going to blow up in the next month."

"My workload is increasing at Analytics," Tom said. "I'll do what I can. I may ask one of my kids to help with the routine work."

Jim said, "We can't thank you enough."

They went back to their cubicles and faced the project files stacked up on their desks.

Sue held her cell phone to her ear. "This is her. Yeah, I made our airline and hotel reservations for next month. It's been a long winter. Three whole days in the sun. California beaches, here we come! I'll text you when I get there."

"Well, ain't you the golden child," Amber said.

"I'm gonna buy me a swimsuit. Dusty wants it to be a bikini."

"Then you should get a bikini wax."

"I'll think about it. I thought about it. Nope."

Kessie called out over her cubicle wall, "Don't worry, Sue! I'll help out when you're gone. You can take a good vacation far away from this place and not worry."

"Them Principal weirdos need something to keep 'em busy," Amber huffed. "I have no clue what they do all day. Beth wanted to show me how to do some of her tax returns. Omigod!"

Sue said, "Did you see her old-timey shoes?"

Amber grinned. "Beth saves her hoochie shoes for the clubs."

Chapter 13: Wednesday, May 17

Beth's voice was faint. "I can't make it this morning, Jim. I'm light headed and chilled. I'll be in later today, if I can. I left a voice message for Judy."

"Beth, get some rest. If you keep pushing yourself too hard, your body will force you to take a break."

"I need to go."

Jim processed tax returns, listening to a mix arranged to enhance focus. He would layer the basses and add low strings later. Sensing someone behind him, he dismissed the green-haired annoyance that he assumed was Amber.

After a few minutes, he snapped, "Okay, knock it off, Amber." He glanced behind him and jumped to his feet, his earbuds flying to the floor.

Corabell stood inches from the back of Jim's chair, eyes on his computer screen, her black dress amplifying her formidable figure. "You've been selected for random drug testing," she barked. "Go to the lab."

"I know where it is," Jim replied.

"Then get over there." She clumped away.

Jim sat back in his chair, staring straight ahead. *The small dose of Prozac I'm still taking will show up as a controlled substance. The test will identify the Adderall I took this morning as amphetamine. Last night's sips of vodka are present as alcohol in my urine for nine to thirteen hours. A failed drug test will follow me around for years.*

Amber, Sue, and Kessie huddled, whispering in the aisle.

Jim put on his jacket and left. From the driver's seat of his car, he made a call from his cell phone. "Tom, Corabell ordered me to report to the lab for a random drug test. Would you meet me at the lab in fifteen minutes? I'll pay you $1,000 to take the test for me."

"Didn't you report your medications before your pre-employment drug test?"

"I did. No one said anything to me about that test. I suspect Amber got into my records and made a stink with HR. You and I look enough alike that it shouldn't be a problem for you to use my ID card. If you're caught, I'll contact my lawyer and take full responsibility."

"I'll be there in fifteen. And I'll do it for free."

"Thank you, Tom." Jim hesitated. "Hey, Tom?"

"Yeah."

"I changed my mind. I'll take the drug test myself. I'm ready to deal with HR."

Beth stopped at Jim's cubicle a few minutes after noon.

Jim said, "What are you doing here? I can tell you're sick. Go home and take care of yourself. We'll all get sick."

"I'm better. This morning I received a certified letter from the State Board of Accountancy. Amber filed an official complaint accusing me of substandard practice. It's bizarre."

"I got one yesterday."

"Those accusations could land us in hot water. The Board could revoke our right to practice. We'd lose our ability to make a living as accountants."

"I'll call the Board," Jim said. "I'll explain that a disgruntled coworker filed the complaints and insist that they be dismissed."

"Thanks. I'm up to here with Amber. My attorney friend who handles these cases would love to go after her and win us a nice settlement. We should keep him in mind. Right now, I have to call the downtown health club. Amber registered me for a Zumba class."

"You should go! It'll keep you in shape for pole dancing!"

Amber faced Judy across the small conference table. "Yeah, I filed 'em." *Betcha they're in HR doing exit interviews right now.*

"Amber, you will withdraw your complaints immediately. We're not pleased to have you complaining to a state agency. Heenehan doesn't need that kind of publicity."

"Go look at Jim's computer. It's full of toolbars he shouldn't have. Him and Beth ain't keeping up with their work. I wrote down all the facts on the forms." *What more proof does Judy want?*

"Heenehan's management is fully aware of any and all issues. We will handle them. Don't involve any other organization in Heenehan's private business. Am I making myself clear?"

"Yes, ma'am. Thanks for being totally fair about my mistake. I'll call the state this morning." *Judy's a muckety-muck with a big ol' butt.*

Beth stopped in the restroom. A few moments after she entered the stall, the restroom door opened, the lock clicked, and the lights went dark. Beth remained frozen behind the stall door.

Amber spoke in a low voice. "I'm gonna wipe every trace of you off the planet. Nobody's gonna know you ever existed." She flipped on the light switch, unlocked the door, and left.

Shaken and feeling faint, Beth exited the stall, washed her hands, and hurried to her desk.

After an hour, Beth told Jim about the restroom incident. "It was super scary. From now on, I'll use restrooms on other floors."

"How much more are you going to tolerate? You're not serving a jail sentence. I advise you to ghost this company. Cut off all contact."

"I told you before, I'm staying as long as you're here."

"Gather your personal items. Make a run for it." *Beth is pigheaded to the point of stupidity.*

"Why don't YOU leave?"

"How would I take care of Mom if I quit working when companies aren't hiring? I need a steady income. I have a job to do, and I do it. I'll move on when I can. You have options."

"I'm not leaving. End of discussion."

Kessie stopped at Sue's cubicle, purse strap slung over her shoulder, bus pass in hand. "How come you ain't leaving at 3:30 no more? You already shifted most of your work off to them Principal freaks."

"Judy's making me work on a project for the system auditors. It's real complicated. She wants it done in a few days."

"Okay, gotta go. Jack's mad. My grandson and three of his friends are making water balloons in my kitchen."

In the fourth-floor conference room, Gary Hudson nodded at Spartak and Ludmila.

Li Chang regarded him with interest. "Gary, as network administrator, you're in an excellent position to help us expand our sphere of operations. We're delighted you're working with us. You have the big picture. Can you recommend a course of action?"

"I can bypass Heenehan's and Analytics' security systems and set up a backdoor program that will give us a continuous data feed. I'll activate it later today."

"Excellent," Chang said.

"This afternoon I have to change out monitors in the tax group. Brad's an idiot for putting his staff through this time waster, but it's an opportunity to install our software on all the computers in the group."

"Keep me posted."

"Hello!" A stocky, middle-aged man with a buzz cut and dark hair and wearing a black polo shirt and black slacks stood in Amber's cubicle doorway. He extended his right hand. Amber jumped to her feet, accepting his firm handshake.

"I'm Gary Hudson, your new network administrator. I took Andy Price's spot."

"Hi, I'm Amber. I'm the tax point person, so if you think of any questions, just ask."

"I will, thank you."

Jim and Beth came over and introduced themselves.

Jim said, "Gary, did you receive my urgent email about the security breach at the state? All signs of its origin point to Heenehan."

"I did read your email," Gary said. "The problem was on the state's end. Sorry I didn't get back to you, it's been a crazy week. Thanks for the heads up. I need to know about those types of issues."

"Thanks for checking it out, Gary," Jim said.

Returning to their cubicles, Jim said in a low voice, "The state's system was the problem? No way."

"He did not sound convincing," Beth whispered.

Gary said to Amber, "I'm going to swap out your group's small monitors for the new wider ones, then reformat your computers. I'm starting with yours."

"Okay." Amber logged out of her computer. She reached into her top drawer, pulled out a plastic baggie containing small, red candies, and held it out to him. "I love these cherry gummy bears. I've been eating them all morning. Would you like a couple?"

"Sure, thanks!" Gary took two out of the bag, popped them into his mouth, and disconnected Amber's monitor. "Those gummies are good. Give me a couple more." He began examining the cables with wonder, as if each one were strange and new.

Corabell appeared at Amber's cubicle door. "Human Resources is conducting employee drug tests this morning. The random generator program selected a drug test list that includes your name, Gary. Please go to the lab where you'll be given instructions. You were there prior to your offer of employment."

"Oh, yes, of course," Gary said, squinting.

Corabell turned and left. Gary wobbled toward the stairs.

Chang's black eyes bore into Amber with cold rage. "Did you give Gary Hudson marijuana edibles?"

Amber lowered her head, looking into his eyes. "No."

Chang smacked the table with his hand, making Spartak and Ludmila jump. "You're lying to me! This company has a zero-tolerance drug policy. What's wrong with you?"

"I didn't know they was gonna do random drug tests today."

"What were you doing with marijuana candy in your desk?"

"I passed my drug test when I got hired."

"Throw that stuff away! Weren't you listening when I informed the group about our new assistant? Didn't you realize he holds a sensitive position? He's developing a bypass to the security channels."

"Nobody told me Gary was working for our team."

"The hospital released him a short while ago. He had over 10,000 milligrams of THC in his system. His body couldn't handle it."

"I'm really sorry, Li."

"Gary failed the drug test. Heenehan fired him. We have to finish the project without his expertise or proximity to the IT group."

"I just wanted him to quit messing with my computer. A huge monitor would've, like, screwed me up."

"Get out of here!" Chang shoved Amber out into the hall and slammed the door shut. He sank into his chair, drawing sympathetic looks from Ludmila and Spartak. "She's the most energetic, creative member of our team. A little wildfire is better than no fire at all. But she's out of control. She scares the life out of me."

Striding along the walkway next to the pond, Sandra Young spoke into her phone. "A shame about Agent Hudson. Gary's a good man. We'll have to rely on our other informant. It won't be easy for Sue. I'll contact you if I observe anything out of the ordinary."

Amber stopped at Kessie's cubicle. "The new network admin flunked the drug test and got fired. Gary something."

"Oh, razzlefratz! I was looking forward to two big new monitors. I don't care if my computer's down a few days to put the crapware back on."

"You're the one who's always ragging on us to keep up a good attitude," Amber said.

Kessie sighed. "Jack spent last night in jail on a drunk and disorderly. I need a break."

Beth took Jim's mouse from him. She scrolled across his computer screen, examining Sue's spreadsheet. "Her procedures aren't easy to figure out. It appears she enters bottom-line amounts from two reports. If the amounts aren't the same, she plugs the difference in purple on the next line."

Jim stood, looked around, and sat back down. "Yesterday I dropped a report on Brad's chair," he whispered. "A manila envelope was sitting on his desk. A yellow Post-it note on the envelope said, 'Exit Process.' This morning, Judy was in Scott's office with the door closed."

"Could this be the day Amber is finally escorted out the door?"

"I'm keeping my fingers crossed."

They continued analyzing Sue's procedures.

Sobbing, howling, and wailing shattered the garden level. They peered over the cubicle wall. A uniformed security guard stood outside Kessie's cubicle entrance. She was flinging her personal items, one after another, into a large cardboard box on her desk.

Amber handed Kessie a tissue.

Hands on hips, Sue shouted, "What the Sam Hill is going on here?"

Judy and Cody worked at their desks with heads down.

At Kessie's cubicle, Beth asked, "What happened?"

Kessie gasped convulsively. "Corabell gave me a pink slip. What am I gonna do? Dadgummit! My husband ain't working. I'm helping out my grandkids. I need this job!"

"What a bad break," Jim said.

"We're so sorry." Beth gently patted her hand.

Eyes full of tears, Kessie turned to Beth. "Here, I have something for you. I was gonna give it to you later for your granddaughter to wear next weekend. It's like the one I made Starla." She opened the bottom drawer of her desk. Pulling out a neatly folded lavender sweater, she handed it to Beth.

"Oh, thank you, Kessie." Beth unfolded the sweater and held it up. "It's perfect. Claire will love it." Beth gave Kessie a hug. "I'll send you the money to cover your time and materials. Write down your address for me." Taking a scrap of paper from the wastebasket, Beth put it in front of Kessie, who scribbled her address in shaky handwriting.

"I can't believe they gave you the axe," Sue said. "You do more than your share of work around here."

Kessie's voice quivered. "Corabell said the company that wants to take over Heenehan thinks we got too many tax people."

"Analytics Telco hasn't made any staffing recommendations," Beth said.

"Ain't Analytics. Some other company."

"We should all go on Monster.com because we're next," Sue said.

"What company, Kessie?" Beth asked.

"Bom Cat, sumpin' like that."

"Bomkamp Management Group, the private equity firm?" Jim asked.

"Yeah, I guess."

"Where's Brad?" Jim asked.

"He left to go golfing with the other managers," Sue said, putting an arm around Kessie's shoulders. "You can still hang out with us, no matter what."

Kessie burst into tears. "It's all my own fault. I should of worked more and not took my vacation."

"Ain't your fault," Amber said. "Take 'em to court. Sue Heenehan for all the money you can get. Even if you don't get money or your job back, you'll feel better."

"I don't feel good about nothing." Kessie started crying again. She hurled her belongings from her overhead bins into the box, pushed the flaps down, and shut it. Amber carried it out the door, followed by Kessie, Sue, and the security guard.

"Poor Kessie," Beth said, sitting in Jim's side chair. "She wasn't a perfect employee, but I'm sorry to see her thrown out the door like that."

"I wish management would tell us their plans. If Bomkamp acquires Heenehan, things are going to get interesting. It's one powerful firm. Skip Bomkamp calls himself the senior managing director. He's amassed a fortune."

"Heenehan will be one of dozens of Bomkamp companies," Beth said, mounting pressure squeezing her head.

Jim rested his elbow on the table, chin in hand. "When Bomkamp buys a company, he normally pays cash for 20 percent, and borrows the remaining 80 percent. The responsibility to repay the debt falls on the acquired company. So Heenehan will be on the hook to pay back all that borrowed money."

"You don't need an MBA to know that's a bad deal for Heenehan," Beth said. "Bomkamp will grow Heenehan's revenue and pocket the profits. They'll downsize staff, reduce marketing, and cheapen the products. Anything to slash costs. Employees will lose their minds without the resources to do their jobs. Bomkamp's loyal to the money, not to the business."

Jim shook his head. "Heenehan will default on any large debt. Bomkamp will sell Heenehan's assets, pay off the debt, and make a nice return on their investment. They do that to all their companies."

"Heenehan's board and officers must expect attractive pay packages. Bomkamp's telling them Heenehan can keep its name while staying independent, so the company can continue business as usual. But not for long."

"The VIPs are counting on a bonanza, no doubt," Jim said. "It's a money grab."

They sat silently for a moment.

"This acquisition will hand the Tech Team access to all the companies under Bomkamp's umbrella," Jim said. "They'll vastly expand the scope of their operation."

Beth rubbed her aching temples. "I thought the same thing the minute I heard Kessie say Bomkamp. The Tech Team's going to hack into Bomkamp's servers. Spy on the computer systems of all its companies. Elly might know why Heenehan's executives no longer plan to sell its assets to Analytics."

In a third-floor huddle room, Jim called from his phone.

"Elly, we have big news," Beth said. "Bomkamp Management Group plans to acquire Heenehan. This afternoon Kessie Hinkle was laid off. We assume that this is just the first round of job cuts."

"It doesn't surprise me. Bomkamp is always searching for companies to buy. I hope it works out. Bomkamp's tough on employees. Kessie has my sympathy. Analytics doesn't need Heenehan at all. Or Bomkamp."

"Your perspective is helpful, Elly," Beth said. "We were stunned." *So Bomkamp has been circling Heenehan for some time.*

"Sorry to interrupt you when you're so busy. We wanted to give you advance warning," Jim said.

"Don't worry about interrupting me. I'll be in a position to make offers shortly. Feel free to call anytime."

A smiling Brad Mitchell sat at the head of the conference table. "I called this meeting to give you some excellent news. I'm pleased to announce that Bomkamp Management Group has agreed to acquire Heenehan. Bomkamp is a great company."

The staff sat expressionless.

"Heenehan's senior management decided to go in a different direction. They no longer plan to sell Heenehan's assets to Analytics Telco. They're working out a process to integrate Heenehan into Bomkamp's systems and company culture. This includes 10 percent salary reductions across-the-board for manager level and below. Sorry. It is what it is. But Heenehan is going to stay in business, and Bomkamp will boost our revenue. The transition team says our future's so bright, you gotta wear shades!"

The group laughed, but not much.

"Who are those people walking outside our building with signs?" Sue asked.

"Bomkamp has instructed us to ignore any picketers. They're disgruntled employees from other Bomkamp companies."

"They're blocking our sidewalk."

"There's only about a dozen of them. Walk around them."

"Okay."

"Our computer monitor replacement project has been delayed until HR hires a new network administrator. We'll continue to use our standard-size monitors. Bomkamp's contract requires Heenehan to adopt a tax platform that one of its companies developed. It's called BomTax. I'm told it will interface nicely with Judy's database. We'll start the rollout right away. So, we can look forward to a great new tax system conversion."

The staff stared daggers at Brad.

Beth opened her mouth to speak, then fell silent. *A system conversion will be a time-consuming, expensive undertaking, causing enormous upheaval, even if it happens exactly according to plan.*

Brad made a downcast expression. "I'm sad to say that Kessie was resource-actioned because our quarterly earnings didn't meet projections. She was a valued employee. We wish her nothing but the best. Bomkamp demands optimal efficiency. They plan further reductions in force through curtailing redundancies and streamlining operations. Kessie's job duties will be absorbed by the tax group. Our teammates are quick learners who help each other find a way."

Jim glared at Brad.

"On a lighter note, Bomkamp is going to sponsor a teambuilding day for all its companies. We can choose to play softball or to cheer our company team."

The group sat stone-like.

"Bomkamp has provided a job description form for each of you to record your job duties. Take one and pass them along. Sue, please collect them later this afternoon and put them in my in-box. In the next few days, Sam from Bomkamp will stop by to discuss your job duties with each of you. He'll recommend improvements to our processes."

Brad spoke with authority. "I expect you all to cooperate fully. It is in your best interest to do so. Make sure every job duty you report impacts shareholder value. Are you with me?"

They looked over the forms.

"These are half-page templates," Beth said. "Even a brief summary of my job would take more space than this form allows."

"It's their form," Brad said. "Do your best. You'll have a chance to talk to Sam. Any more questions?"

No response.

"We're shifting to a whole different paradigm. I'm counting on all of you to make this a seamless transition. The entire team of Bomkamp welcomes us aboard."

"Andy told me BomTax is a nightmare," Jim said, filling his coffee cup in the small kitchen. A man from another work group removed a lunch sack from the refrigerator and left.

"I've heard disturbing stories about it in my women's accounting group. Bomkamp's peddling that software around to its companies, pressuring them to buy it and beta test it. The tax rates are wrong, and the return forms aren't accepted by the taxing jurisdictions. Most data has to be entered manually because the programming doesn't work. Brad's got to be aware of that."

"Andy told me the BomTax programmer left, and no one else would take on his work because it's a time-sucking mess. Skip Bomkamp opted to market BomTax as is and let the companies that use it fix the problems. He hired some tall, blonde woman who's pushy and full of herself to take charge of marketing. She makes all kinds of pants-on-fire promises. She sounds like you-know-who."

"Vanessa, your ex," Beth said. "Let's hope we never cross paths with Vanessa or with BomTax."

"I figure Scott's enjoying his bonus for cutting Kessie's position."

"I'm sure he is."

Sue and Amber stopped at Jim's cubicle. "I'm here collecting job description forms," Sue said. "Hand 'em over."

"Here's mine," Beth said. "Jim's finishing his."

Amber took Beth's form and gave it to Sue. "We ain't done ours yet."

"Brad wants them this afternoon."

"Wha-evah. It'll take us five minutes to fill out that lame form." Amber sashayed out the door.

Jim handed his form to Sue. "Here you go."

Sue put the form in her stack, pulled a wad of gum out of her mouth, dropped it into Jim's wastebasket, and carried the forms out the door.

"What a pair. Katie told me another woman applied when HR was hiring for Amber's job. That woman dressed professionally, was sensible and friendly, and had over ten years of tax experience. Scott rejected her because she was overweight and not pretty."

"She was obese?"

"About fifteen pounds overweight."

"This group would be in a heck of a lot better shape if Scott hired that imperfect woman instead of Amber. Or a random person off the street," Jim said.

"I can imagine the snow job that Amber did on her online application form. Scott got catfished, and Brad knows it."

Jim pulled his car into the garage, pressed the button to close the garage door, and sauntered into the kitchen.

Doris, a gray-haired matron in a yellow-flowered housedress, was seated next to his mother on the blue living room couch.

"Mom? Doris? What's going on?" He dropped into the blue paisley recliner chair across from the couch. Hannah was curled in a ball on the chair's padded arm, her eyes wide open, her tail twitching. She eyed Jim and made a silent meow.

"I had a doctor appointment, so I came over a bit later than usual to check on Rose," Doris said. "A young woman was at the front door with a pistol in her hand, talking to Rose. She tried to sell Rose a gun." Doris stretched out her hand and patted Rose's arm. "Didn't she, Rosie?"

"The girl told me I can shoot anybody who comes into my house. Anybody!"

"Oh, no!" *I can't leave Mom alone anymore.*

"You don't need a gun, dear," Doris said.

Jim leaned toward his mother. "Mom, I love you, but I won't allow guns in the house."

"I told you I want a gun!"

"No guns! Doris, can you describe this woman?"

"Slender. Strong. Green hair. Are you all right?"

"Her name is Amber. I expect she'll be back. If you see her again, please call me right away."

"I will. I told her Rose had to talk to her son first. She kept giving Rose the hard sell, so I had to get quite forceful with her."

"I can't thank you enough, Doris."

"You're welcome. If you report this person to the police, I'd be happy to provide a witness statement."

"I'll keep it in mind."

"I heartily agree with you that a gun in the house isn't a good idea," Doris said. "When I come over to visit, Rose needs a moment to recognize me."

"She's doing that with me, too," Jim said. "I checked out the place you recommended, and I'm sure Mom would be comfortable there. I'll think it over." *No way can I afford it.*

Rose shouted, "Jimmy, don't talk about me like I'm not here!"

Doris stood. "I'm sure you'll do what's best, Jim. I have to scoot. Rosie, I'll see you tomorrow."

"Bye, Doris."

Doris opened the front door, turned the deadbolt switch clockwise, and shut the door behind her.

Jim stroked Hannah, who stretched out flat on the arm of the recliner. "Mom, I don't want you to open the door to anyone. That girl will hurt you. Do you remember what she looks like?"

"She wore a green hat."

Chapter 14: Tuesday, May 18

Li Chang was seated at the head of the conference table. Ludmila and Spartak were sitting on one side. Amber, Sue, and Hwan sat on the other side.

"I want to impress upon each of you the importance of our mission at this point in time. Bomkamp Management Group is a private equity firm that controls dozens of companies. Each company has its own computer system, connected to a server at Bomkamp's headquarters. Ludmila, Spartak, are you familiar with this structure?"

They nodded.

"Are your backup devices in place?"

The Russians replied, "Da, koneshno!"

"Good. Hwan will embed code into Heenehan's network. It will spread to Bomkamp's headquarters, and from there out to all its companies."

"So we're getting access to the computer systems of all the Bomkamp's companies," Sue said.

"Right. Amber, I'm reluctantly giving you another chance. Sue has accepted responsibility to oversee your work. I have instructed Sue to make you aware of your behavioral problems. Serious consequences will befall you if you cause trouble or do anything else to impede our mission. Am I getting my point across?"

"Yes, sir! Thank you, Li! Brad asked me to help him with special projects for the Bomkamp deal. It's a totally important job."

"Good. Keep me updated."

Amber pointed at Sue. "I don't need no overseein' from her."

"We're not convinced you bring the right skills to this job," Sue said.

Amber looked away. *I have the right skills to take down this bossy bitch.*

Chang said, "Hwan, I want you to be available for anything Sue and Amber tell you to do."

"Right."

A grating noise came from a narrow L-shaped aisle in the far corner of the room. Chang stood, moved toward the turn, and peered around it. He spotted a man in beige work clothes lying on the floor, facing the beige wall. "Who are you?" Chang demanded.

Tom said, "I'm from the utility company working on boosting the electrical system." He turned a screwdriver into the wall plate. "I'm about finished here." He put his ear next to the electrical outlet and tapped the wall twice. "It's working." He stood, momentarily making eye contact with Sue, who stared at him. He picked up his toolbox and sauntered out the door.

Outside the building, protesters marched single file on the sidewalk carrying signs. Tom stood on the grass and dialed his cell phone. "Hey, Andy, the job's done. I installed several cameras in the Tech Team's conference room. A professional-grade detector might find them, but they're tough to spot. The cameras livestream audio and video when sound or motion is in the room."

"You're doing a fine job, Tom."

"I was installing the last electrical outlet camera when they all trooped in for a meeting."

"Yowza."

"I laid low, but Chang caught sight of me. I told him the utility company sent me. I think Sue recognized me."

"Let's hope not. Send me any close-up photos of their screens you take."

"Sure thing. I'll update Jim and Beth."

A muscular young man, wearing dress jeans and a black ribbed T-shirt, greeted Amber cheerfully. "I'm Sam from Bomkamp. I'll be here this week to meet with each of you. We'll discuss your jobs and brainstorm ideas for streamlining. I need you to show me the basic steps you go through to complete your daily work. I borrowed a chair." He set his laptop on Amber's desk and rolled a chair into her cubicle.

"Nice to meet you. This is Hwan Cho sitting next to me. He's helping us out," Amber said.

"Hello, Hwan."

Hwan rolled his chair back. Sam pushed his chair around the clutter on Amber's cubicle floor and sat next to her.

"You can use my laptop, Amber. Your IT department gave me access to your network, so your screens are the same as mine."

"Okay." Amber pulled Sam's laptop in front of her. "I do lots of work, so it's gonna take time to run through it all. Hwan's our support person who's better with computers than me. He can explain some stuff."

"Let's start with the accounting reports," Sam said.

"Some reports are in hard copy," Amber said. "Come with me. I'll show you where I get 'em in the accounting department."

After they left, Hwan sat at Amber's desk, installed the Tech Team's code on Sam's laptop, and moved back to his chair.

Amber and Sam returned. Amber launched into rambling stories about her job duties, opening and closing screens on Sam's laptop. Hwan cackled at Amber's fictional narrative, drawing odd looks from Sam.

After Sam left, Amber and Hwan stopped by Sue's desk. Sue whispered, "I talked to Li. The Tech Team's connected to Bomkamp's server. Nice going, Hwan!" She high-fived him.

"No way he did it without me," Amber said.

"Of course. You both did it together."

Judy materialized from the corridor shadows. "How did your session with Sam go?"

Amber grinned. "Great! He seen all the work I do. Hwan helped me explain a few things."

"Super." Judy spun around and left.

Andy opened the bottom drawer of his desk, snapped the cap off a small plastic bottle, and popped a headache pill. He called Jim, then added Tom to the call.

Jim and Beth went to a huddle room on the far side of the garden level to take the call.

Andy said, "I've been monitoring Amber's cell phone, the one you picked up off the floor, Jim. I read all her texts and listened in on her calls. Li Chang congratulated Amber on Hwan's successful installation of the code on Bomkamp's server."

Beth gave a deep sigh. "I figured we couldn't trust Hwan. He's worried about his parents' safety." *Every single Bomkamp employee is screwed.*

"If Hwan had deliberately botched the installation again, the Russians would have taken over," Jim said. "Then Amber would tip off the North Koreans. His only choice was to launch the malware."

"It's already spreading out to Bomkamp's companies," Andy said. "Their computers should be disconnected from the internet, scanned, and disinfected. It's an impossible job. I can't remove the worms and spyware from all the systems they've infiltrated. I can only protect my own company. I plugged all means of access between Heenehan and Analytics. I set up continuous monitoring of Analytics' network and tightened security."

"Do we still need the cameras I installed in the Tech Team's conference room?" Tom asked.

"The cameras can stay. They're connected to a burner phone I bought with cash. Since the Tech Team invaded Bomkamp's companies, I see them observing the network, maybe waiting for a command to disrupt the infrastructure. It stinks."

"The FBI or NSA or some other agency must be involved," Beth said. "Sandra told us the authorities are monitoring the situation.

Jim said, "We can't believe anything Sandra says after she gaslighted us about Hwan's incompetence."

"Sandra was protecting Hwan," Beth said.

"Or herself."

"I did a gut check, and I believe her that the authorities are involved."

Andy asked, "Could Sandra be working with the Tech Team?"

Beth said, "I'm having a hard time making out what you're saying, Andy. I hear dogs barking."

"Hang on a minute." His voice became distant. "Max, Sneakers! Quiet! NOW Max!" He returned to the call. "Sorry about the barking. I'm working from home today. The dogs want to chase a squirrel in the backyard. I need to put in more training time with them."

"Sandra's respected in the accounting community," Beth said. "She wouldn't have the slightest interest in the Tech Team. She's way out of their league. I believe she's credible." *Whoever she's working for.*

"Okay, we'll assume Sandra's telling the truth. There must be a reason those authorities haven't intervened."

"It might be a delicate situation they need to handle carefully," Jim said.

"Understood," Andy said. "This is a small part of an international situation. If law enforcement or the intelligence community didn't want us to continue what we're doing, they would have told us."

"We're on the right track," Tom said. "We have to keep moving."

"I agree," Andy said. "Tom, about those documents I thought you sent me, they're key to the Tech Team's conception of Heenehan's network. They were wrong about some of the design elements. They worked around what they didn't understand and pushed ahead with their agenda. Who do you suppose sent me the documents?"

"I'm positive it's Sue's handwriting on the envelope."

"Sue joined the Tech Team?" Jim asked.

Beth said, "Hmm, it's possible. Sue's half on and half off the job. Kessie's gone. Cody's marking time until Brad makes a move. Amber and Hwan are turning company data over to the Tech Team. Brad keeps the two of us working our tails off with impossible performance expectations."

Jim said, "Scott's pushing Brad down, making every day a living hell for him. Brad's hanging loose, playing it off like it's no big deal."

"Brad's undermined Heenehan in ways the Tech Team can only dream about," Andy said. "Thanks to Brad, the company is a ticking time bomb."

Scott Campbell arrived at the conference room twenty minutes late. The tax staff put their phones away. Wearing an open-neck white shirt and navy blue jacket, Scott studied the tax group and spoke rapidly. "Bomkamp Management

Group has ordered us to shrink our workforce in an effort to flatten the hierarchy. Yesterday Brad Mitchell accepted a buyout package. I will assume Brad's responsibilities going forward."

Cody made a little smile.

"Brad's management level has been eliminated. The position will not be backfilled."

Judy said, "You will continue to do your jobs as usual. Are there any questions?"

"Scott, will you be available to represent the company in the tax audits?" Jim asked. "Amber's state audit and our city audits require a sign off by a manager or director."

"If you need help, make an appointment on my online calendar, Cody. I've told this group my availability is limited. Remember?"

"My name is Jim, not Cody. I had a meeting scheduled with Brad."

"Brad provided me with his calendar and a list of his job duties. Don't worry about audits. I have ways of dealing with auditors."

Beth said, "Cody and Jim and I are preparing about five hundred returns. Judy transferred Amber's and Sue's returns to Jim and me. And half of their projects."

Scott's face tightened. "Forget about the projects. Get the returns out the door."

"Amber and Sue, you will each take a dozen returns," Judy said.

"Thank you," Jim said.

Beth said, "What if we decrease our orders for office equipment instead of cutting staff? We could share with other groups."

Judy narrowed her eyes. "Those expenses are already cut to the bone. Our highest expense is salaries."

"What about the company plane?" Beth asked.

"That's off the table," Scott said.

"We spread out Kessie's work to all of us," Sue said. "Are there gonna be more cuts?"

"Yes, you can handle it," Scott said. "I expect more effort. All you do is plop numbers on the returns. If you can't get your work done during the week, then work evenings and weekends. I need each of you to work a few hours on Sundays." Scott lowered his voice. "It's amazing what you can do when you're under pressure. Hard work makes a top performer."

Amber's phone vibrated, drawing startled looks. She shut it off.

Beth crossed her arms, ignoring butterflies in her stomach. "You're saying you want us to work more than our normal ten-hour workday to absorb the work of the staff you laid off?"

"I don't see anyone working ten-hour days. You love tax work, don't you? You're passionate about it? We want you to be challenged. It's our company culture. People work long hours because they choose to. The workday ends at five o'clock. I don't want you working ANY overtime. Got it?"

"You just said we should work evenings and weekends and a few hours on Sundays."

"You're conflating different situations. I'm asking your group to pull together as a team and get your jobs done."

"We can do it!" Amber exclaimed. "We're all about helpin' each other."

"That's the spirit! Judy, please write a recap of this meeting and email it to each person present. You may return to your cubicles. That's all for today," Scott said. He bolted out of the room, followed by Judy.

The group shuffled to their work area.

Sue emitted a heavy sigh. "I can't believe Scott's our boss. He don't have the dimmest idea about taxes. Having fun yet, Amber?"

"I found a rad place for lunch."

Sue and Amber grabbed their jackets and left.

"So Brad finally threw in the towel," Beth said to Jim.

"I guess that explains the banner taped across Scott's door that Corabell was peeling off this morning. The yellow one with black letters saying, 'SUCK IT, CAMPBELL!'"

About an hour later, Amber and Sue stood chatting in the aisle. "You looking for your binky?" Amber asked Jim.

"Where's Cody?"

Sue sniffed. "Why do you want to know?"

"I have a question," Jim said.

"Brad got a job as a VP at another Bomkamp company and hired Cody, yesterday, in fact," Sue said. "Cody took all his stuff home last night. Turned in his resignation after the meeting. Judy's gonna bring Cody's work over to you and Beth."

"I'm going to tell Judy to turn around and put it on your desk," Jim said. He returned to his cubicle, frowning and biting his lip.

Amber went to her cubicle, then strolled into the aisle, wearing a glittery dark green wrap with a fringe. "Scott's freaking out."

Sue eyed Amber. "Did you inherit that from your great-grandma?"

"Haha and ha. You're, like, so annoying. It matches my hair."

"I like giving you a hard time. I'm sure that thing conforms to our employee dress code."

"What's happening with Scott?" Beth asked.

187

"Some gnarly blowup with the system," Amber said. "Good thing Andy left. Scott's all bent out of shape, giving the new guy hell. We can't file and pay returns online, so they'll be late and we'll get fines. Judy said we gotta file paper returns, and she was looking for checks. I thought she said she was looking for sex. Ha! And eww!"

Jim walked beside Beth. "Brad must've been ready to blow this place to kingdom come."

"He left the department in ruins," Beth said. "To cap it off, he jumped up to the next rung on the corporate ladder. Brad's now a vice president at one of the Bomkamp companies, at a higher level than Scott, and he took Cody with him."

They passed Scott's office and stopped beside his door. They observed Raj sitting woodenly in front of Scott's desk.

"Haven't you got your head around your job yet?" Scott bellowed. "Your number one priority is to fix performance issues before the entire system spins out of control."

"I understand your concerns completely."

"Every one of the states' systems blocked out Heenehan. How could this be?"

"The states are telling me our uploaded files and bank accounts are fine," Raj said. "Until we resolve the issue, the tax group will have to file paper returns and pay by check."

"That won't work. The states require online filing and payment. What's more, paper returns with checks take too long. We'll miss our due dates. We'll incur penalties and interest. What do you plan to do about this?"

"I'll need to replicate the process to figure out the cause. I've never encountered anything like this. It may be a temporary glitch in the system. I honestly don't know."

"You don't know."

"The IT group has been working on it nonstop. We will continue to work on it."

"On top of that, I expected you to be further along with the BomTax implementation," Scott said. "Bomkamp's sales rep showed us how easy the system is to install. It should be fully functional."

Raj looked directly at Scott. "Your current tax preparation software is working well. I advise you to keep it. BomTax is expensive, slow, and cumbersome. It's badly designed. I don't recommend its use by Heenehan's tax department."

Scott sat erect. "I see we're not on the same page. If I had known you'd resist our requirements, I would have hired an American. If your employment here ends, it will be the end of your visa. We'll comply with all the legal requirements of a bona fide termination and pay your transportation home."

"Please allow us to work out this system hiccup," Raj pleaded. "Losing my visa would be a catastrophe for my family and me."

"You've lost my trust, Raj. Thank you for your time."

With head down, Raj passed Jim and Beth.

Grumbling and soft curses filled the garden-level offices. Employees began ascending the stairs.

"What the hell!" Amber shouted. "I can't do nothing. The stupid, buggin' system ain't working right."

Sue hurried to Amber's cubicle and whispered, "The Tech Team's doing a dry run today. The whole network's acting funky doodle. Tomorrow the online returns and payments will go right through."

"Li picked a bad time to do his damn test. We got deadlines this week, and the system goes bye-bye."

"A busy time's the best time for testing. I'll file and pay all my returns in the morning. I'm leaving early. Me and Dusty are going four-wheeling. We like to spin around in the mud and get filthy."

"Gu-ross!"

"Don't knock it 'til you try it."

"I'm gonna beat your ass out the door," Amber said. "Hey, check out my new tattoo." She lifted her shirt tail. A werewolf baring its fangs covered her back.

"It would kill your mother. You look like a street thug."

"That's me. What's the rope sticking out of your desk drawer?"

"I bought me a horse for our property in the mountains," Sue said. "She's still a tiny bit wild, so I'm gonna make a lasso."

"You do that. Have fun, mountain girl."

"I will, tat girl."

Jim said to Beth, "We'll have to work offline at home, since the internet connection is unstable and we can't file or pay returns today."

Judy carried a large stack of documents to Beth's desk, where she unloaded half. She dumped the other half on Jim's desk.

"I've split Cody's work between the two of you," Judy said. "Brad left a few urgent projects I'll let you handle once the returns are filed." She turned to leave.

"Judy! We can't assume Cody's work!" Beth. "Assign it to Sue and Amber. You gave each of them a dozen returns. We're responsible for over five hundred."

"I told you, they're busy. Have Hwan help you. It'll go fast. Knock it out." She trundled to her cubicle.

"I'll ask Tom to take a few more," Jim said. "Hwan's here. Let's grab him and go for a walk around the pond. He has some explaining to do."

Jim, Beth, and Hwan strolled along the walkway.

"Hwan, you promised us no more computer hacking," Jim said. "What's going on? We can't file or pay returns online. We overheard Sue and Amber saying the Tech Team's testing Heenehan's system."

"They test Heenehan today. They going to test other Bomkamp companies before they do anything bad."

"Did you put another code on the network?" Beth asked.

Hwan avoided their eyes. "When Sam from Bomkamp here, Amber show him where reports come from. When they gone, I put code on his laptop. It connect Tech Team to all Bomkamp companies."

Jim threw up his hands. "Hwan! Why did you do that?"

"If my parents go outside, a man always stay behind them. They not know him. Probably Amber know him."

"What are you going to do?" Beth asked. *We can't expect him to put himself and his parents in danger.*

"We move far away. We change our names. Sandra help us. We stay there, never come back here."

Sun sparkled across the pond. Light green leaves fluttered in the warm breeze, defying the dark gray clouds spreading across the mountains on the west. Protestors chanted something inaudible, carrying picket signs along the far side of the office park.

"Where are you moving?" Jim asked.

"We go where they take us."

"What about the code you put on Bomkamp's network?" Jim asked.

"If I not do it, Russians will. My code much better. I can delete lines for malware."

"You should delete those code lines before the malware causes more damage," Beth said.

"Might not matter," Hwan said. "Russians make backups. They can find code lines I delete. They did that before."

A silver fish swam below the surface of the pond, blending into the soft ripples.

"Regardless, you need to delete the code, Hwan," Jim said. "The Tech Team might give out Bomkamp's sensitive information. Or worse."

"First, they watch everything in companies and test. Amber want to play with Bomkamp companies' finance numbers, but Li tell her no."

"So if we see strange numbers in the financial statements, it's Amber's work."

"If Amber do that, I not surprised. She not do what Li tell her. And she leak out information to anybody who pay her."

Beth said, "So at this point, you're useless to the Tech Team. The North Koreans are trying to assassinate you and your parents. For heaven's sake, take off!" *His lack of urgency boggles my mind.*

Jim said, "Hwan, after you delete those lines from the code, tell Sandra to move you and your parents out of here."

"I get out fast as I can."

Chapter 15: Friday, May 19

Amber stopped at Judy's cubicle. "System's working again. No biggie."

Eyes on her computer, Judy muttered, "Congratulations on your promotion."

"Thanks!"

Sue studied her phone as she passed Amber in the aisle. "Way to go."

Judy stood and walked heavily to Jim's cubicle door. "Scott wants to talk to you and Beth in his office."

Scott cradled the black desk phone receiver to his ear. He glanced at them and held out his palm. They waited outside his office door.

Scott spoke into the phone with impatient authority. "Add an administrative charge to their bill. It's an easy price hike. Let them file a class action and take us to court. The lawyers will walk off with the money. Fine." With a snort, he slammed down the receiver.

Scott swiveled in his executive chair and motioned for Jim and Beth to enter. They sat on armless office chairs facing Scott. His blue blazer and blue pin-striped shirt complemented his silver hair. Tilting his head back, he spoke in a baritone voice. "What are your names again?"

"Jim Dennis."

"Beth Madison."

"I want to inform you that I promoted Amber Wolfe to the position of senior tax accountant. Brad thought highly of Amber for her contributions to the tax group. I agree. Amber will assist Judy in reviewing your returns."

"You can't be serious," Beth said. "Amber has no tax background. She's immature and absent more days than she's here. You're doing a disservice to the company."

Scott sat back in his chair, fingertips held together like a church steeple. "Amber shows strong leadership potential. That's more important than any degree or years of experience. I expect you to give her your full support. She's young and lacks technical expertise, but she'll learn everything she needs at the next seminar."

Jim gave Scott an incredulous stare. "Tax work is nowhere near that simple. How can Amber review our work? She wouldn't have the slightest clue what she was looking at. Millions of dollars in tax liabilities are at stake. Why didn't you promote Sue? She's been with the tax group for years."

"Let's be honest. The rest of you aren't leaders. You're followers. Amber has the killer instinct necessary to succeed."

"You could hire a qualified adult from outside the company," Jim said. "What do you mean by 'killer instinct'?"

"If you don't know, I'm not going to tell you. Amber's can-do spirit is a winner. We need a sparkplug in this group to incentivize the rest of you."

"There's a huge disconnect here," Beth said. "Amber isn't anything like you described. She's apathetic, and her work is full of mistakes."

"Let's get something straight. Your mistakes are more of a problem to us than hers. This morning you filed a return with a transposed number. Have you considered retiring? You're a bit advanced in years."

"The transposition was on the accounting report," Beth said. "I didn't know about the error before accounting notified me. The correction will be reflected on next month's return. There's no need to file an amended return."

"Regardless, your performance is suboptimal. You and Sue trained Amber. She couldn't be more prepared to lead the group."

"We were willing to set aside any time Amber needed to learn her job," Jim said. "We tried to train her. She's unteachable. For Beth and me, returns are assembly-line work. We're responsible for so many mundane tasks that we don't have time for strategic planning. We can save Heenehan serious money if we dig into the tax issues and lay them out for you."

Scott spoke with authority. "Bomkamp directed me to push the work down to available staff. Work harder and finish your returns first. If you want to take a deep dive into research, find time to do it. I assume you're free of family obligations at this stage of your lives. Amp up your engagement level. Put in overtime to meet the needs of your company."

Outside Scott's picture window overlooking the office park, Canada geese flew in a V formation, honking at the lead goose flying point.

"I also extended the contracts of Li Chang and his staff of two internal auditors. Amber will continue as their contact person."

Alarm overtook Jim's controlled demeanor. "Do you understand what these people are doing? Those auditors aren't who they say they are. We have a lot to tell you, if you'll listen to us."

"Scott, he's right!" Beth said. "We can't overstate how insidious this group is. Amber is a member."

Scott's mouth twisted. "Oh, for Pete's sake! Don't let jealousy get the better of you. I expect you to behave as professionals and contribute to a productive office environment."

Beth clenched her fists. Jim rubbed the back of his neck.

"I have another important issue to discuss with you," Scott said. "Bomkamp borrowed money to acquire Heenehan, using Heenehan's assets as collateral. The details of the transaction are over your heads. It's called a leveraged buyout."

"We're familiar with that type of acquisition," Jim said.

"The loan payable was moved to Heenehan's balance sheet, so now it's our debt. Heenehan has to repay the money to Bomkamp. We expect huge future growth. At the present time, we need to conserve every dollar to pay off our debt."

Jim leaned forward. "It's our job to save the company money. We can help you do that."

"I want you to minimize our tax payments," Scott said. "You will pay tax on a portion of the accounting reports, such as the first through the fifteenth of the month. If the states challenge us, tell them our business decreased and we already gave them all the records."

Jim moved his chair back several inches from Scott's desk. "That would be a serious ethics violation."

Beth said, "Underreporting for even one month will raise a red flag! If it came to light, we'd have trouble being employed in our profession. No one is above the law."

Scott fixed Beth with a dead-eyed stare. "That shrill voice of yours grates on my nerves."

"I'm speaking to you in a normal tone of voice. Jim is right. If we had time for research, we could minimize the company's tax payments legally."

Scott's face reddened. "Let me be clear. If you do not adhere to this directive, you will be terminated. And don't be truth warriors and phone the ethics hotline. It's designed to flush out troublemakers."

"Heenehan's code of conduct prohibits retaliation for reports of misconduct made in good faith," Beth said. "We should be allowed to communicate our concerns without fear of the company extracting retribution."

"Don't lecture me. Everything will go smoothly if you cooperate. Any pushback and you'll be in the same situation as Brad, but without his generous severance package."

Beth looked away.

Jim maintained a neutral expression. "Scott, I read the quarterly audit report. Why did the external auditor indicate doubt about Heenehan's ability to continue as a going concern?"

"You are not privy to that information. I'll check on your progress after I return from my annual bike race over the mountains." Scott began typing at his computer, as if he had turned on a neon arrow pointing to the door.

They rose and left Scott's office.

"What a horse's ass," Jim said. "We don't need to waste our time worrying about Scott's strategy to underpay our taxes. He's so distracted by all the departments in his empire, odds are he'll have no memory of our conversation."

"I won't change my process," Beth said. "I refuse to support that man with his power plays. I'm concerned Amber's promotion will give her more scope for mischief. Brad was her strongest supporter. Maybe his departure will slow Amber down."

"It's possible, but only if Scott falls off the mountain."

At 10:05 p.m. Beth double-checked her home computer. She buried her face in her hands. *I forgot to scan the accounting report. I left it lying on my desk at work. The filing deadline is midnight. I'll make a quick trip to the office.*

She pulled into the shadowy lot and made her way downstairs in the dim security lighting.

In the brightly lit kitchen, Amber was spraying liquid from a can onto the floor, back and forth in a sweeping motion. *What in God's name is she doing? I don't see a security guard. Amber would concoct a wild cover story for me.* Beth gathered the report from her desk and returned to her car.

Chapter 16: Monday, May 22

Red-faced, Judy roared into her speakerphone. "Why the HELL did he wax the floor and leave it so slick? No, he will clean it NOW. Not later this morning. Not this afternoon. NOW."

Mary in the facilities department said, "I'm so sorry! I take full responsibility for your mishap. The janitor will be there within the hour to wipe the floor. I promise I'll get to the bottom of this incident."

Having observed yellow caution tape secured across both kitchen entrances, Beth entered Jim's cubicle. "The one morning I'm late, I walk into a crime scene."

"Yesterday Judy and Amber were planning today's meeting with the Bomkamp companies' managers. I'm usually here early, before anyone else. This morning they came a few minutes ahead of me to prepare for the meeting."

"I have an idea of what happened next."

"When Judy stepped onto the kitchen floor, her feet flew out from under her. She fell flat on her back. Amber rolled her over to the carpet and helped her up."

"Oh, my."

A slightly amused expression flashed across Jim's face. "Judy said she's all right. She's going to get checked out when her doctor's office opens."

"I'm glad it wasn't you or me," Beth said. "That nosedive would've sent me to the nearest orthopedic surgeon. Last night I came in here to pick up a report for the deadline. Amber was spraying something across the kitchen floor. I left without drawing her attention." *Good thing I didn't interfere.*

"I assume Amber's whole idea is to replace Judy at the Bomkamp managers' meetings," Jim said. "For some reason, Amber wants to serve on the teambuilding committee."

"After Amber slammed me into the wall, Judy insisted it was an accident. Judy's tumble wasn't any more of an accident than mine."

"A karmic slip for Judy."

Mary walked briskly to the kitchen entrance, Judy hobbling behind her. Extending her index finger, Mary bent over and took a sample of the oily substance on the glistening floor. "It has a rancid odor. Here, smell it." She put her index finger close to Judy's face.

Judy wrinkled her nose. She reached over the yellow tape to grab an empty can on the countertop. "We've been using this spray to fix our squeaky office chairs."

Mary examined the outdated container. "Olive oil spray. It's on the floor."

"The cleaning crew should have mopped the floor yesterday!"

"The janitor finished his work in this building late yesterday afternoon," Mary said. "I verified he did not enter the building yesterday evening or this morning. He is aware of the situation. He will clean the floor when he comes in, which should be soon." Mary attached cardboard signs to each of the two kitchen entrances stating, "Please use the treasury department kitchen until further notice."

"What's going on here?" Sue asked.

"Judy had an accident," Amber said. "Now that I'm the senior tax accountant, I'm taking over for her at the Bomkamp managers' meeting. Li told me to get the managers' email addresses and phone numbers for the softball activity. I'm gonna let you organize it."

"Sure, boss. Anything else I can do for you?"

"Did you tell Li I'm a smart girl who's gonna help him out with the Koreans, like I asked you?"

"I plumb forgot. You tell him."

Walking toward a nearby shopping district during the noon hour, Jim said to Beth, "Doris and I are in the process of moving Mom to Sunny Senior Care."

"Oh, Jim, that's a huge undertaking! A whole new environment for Rose. So much to consider."

"Doris has been handling the details. She's an angel. I'm sad, but relieved. I can't take care of Mom anymore. I worry about her all the time. She'll be safe at the facility. It's the best, most affordable place we could find."

"You're a good son. Let me know how she does there."

They joined Andy and Tom at a fast casual restaurant. They carried their lunches to a round table on the outside terrace near the sidewalk. Cheerful young adults prepared tables, canopies, and banners for a street fair. Craftspeople erected booths, arranged handmade items, and attached price tags. Artists hung paintings and photographs inside their stands. Food vendors assembled pop-up tents, placing tables and chairs underneath.

Andy brushed a wet chestnut brown curl from his forehead. "I took a quick shower after my ten-minute workout at the gym. I checked Amber's cell phone. The Tech Team's done at Heenehan. They gathered all the information they needed."

Tom took a big gulp of iced tea. "I say good riddance to the whole gang."

"I'm curious about Sue's role in all of this. She and Amber aren't as tight as they used to be." Beth swallowed a bite of her vegetarian wrap.

"Sue's playing footsie with the Tech Team. We saw her in the fourth-floor conference room on live camera feed, thanks to Tom's excellent work." Andy bit into a turkey sandwich.

"That's odd. I never would have thought that Sue was part of the Tech Team," Beth said.

Perched on a tree branch overhead, a large black-and-white magpie warbled. Another one responded with raspy chatter.

"Hwan said that after the Chinese finish their work, the North Koreans will move in," Jim said. "He didn't say whether they would physically move into the conference room, or work inside the Bomkamp companies' systems from a remote location."

"Chang has an agreement of some sort with the Koreans," Andy said.

Tom moved his chair a few inches from the sidewalk, making room for the street fair underway. "I took a screen grab of their contract. It was in English, written in legalese. It looked as if Chang agreed to pass along some of the Tech Team's intelligence."

Jim said, "They used Heenehan's network to burrow into the Bomkamp companies and all the organizations they do business with."

"The Bomkamp companies' trade secrets are in the Tech Team's possession," Beth said. "They don't need to be at Heenehan or Bomkamp in person anymore. I believe they'll do their work somewhere else. I'd like to hear what Amber says when Scott asks her where the consulting group went." *If Scott even notices the Tech Team is gone.*

As more people arrived, browsed booths, and gathered to watch performers, the noise level increased.

Andy took a look around before speaking louder. "Amber had a lengthy phone chat with one of the Koreans. They plan to activate a section of the code Hwan put on the system. It will delete all the Bomkamp's companies' records, bank accounts, internet files, everything. And they won't be able to restore their backup data."

Tom spoke in a pained tone. "Bomkamp's systems will be useless. Except for paper copies in storage or in an employee's possession, companies will be erased. So the Koreans are preparing for a successful hit."

"Here's the thing," Andy said. "If the Koreans wipe out Bomkamp's network, all the companies, government agencies, banks, and individuals doing business with Bomkamp would be affected, too."

Jim said, "From what I've learned about North Korea, we could experience random events with no particular target that are, in fact, cyber-terrorist attacks."

Andy nodded. "That's the sort of thing those gangsters do in their own country. And they send innocent people to prison camps, assassinate anyone in their way, detonate bombs, and hijack aircraft. Thousands of men, women, and children disappear without a trace. Those crackpots isolate and misinform their own citizens."

"Their propaganda posters are ridiculous." Jim popped the last bite of the grilled cheese sandwich into his mouth.

"If the authorities are monitoring the situation, where are they?" Beth asked. "I'm afraid something will happen to Hwan."

Jim said, "We told Hwan he needs to delete the code. We warned him to leave before the Koreans come in."

A long-haired young man skipped along the sidewalk juggling three bright red balls, tossing them high in the air.

Tom sighed. "I don't care about foreign wackos. I just want to focus on my job at Analytics. I want regular hours at a normal company so I can be home for dinner and spend my evenings and weekends with my family. Have some fun like that juggler."

"I'm with you," Andy said. "I'd lose my sanity if I didn't pay attention to my normal life. Hey, a great little acoustic duo is playing at the Hideout tonight. I'm going to stop by for about an hour. Anyone care to join me?"

"Sorry. It's my night to help the kids with their homework," Tom said. "Sherry's going to a PTA meeting."

Beth said, "I need to turn in early." *I'm about ready to drop right now.*

"You won't be tempted to make a night of it, Andy?" Jim asked. "A good-looking single dude like you?"

"You know me, the white sheep of the family. My favorite drink is iced tea. I'd offer to pick you up, but you wouldn't want to ride in my dogmobile. Hair embedded in the seats, paw prints all over. I haven't had time to clean it."

"Doris and I are going to visit Mom at Sunny Senior Care late this afternoon. I'll meet you at the Hideout at 8."

"Great! Hey, swing by Analytics when you can. I'll show you my cool new platform. Our customers use it to shop for products and services, compare prices, place their orders, and view their account activity. I added continuous monitoring to catch any fraudsters inside or outside the company."

Beth said, "You're amazing, Andy. We'd love to see it."

They emptied their trays into the trashcan.

Andy and Tom headed back to Analytics.

Jim and Beth negotiated the busy pavement. Jim shouted into his phone, "Sorry, Doris. I'll call you in a few minutes. It's too noisy. I can't hear a word you're saying."

A man in a plaid jacket played boogie-woogie with joyful energy on a street piano.

Jim knocked, waited a moment, and opened the door. Rose sat in a chair next to the picture window, wearing a clean flowered robe, her long, gray hair combed neatly. "Hi, Mom! Doris and I came by to visit you. How are you doing today?" *I can see that the staff is taking care of her.*

Rose glared at him. "Jimmy, I told you I don't like it here. I want to go home!"

"Okay, we'll go soon," Jim said. "It's nice here at Sunny Senior Care. Your room's light and airy. I heard you did arts and crafts and took a walk this morning." *I wouldn't mind living here myself when I'm old.*

"I don't know who these people are."

"Your nurse said you enjoy talking to the other residents," Jim said. "You told her the food's tasty."

Rose's face grew pale. Her hands shook. She looked up at Jim, eyes wet with tears. "Those old biddies are trying to kill me!"

Doris rubbed her arm. "Rosie, you feel like they're trying to kill you, but they're not. Moving to a new home is scary! You're safe here. We won't let anything bad happen to you."

"Look out the window, Mom. The flowers and birds are so pretty."

"The flowers are different colors. I like the bluebirds."

"We brought a few photos with us," Jim said. He and Doris pulled up chairs beside Rose. "These are from your schooldays. Tell us about this picture."

"I remember. Our school nurse made us line up for polio shots. That girl was in my class. She screamed and screamed. Such a baby! She made us all upset. Our nice teacher hugged her and talked to her, so she stopped crying." Rose studied each photo, telling stories about her childhood. After a half hour, she spoke slowly, her eyes heavy and head nodding.

"Mom, we need to leave so you can rest."

They assisted Rose to her bed, helped make her comfortable, and covered her with a light blanket. She closed her eyes.

Doris patted her hand. "I'll be back soon, Rosie."

"I love you, Mom." Jim hugged his frail mother gently.

Chapter 17: Tuesday, May 23

Hwan stopped at Jim's cubicle, where he and Beth were working.

"Sponsors call me," Hwan said. "They ready for my parents and me, someplace north. They have our new names. Amber and the rest of them not ever find us. I go today. Sandra drive us to airport. I watch for her car outside front door. Safer to leave middle of day."

"Hwan, best of luck," Jim said. "I wish you and your parents a much better future in your new life. Did you delete the code?"

"I did my best. I cannot do it."

"Thank you for helping us, Hwan," Beth said. "But you must delete the code before you go. If you don't, it will cause great misfortune for thousands of people." *Deleting the code might cause great misfortune for Hwan.*

"Okay, I try. I call you when Sandra here. Please walk me to her car. I afraid Amber or somebody stop me."

"We'd be happy to walk you to Sandra's car," Beth said. "We wish you the best in your new life."

"Thank you for helping us figure out what's going on here." Jim tapped Hwan's forearm. "Good luck."

Amber arrived a few minutes before noon, complaining about a furnace issue at home.

Jim answered his phone.

"Time now," Hwan said. Jim observed a car parked outside the front door of the building, with Sandra in the driver's seat. In the back seat, an elderly Asian couple sat facing forward. Jim signaled Beth with a wave. Hwan arrived at Jim's cubicle carrying a small plastic bag filled with his possessions. Jim and Beth joined him on either side as they walked toward the staircase.

Amber peered over her cubicle wall, her face hardening. She shot out of her door, running full tilt toward Hwan. Jim and Beth pulled Hwan aside. They braced for the impending collision.

A lariat circled the air, settled around Amber's waist, and tightened. She lunged for Hwan and fell, the wind getting knocked out of her. Strong feminine hands grasped Amber's fists behind her back and tied them to her feet. A red paisley bandana covered her mouth and knotted behind her head. Sue dragged Amber down the corridor. Hogtied on Sue's cubicle floor, Amber thrashed and made muffled grunting noises.

Standing over Amber, Sue said, "Don't worry. I'm gonna bring you out alive. I know how to handle wild animals like you."

Jim and Beth accompanied Hwan upstairs and out the front door to Sandra's car.

Beth asked, "Hwan did you delete the code?"

Hwan shook his head.

Jim opened Sandra's car door, helped Hwan into the front seat of the car, shut the door, and pulled the handle to ensure the lock was engaged. They waved goodbye as Sandra drove away.

"I really didn't expect Hwan to delete the code," Beth said, descending the stairs back to the office. "I'm just relieved he made it out of the building safely."

"Hwan will be responsible for destroying Bomkamp's entire network," Jim said. "We should have put more pressure on him. When are the authorities going to do something?"

"Hwan said if he deleted the code, the Russians would re-enable it," Beth said. "We can't control the chain of events that's going to happen."

"You're right, we've done what we can. I'll delete the spreadsheets on Hwan's computer and toss the old accounting reports into the shredder."

"Thanks, Jim."

They paused at the immobilized figure on the floor of Sue's cubicle. Sue turned from her computer and winked. They returned to their desks, ignoring Amber's muted howls.

After an hour, Sue said, "Well, looky here! How long have you been down there?" She whispered, "One peep out of you, and I'm calling Li Chang. He'd be mighty unhappy with you." She untied the bandana around Amber's mouth and loosened the rope from Amber's feet and hands.

"You're gonna pay for this, you two-faced bitch."

"Simmer down, girlfriend. I don't know WHAT you did to make somebody do this to you."

The sun was setting when Jim and Beth wrapped up their work for the day. As Jim shut down his computer, Amber stood at his cubicle door, purse slung over her arm. The stocky, round-faced man by her side wore an olive green shirt, loosely fitted brown pants, and boots.

With a dark glint in her eyes, Amber said, "Jim, this is Minjun Mook. He's the auditor over all the Bomkamp companies." She turned and clomped toward the stairs.

Jim held out his hand. "Hello, I'm Jim Dennis, tax accountant for Heenehan Telecom Company."

Mook gripped Jim's hand, pulled him forward, grabbed him by the collar, and shouted, "Where is Hwan Cho? Where is he?"

"I don't know! No one knows!"

Mook threw him against the wall.

Beth hurried out into the corridor. "Who are you?" she demanded.

Mook raised his hand. Beth moved aside as he took a hard swing at her. He stumbled, then regained his balance.

Beth shouted, "Hwan's whereabouts are known only to the U.S. government!"

Mook poked his index finger into Jim's chest. "My men are out searching for him. If I find out you or the lady here are hiding Cho, you'll spend the rest of your sorry lives in a nice camp where we welcome our guests by cracking their kneecaps. Or we'll string you up in public. That's how we roll, buddy." He barreled down the hall and charged up the stairs.

Jim walked unsteadily to his desk chair. "Are you all right?"

Beth sank onto the side chair. "I think so. How are you doing?"

"Still shaky."

They sat for a minute.

Jim spoke with effort. "Hwan might have been involved in subterfuge before he left North Korea. Or he's in trouble for leaving the country. Most North Koreans can't travel freely around their own country, let alone travel abroad."

"So Amber's working with this lunatic Minjun Mook, as well as Li Chang."

"Mook must be picking up where Chang left off. Amber's in the middle, transferring Chang's data to Mook. If Heenehan hadn't hired Chang, Bomkamp wouldn't be dealing with Mook."

"Amber is Chang's loyal fan, so the Mook gig has to be temporary," Beth said. "Mook must be aware that Sandra took Hwan to the airport. He'll have Sandra's head on a stick."

"Hwan's not a big deal to the Koreans, neither are we, but Sandra's disappearance would touch off an international incident. At any rate, Mook's running the show. Grab your jacket, and let's go."

Beth returned to her cubicle and shut down her computer.

Jim stopped at Beth's cubicle. She was sitting at her desk, head down, fingers pressed to her temples, staring at her phone.

Jim sat in her side chair. "What's wrong?"

Beth slid the phone on her desk over to Jim. "Breaking news."

Jim read the report. "Police have launched an investigation after three bodies were found in a field near the airport. They were identified as Hwan Cho and an elderly couple believed to be his parents. The manner of death has not been released."

Beth said, "Horrible. That crazy, fearless man."

They sat in silence.

Jim cleared his throat. "Making it out of here alive was a long shot for Hwan and his parents. The North Koreans must have abducted them at the airport."

Beth took a tissue from the box on her desk and wiped her eyes. "He tried to keep his parents safe. The North Koreans murdered all three of them."

"Amber might have tipped off the Koreans after Sue untied her. Or the Koreans followed Sandra's car. He almost escaped."

"Surveilled by sinister people, living every day in mortal danger. Poor Hwan."

"None of us are safe."

Chapter 18: Wednesday, May 24

Jim entered a small building on the outskirts of the city. He found Derek sitting behind a table covered with clusters of electronic equipment. "Hey, Jim! Haven't seen you forever. Take a seat. You must be wondering why I asked you to stop by my office during your lunch hour."

"Tom told me he ran into you at the hardware store. We're reviving our old high school band. Did he ask you to play with us?"

Derek chuckled. "Not exactly. Tom told me about your work with sonification. We do music media production here. We design and sell our own products, and we provide services for larger companies. My company needs someone with your technical skills. I'm looking to fill a new position of senior multimedia technician. I need someone to update our app for musicians who build songs and create their own music and to teach group tutorials for the app. The person in this position will write algorithms to learn users' tastes and help artists tap into that information. You'd have the opportunity to release your own songs on the streaming services. You can read the full job description and salary range on our website. We have a competitive benefits package. Would you be interested in this position?"

Wide-eyed, Jim said, "I wasn't expecting a job offer. I need time to consider it."

"How about a quick tour of my company?"

"Sure."

Beth appeared at Elly Burke's office door. "My apologies for popping in on you so late in the day. Do you have five or ten minutes?"

Elly's shoulder-length blonde hair brushed her purple, sleeveless blouse. "Of course I do! Have a seat." She motioned to a mesh office chair in front of her oak veneer desk. "What's up?"

"I want to thank you for offering me the senior tax accountant position at Analytics. After careful consideration, I concluded it's not the right fit for me. After I'm finished at Heenehan, I plan to fully retire." *This conversation is too difficult for me.*

Elly leaned forward with an expression of concern. "I'm truly sorry to hear that, Beth. What influenced your decision?"

"I'm ready for a new chapter in my life. Before Jason came along, I loved doing artwork, especially drawing and painting. I haven't touched it in years. Recently I entered several of my old paintings in the Downtown Gallery art fair. I sold the ones with patterns, repeating colors, lines, and shapes. Now I have big ideas. I want to create designs."

"Wow! That's bucket list!"

"It makes me happy. Elly, I'm grateful to you on so many levels. It was a privilege to be a member of your staff. Your leadership has been an inspiration to me."

"Thank you, Beth. Would you be interested in working part time, say, ten hours a week? With your expertise, you'd be an ideal mentor for a younger staff person."

Beth shifted in her seat. "Elly, I'm not up to it. At almost sixty-five, my energy is a finite resource. Time is precious to me. I'm hoping for fifteen good years of retirement. I don't want to cut short my potential as an artist. I won't run out of money if I'm frugal."

"You might just have decision fatigue coming from burnout. I know burnout; I've been there. The career you worked so hard for feels like a mistake. The work you do all day isn't important or worthwhile. Your workplace is beyond unpleasant. Nothing turned out the way you expected."

"Exactly. I'm frustrated with everything. It's beyond my ability to cope with it. I'm at retirement age. I don't need to work."

Elly regarded her with concern. "Beth, it may take a while to get back to normal. Your expertise won't disappear. Since Analytics is a new venture, we're sucked into hard work, long hours, late nights. That wouldn't be good for you. A fixed, part-time schedule, when you're ready, is a solution we both could live with. What do you think?"

Eyes brimming with tears, Beth stared at her hands. "I don't believe I can or should work anymore." *I promised myself I wouldn't cry.*

"I understand," Elly said. "It's a hard decision. I'll assume you're confidently turning the page and moving on. Let me know if you change your mind."

Beth stood. "Thank you for everything, Elly."

"Keep in touch."

"I will."

They gave each other a warm hug.

Scott Campbell exploded with rage. "Another calamity, Raj! We're looking at millions in fines if we can't pay our taxes on time. How long will the internet be down?"

"Something is loose in the company's network."

"With all your schooling and experience, what do you believe is going on?"

"I don't know what to believe."

"A pathetic statement. I'll speak with George Weston to discuss ways treasury can make our tax payments," Scott said. "Shontae Williams in his group is an expert at working with the taxing jurisdictions' banks."

"Um, Shontae left Heenehan for a position in the Analytics Telco treasury department."

"Great. That's just great. And what happened to BomTax? Raj, your work here at Heenehan has been unsatisfactory. I will discuss this with your director. Expect consequences for your substandard performance."

Raj straightened his shoulders. "Sorry, I won't touch BomTax. This morning I submitted my resignation to my director. I accepted a position at Analytics Telco. I'll be working for Andy Price. My visa will not be affected by the change. Andy's already initiated my visa transfer." He flashed a beaming smile, which he quickly suppressed.

"Get the hell out of my office."

Sue stood in the aisle, putting on her jacket. From her cubicle, Beth asked, "Where's Amber?"

"Off for the rest of the day. Scott sent her to a basic tax seminar." Sue walked toward the stairs.

Entering his cubicle, Jim took the stapler from his chair seat and set it on his vacant desk. He mumbled, "Where are my office supplies?" Taking a seat, he faced a Post-it with a smiley face stuck to the center of his computer screen. He peeled it off, crumpled it, and threw it toward his upside-down wastebasket, where it bounced to the floor.

Beth stopped at Jim's door. "I found my supplies strewn all over my cubicle. It looks like you're dealing with the same problem."

"Amber." He turned his wastebasket upright and deposited the Post-it note into it.

Beth lifted his empty desk organizer from the floor and placed it on his desk. "I talked with Elly. I told her I'm going to fully retire."

"You're not going to work part time?"

"No. I told Elly I want to pursue my artwork. We had a tough talk."

"You're making the right ... the right ..."

"Hey, what's happening with you?"

Jim stared blankly at the computer screen, his face colorless.

"You're having another brain zap." Pulling up the guest chair, she gently rubbed his arm. "It's so cold in here. Try to breathe. Big, slow, dragon breaths."

Jim continued to sit motionless, breathing slowly, his color returning. "This one wasn't bad," he said. "A few electric shocks and lightning flashes in my head. My stress level is off the charts. I have too much on my mind. I can't make all the moving pieces fit together."

"Tell me about it."

"Well, this morning I saw an opening for a senior tax accountant posted on Analytics' website. Elly said it's their policy to post open positions."

"It's about time!" Beth exclaimed. "We'll be out of here before the sky falls!" She pulled out a spiral notebook and file folders wedged behind Jim's computer and placed them in the organizer.

"I'm considering another offer."

"What?"

"Something came up. When Tom and Andy and I played in our high school band, we met a few local musicians. Tom ran into one of them at the hardware store, Derek. He owns a small music media company not far from here. Their conversation was cut short because Tom had his kids with him, but he mentioned my work with sonification. Out of the blue, Derek called me. I stopped by his office. After we talked for a while, he offered me a full-time position."

Beth clapped her hands together. "Oh my gosh! This calls for a celebration! What will you be doing?"

"The company's making music in new ways. They design their own products and provide services for larger companies. I'll have lots of potential opportunities. Right now Derek needs me to update an app for music lovers who want to build songs and create their own music. And I'd roll out my own music."

"It's a perfect fit for you."

"I'd love to release my songs on the streaming services. A few are good to go, and I saved lots of raw sound that's ready to arrange. I want to write music people will listen to now and forever. I want bands to play my music live. I'm dreaming big. I'm terrified and slightly numb."

"You've been working on your own music for years. Are you having mixed emotions about the position?" *Why would Jim even consider declining Derek's offer?*

"It's a big decision. I can't make a mistake. It's a better job than I ever imagined. But the starting salary isn't enough to cover Mom's care and my living expenses, even after I sell the house. I won't put her in the county nursing home. At Analytics, my salary would provide the memory care Mom needs. I can't always do what I want to do."

"What if you made Elly a counter offer? Maybe part time, a couple evenings during the week and one day on the weekend." *Not ideal, but a workable solution.*

"It wouldn't be fair to limit my hours when everyone else at Analytics is on call or working round the clock. Plus, I'm completely burned out."

"Analytics is a different world from Heenehan. Working part-time for Elly would be energizing. She needs you. You like that wonkish work your coworkers go out of their way to avoid."

Jim made a tight smile. "Okay, you win. I'll talk to Elly and run the numbers to see if it could possibly work out. It would be a heavy schedule with limited flexibility. I think I'm up to it. In any case, it would be an improvement over Heenehan. I wouldn't drive to work every day half-expecting a pile of smoking rubble where the building used to be."

"It's worth a try." Beth retrieved his scissors and Scotch Tape from the top of his cubicle wall and set them on his desk.

"Analytics has great potential, but most start-ups fail. The media company's in the black. I expect Derek will sell it eventually. If something happens to Analytics or the media company, what then? I could be shuffled off to another Heenehan."

"I bet you'd be safe for some time." Beth flipped his wall calendar, which was turned toward the wall.

"I know Elly. As for the media company, I'm not sure what I'm walking into. Not everyone has good intentions. I've seen enough backbiting and scheming for ten lifetimes. The music business produces winners and losers."

"I'm guessing it would be a more collaborative environment than you're used to," Beth said. "Derek wouldn't throw you into a group of combative strangers. You might find yourself exchanging creative ideas." *Don't overthink this, Jim.*

"This change is nuclear for me. Do you get why I've been pressing the snooze button instead of making a hasty decision?"

"Of course. I'm going to love your music."

"Tom doesn't know about Derek's offer, so please keep it confidential until I decide what I want to do. I don't want Elly or anyone else to hear about it yet."

"I won't say anything." *Darn, I was going to text Katie.*

They plucked out a colorful array of pencils, pens, and highlighters sticking up from Jim's desk plant.

Judy dropped into her chair at the head of the table in a conference room. "I called this short meeting to inform you that Sue Gatling resigned."

Amber gasped. "Sue never told me nothing about leaving!"

"Sue and her husband will manage a farm and home supply store with a small grocery. Unfortunately, Sue fell behind in her assignments. Jim, Beth, you will take over Sue's work. You can access her files on the network. I will bring her paperwork to you."

"That makes us responsible for all the returns, audits, and projects," Beth said. "No way can we handle the whole group's workload."

"We can't do it," Jim said.

"Amber has been working diligently on the state audit and her projects, as well as reviewing your returns, so she's carrying a heavy workload. Make a list of your job duties. Sandra can pull someone from her group to help us on a temporary basis."

"Sandra's group is swamped," Beth said.

"You are expected to maintain the quality of your work, which Amber and I will review. You must complete all your work within a normal forty-hour workweek."

Jim and Beth called Tom from a quiet area on the sidewalk across the street. Jim put his phone on speaker.

"Tom, Sue left the company," Jim said. "Since Amber doesn't produce any work, we're responsible for all the work in the department. Can you take more of our returns?"

"If I do, Sherry won't be happy. My job at Analytics is full time now. I've missed more than one family activity because I was working on a Heenehan deadline. I need the money you're sending me, but I can hardly keep track of all my responsibilities as it is."

"Would you take ten more returns?" Jim asked. *I hate putting more pressure on Tom.*

"Well, all right. I guess ten more won't make any difference."

"Thanks, Tom. I promise this is coming to an end." *I hope we're still friends when it does.*

"You're welcome. You made good improvements to Judy's database. Andy ran performance analyzers and made a few more changes. It should save us at least five hours a week."

"That's great. Judy won't detect any changes. She'll think those features were in the database before she stole it."

"Andy customized the database for Analytics, too. It's more highly developed than the one we're using for Heenehan."

"Andy's first class." *What did I ever do to deserve these wonderful friends?*

"What else is happening?" Beth asked Tom.

"Andy's keeping tabs on Amber's phone. We believe she has plans of her own, but she won't wander far from Li Chang. Hang on, Andy's calling."

After a minute, Tom returned to their call. "Andy found new texts. Chang told Amber they don't need Sue anymore. Sue cut all ties to the team. Chang said they have everything they need. Amber's not supposed to go back to the conference room after she leaves the building today."

"Interesting," Jim said. "Keep us posted. Sorry to push more work on you, Tom."

"That's okay. As long as you're suffering more, I'm good. Ha! Talk to you later."

Amber entered the vacant fourth-floor conference room. She surveyed the conference table, clear except for a few papers stacked in a neat pile in a cardboard box. She lifted the box, smiling at the empty champagne bottle in the wastebasket as she left the room.

Chapter 19: Thursday, May 25

Judy sat at the head of the conference table, Jim and Beth on either side.

"Amber has taken a few hours off to deal with a family emergency," Judy said. "I was asked to notify you that we anticipate sporadic internet outages. Our building is having electrical problems related to the internet issues. I expect you to continue your normal work. The situation should be resolved shortly."

"Are any of the other Bomkamp companies having these issues?" Jim asked.

"Certainly not. Why do you ask?"

"Just a hunch. Are you sure?"

"None of the tax supervisors in the other companies reported any problems to me."

"All right. We'll do our best."

"This morning Heenehan's management informed me that some employees are picketing Bomkamp's headquarters downtown," Judy said. "Tomorrow they plan to picket each of the suburban offices. If any Heenehan employee participates in the picketing, they will be immediately terminated."

"Why are they picketing?" Beth asked.

"I have no idea. Heenehan's leadership team is committed to keeping you well-informed about important developments. Stay focused on your jobs."

"Is the softball teambuilding activity going to happen tomorrow?" Jim asked.

"Yes. I expect you both to be in attendance, if your work is done."

"It's supposed to turn cold and rainy tomorrow afternoon," Jim said.

"In case of inclement weather, our teambuilding activity will be held indoors."

"What will we be doing if it's indoors?" Beth asked.

"The Bomkamp teambuilding committee put together a schedule of initiatives for employees to meet each other, with the goal of having fun."

Judy heaved herself up, threw open the door, and trundled down the hall.

"Hey, Amber, how're you doing?" Sue's phone voice was brightly cheerful. "I'm glad you're free to chat and not tied up."

"Very funny. I was hoping I'd never hear from you again, you bleached rat. What do you want anyways?"

"C'mon, let's start fresh. No hard feelings. Let bygones be bygones. Dusty's idea of our own store was a good one. It's really cool! We're having our grand-opening celebration all day tomorrow. Can you come?"

"The softball teambuilding event's tomorrow. I'm in charge of the vans and drivers."

"Kessie will be at the party. She works for us now. We pay her good and give her a discount on anything she buys, so she's happy. She picked out our in-store country music."

"Okay, I'd like to see Kessie. You, not so much. I'll stop by during the games when the drivers don't have anything to do."

"Grab one of the vans and bring the drivers along!" Sue said. "We've got a ton of food and craft beers. The more the merrier!"

"If the weather's bad, we're going to some indoor place, so we'll be a little late."

"Okay. Tell the drivers not to lock their vans, and leave their key on top of the dashboard. Not in the ignition, or it will drain the battery."

"Why?" Amber asked. *This bitch is jerking me around again.*

"The drivers might want to switch vans. Or, if somebody needs to move a van while the driver's gone, it'll be easier if the key's still in it."

"Okay, I guess that makes sense. I can tell the drivers to leave their vans unlocked and the keys in the vans." Amber paused. "There's that high-pitched humming again. I hear the weirdest background noises. I swear this phone is hacked. My phone bill's huge."

"The noise is probably the wind," Sue said. "Your phone uses more data because you're so busy. I gotta go. The delivery guy's here with my party decorations. See you tomorrow."

Jim and Beth stood at the garden-level window. They observed people wearing jackets in the chilly morning, carrying placards, walking back and forth on the sidewalk next to Heenehan's office building.

Eight white, fifteen-passenger vans pulled into the parking lot, disgorging more picketers. Signs read, *Job Killer!, No Outsourcing!, Stop Looting!, Wake Up, Minions!*

Jim said, "Over a hundred protesters are out there."

The demonstrators paraded along the sidewalk, on the grass, and around the pond.

"I'm shocked they're so dissatisfied they're willing to stick their necks out against a powerful company like Bomkamp," Beth said.

Jim squinted at picketers who formed lines and began climbing back into the vans. "The van drivers aren't the same as the ones who drove them here."

"They might be taking turns driving."

"The new drivers are all Asian men, except for one woman, who's driving the first van."

"Guess who's the woman driver with the green hair."

"Hey, look at that."

A gray-haired man stood on the lawn, gesturing and yelling at people to get out of the van. The driver tried to drag him into the van. He pulled free, then ran around the pond. He outran the driver, who climbed back into the van.

Jim's phone flashed. He showed Andy's message to Beth. "Someone sent Amber driving directions to a location in the foothills. He says it's an abandoned warehouse."

"Oh, creepy."

They walked to Judy's cubicle.

Beth asked, "Judy, where are the picketers going?"

"How should I know? I was told they went to a teambuilding event. The picketers' plans don't involve me. Or you."

Jim and Beth returned to Jim's cubicle. "Could the North Koreans have kidnapped the Bomkamp picketers?" he asked.

"Impossible. How could the Koreans carry off citizens on American soil without the government knowing?"

By mid-morning, few employees on the garden level remained.

Sitting idly, Beth said, "Work's a lost cause with the internet dropping. I suspect most people either took off for the teambuilding event or went home."

"I've gotten several texts from Andy. He and Tom are following texts and calls on Amber's phone. Yesterday she caught wind of the picketers' arrangement with the van rental company, and she shared it with the Koreans. This morning she and the Korean drivers seized the vans. They drove the picketers to the mountains."

"No activity was scheduled for the mountains. I'm curious what the North Koreans are doing with those Bomkamp employees. Could Skip Bomkamp have told them to get rid of the picketers?"

"Tom wants to drive out to that old warehouse building," Jim said. "Andy has to work late. He asked Tom not to go out there on his own, unarmed, not knowing what he's going to find."

"You know what," Beth said. "It's go time."

"I agree. Let's go with Tom."

Jim and Beth pulled into Analytics' parking lot.

Wearing khaki coveralls and a ball cap, Tom stepped out of his white minivan. "Let's take my van. It's a midsize, but it could pass for a utility van if you don't see the kids' stuff tossed around inside."

Beth opened the front passenger door and climbed in. Tom pressed a key-fob button to open the sliding door. Jim sat in the seat behind Tom.

Tom accelerated onto the highway, passing Sue's store. The cloudy afternoon sky darkened, and he turned on the headlights. After he exited onto a paved mountain road, his van slowed with the rising elevation. Low vegetation turned to thickets of tall evergreen trees.

"I've lost my cell phone service," Jim said.

Beth examined her phone. "I can't get a solid signal."

"We're too far from the nearest cell tower," Tom said. "Good thing you brought your jackets. Looks like a late spring snowstorm coming over the mountains."

A light rain fell, then a rain and snow mix pelted the van, reducing visibility. Tom switched on the windshield wipers and defroster. The wind increased, and the van skidded slightly on slick spots.

"Jim, Beth, get down!" Tom shouted. They bent low. A vehicle passed them going in the opposite direction. "Okay, crisis over." They sat up. "Amber was driving a white van. It was full of Asian men, probably the drivers who dumped the picketers at the warehouse. They must be going to Sue's party. Amber was so busy talking to the guys, she didn't pay any attention to me."

"I can't believe they just left the Bomkamp employees behind," Beth said. *I'm afraid this trip wasn't such a good idea.*

Tom slowed when he spotted white vans parked on both sides of the road. A gray-brown building became visible in a clearing on the left side of the road. "Let's find out what's going on," Tom said. He made a U-turn and parked a few feet in front of the first van.

Beth took a penlight and air horn from her purse and zipped them into her jacket pocket. She set her purse on the van floor. In the darkening dusk, she, Jim, and Tom got out of the van. The wind had subsided, and snow flurries drifted down. Tom locked the van door, put the key in his jacket pocket, and zipped it shut.

They crept around the crumbling brick building, stooping below cracked and broken windows, careful not to step on pieces of rusted metal and broken glass. Brown steel doors on the front, side, and back of the building stood slightly ajar, as though the old latches had been broken or misaligned. They peered through a thick, snow-flecked evergreen branch in front of a window.

Under flickering fluorescent ceiling lights, approximately 100 Bomkamp employees sat on the decaying wooden floor, curled against the chill of the evening. Water dripped from the ceiling between rough wooden beams. Three softballs lay by the front door.

A blond man walked around with a baseball bat dangling from his hand, scanning the room with watchful eyes. Three hard-faced Asian men stood at attention, one in front of each of the three doors. They each held a baseball bat horizontally across their bodies.

A man sitting on the floor leaped up. Screaming, he charged the front door. The door guard lifted his bat and thrusted the end cap into the man's shoulder. The man kicked at the guard, who flipped the bat in front of the man's shin, blocking his foot. The guard dropped the bat, pummeled the man with rapid hand strikes to his shoulders and arms, and finished with a groin kick. The man lay motionless for a few moments before crawling back to his spot on the floor.

Jim, Beth, and Tom crouched down, inching their way past the window.

"You'd think all those people could overpower four guards," Tom whispered.

"He used military baton techniques with martial arts moves," Jim said. "We should get rid of their bats."

"I wouldn't cross those brutes," Beth said. *They'd make quick work of me.*

Tom tried the door on the nearest van. It was unlocked. The key lay on top of the dashboard. He, Beth, and Jim checked the other vans, finding all unlocked, with keys visible, snow beginning to stick to the hoods and roofs.

"How many people can fit into these vans?" Beth whispered.

"Fifteen passengers max," Tom said. "The breaker panel is next to the back door. I'll flip the main switch. When the lights are off, Jim, you open the front door. Beth, you open the side door. Move the people out the doors and into the vans as fast as you can. One of them has to drive each van. The driver can't leave before their van is full. Beth, may I borrow your air horn?"

Beth unzipped her jacket pocket and handed the horn to Tom, who headed to the back of the warehouse. Jim stood before the front door, Beth at the side door.

Tom worked with the breaker box, making noise. The three Asian guards eyed the back door. The blond guard rushed outside. "What the hell are you doing?"

Tom brushed snowflakes from his eyelashes. "The county sent me to repair the lines."

"I don't believe you."

"A major outage was traced to this area. I'm testing power distribution blocks. I'm checking switches, panels, connectors, the wiring in general. It's an emergency. It shouldn't take long, twenty minutes tops." Tom turned toward the breaker box, examining it.

The guard stood with his eyes fixed on Tom, then returned to the building. The lights turned off, on, and off again.

As Jim gingerly opened the front door, its guard turned to the door. An athletic woman took off from across the warehouse and brought the guard down with a flying tackle. His bat rolled across the floor. A man caught the bat, ran to the front door, and threw it outside.

The guard jumped on top of the woman. She pulled up her left knee sharply against his stomach and pressed her right foot against his hip, holding him back. He grabbed both her wrists. She twisted her body forcefully to the left, loosening her right wrist from his grasp. With her free hand, she yanked his ear. He dropped her left wrist. With her right foot, she pushed him hard, propelling him onto his back.

A few people dashed over and held the guard to the floor. Others handed them scarves, a necktie, a belt, and a small roll of First Aid tape. After fastening his legs together and his arms to his body, they taped his mouth and moved him to a vacant corner of the warehouse. The guard lay bound, making low, angry growls.

Jim poked the person closest to the door and pointed to the vans, whispering, "Go! Go! Go!" Others rose to their feet and stumbled out the door.

When Beth opened the side door, its guard began swinging his bat in a wild frenzy. A young man took a thick piece of rotten wood from the floor. He crept behind the bat-swinging guard, hit him hard on the head, clasped his shoulder, and jerked him backward. Dropping his bat, the guard sprawled on the floor. He pushed himself forward, reaching for his bat. A woman seized the bat and handed it to Beth, who stuck it end up in a juniper bush outside the door.

The group rushed forward and rolled the guard face down, stepping on his fingers when he tried to move. They tied the guard's legs together, tied his arms to his body, taped his mouth, and moved him to another corner of the floor. His shouts came out as feeble squawks.

Beth motioned for people to exit the side door. She pointed her penlight along the snowy ground toward the vans. "Full vans! Every van full!"

A line of disheveled Bomkamp employees formed lines at the front and side doors. After exiting, they broke into a sprint toward the vans, their feet slipping on the frozen ground. Snowflakes and ice pellets hit their faces.

The first van's engine revved to life. Headlights on, it pulled out and started down the mountain. More vans with cold engines grumbled in the quiet darkness and took off.

Beth screamed and pointed her penlight at the hands of the third Asian guard. His bat was on the floor, his foot on it. He held a pocketknife in his left hand and was opening the blade. A husky young man threw a one-two punch to the back of his head and arm, sending the knife spinning across the floor toward a neatly dressed, middle-aged woman. She picked up the knife, closed it, and put it in her purse. The group pulled the guard to the floor, held him, tied him, and moved him to a third corner.

Outside, Tom heard the back door opening. In his side vision, he saw the blond boss stepping toward him with a black baseball bat. He dropped onto the icy ground and rolled away from the building. The air horn in his pocket made a short blast. The guard swung the bat, missed Tom, and gave the breaker box a hard crack. Tom rolled toward the guard like a lead pipe, knocking him over, causing his head to hit the ground. The bat flew out of the guard's hands, landing near the building. The guard lay rigid on his back on the ice-covered ground.

Tom held down the air horn button with his left hand, producing an ear-splitting wail. With his right hand, he grabbed the bat and heaved it into the trees. The guard pulled himself to his feet and hobbled into a thickly wooded region beyond the warehouse, his feet sliding on the icy, rough terrain. Tom silenced the horn.

The vans' headlights and taillights glowed as, one by one, they pulled out onto the road.

Tom opened the back door. From his pocket, he handed a roll of duct tape to a woman standing inside, closed the door, and resumed his lookout for the blond guard. The woman ran to the closest Asian guard, bound and lying in a corner. Others joined her in taping his arms and legs securely to his body. They did the same to the other two guards.

Beth called out, "One more van left!"

A small group remained inside the dim warehouse, gathered around a man lying on the floor. Jim and Beth hurried over to the group. The man was motionless, his face ashen, his eyes closed.

Jim knelt next to the man and stroked his rigid arm. "Hey, Ryan! How are you doing?"

Ryan Ford half opened his eyes and spoke in a shaky voice. "I'm sorry, Jim. A friend asked me to walk the picket line with him. I ended up here. I heard the guards talking. In the morning they'd take us into the backcountry. Abandon us. Go for a beer after they dropped us off. We wouldn't make it back to the road in this weather." He shivered. "That blond guard's name is Carson. He's American."

Jim bent close to Ryan's face, looking into his eyes. "You're safe. You have a ride home tonight. Seb and I will be at your house next week for our meeting. We're going to help you into your van now." Jim motioned for assistance. The group helped Ryan to his feet and out the door.

Two young women wearing puffer jackets picked up the remaining bat and the three softballs on the floor. "They forgot the mitts! They ruined our teambuilding day!" Waving to the three scowling guards lying in the corners of the warehouse, they shouted, "Bye-bye!" Grabbing the two bats outside the door, they carried the bats and balls out to the last van.

Beth shone her penlight around the empty warehouse. She and Jim tried to pull their doors shut, but the latches wouldn't catch. They walked to the back of the building and motioned to Tom, standing vigilant next to the back door. The three of them made their way to Tom's van in the rising wind, their feet crunching the icy snow. Tom brushed snow off the van. Jim and Beth scraped ice off the windshield.

Tom drove the van down the mountain at a slow speed, the tires spinning on the icy pavement at times.

Beth rubbed her hands together. "Tom, you must be freezing. You're covered with snow and ice." *My feet are like popsicles.*

"I could use a cup of hot cocoa. I turned up the heater. When our phones are working again, we can check for texts from Andy."

They sat in silence for a few minutes, snow blowing sideways outside the van windows.

Beth yawned as the heater warmed the van. "I'm curious if Amber and the van drivers made it to Sue's store for the grand opening celebration. Amber wanted to see Kessie."

Jim leaned forward from the seat behind Tom. "Sue's phone call with Amber suggested that someone else besides Kessie would be waiting for them."

"They should lock up Amber and those damn drivers and throw away the key," Tom said.

Beth said, "With Kessie around, Sue better keep an eye on the inventory. And the cash drawer."

A powerful gust of wind blew the van a couple of inches across the dividing line on the road. Tom gently steered the vehicle into its lane.

Jim talked louder. "I expect Carson's freeing the three guards from all that duct tape wound around them. He's the blond guard."

"The one who gave me a hard time outside," Tom said.

"Ryan caught his name. I have no idea about his role in the organization."

"Carson could be Amber's counterpart for the North Koreans," Beth said. "Amber follows Chang to the next job, and Carson follows Mook."

Jim said, "A few years ago, I read about something similar outside a big city in the Northeast. Rescuers flew employees out of the woods by helicopter. They never found out who or what was behind it."

Tom turned his head slightly. "You saw an old man yelling at picketers to get off the van? I bet the Asians muscled out the real drivers."

Jim said, "We prevented a major incident. No way could we have done it without you, Tom."

Tom fixed his eyes on the road. "We all made it happen. I'd be pumped about it, but I'm dog-tired."

Beth said, "We're the best." *I'm almost too tired to breathe.*

Chapter 20: Friday, May 26

"Honey, our coffee's ready!" Dusty Gatling shouted from the kitchen.

"Hang on a sec," Sue hollered from the bedroom. "I need to call Amber."

A groggy voice answered. "Hello?"

"So where were you?" Sue asked. "You missed a great party. People were asking about you."

"Sorry, I wasn't in the mood. The drivers dropped me off at Heenehan's parking lot. I drove myself home. I watched some TV and went to bed."

"Those drivers came to our party," Sue said. "Their boss, Min, stopped by. I think he was checking up on them. They all had a good time."

"Their boss, Minjun Mook?"

"That's him."

"Them drivers were supposed to pick up people who did their teambuilding in the mountains," Amber said, a slight edge in her voice. "It was snowin' up there."

"Yeah, but Min changed his mind. They couldn't go anywhere, with the weather and all."

"Oh, no. Really?"

"No worries," Sue said. "The people in the mountains got rides home. Hey, do you remember Gary Hudson?"

"Uh, yeah. He flunked the drug test."

"Bummer. Gary's a great guy. He lives near our store and came over. Before the weather changed, Gary helped out with the Bomkamp people playing softball in the park for their teambuilding event," Sue said.

"Yeah, I heard they got in a few games."

"Gary took Min and the drivers to a nice, safe place."

"So where'd he take them?" Amber asked.

"He didn't say."

"I'll swing by the store sometime when I can."

"Be sure to let me know when you're coming. I want you to meet somebody. You're in for a big surprise."

"Okay. I'm glad your opening bash turned out good."

"Thanks! Bye."

Sue chuckled, poured coffee into her mug from a thermal carafe, and sat across from Dusty at the kitchen table. "Seeing as I'm not on the Tech Team and not working at Heenehan anymore, Amber can't figure out what to make of me. She's got no clue Gary's an FBI agent."

"Good thing you invited Min and his drivers to our party," Dusty said. "That worked out great. Gary and his guys rounded 'em up quick and quiet before they got in the door. The customers didn't even know it happened. I'm proud of you, Sue."

"Thanks! Couldn't have done it without you." Sue blew her husband a kiss across the table. "I'll give Gary a heads up when Amber tells me she's gonna stop by the store. After that, my work with Gary is done. This morning he's meeting with Sandra Young. Me and Sandra love workin' for him. His guys drove out in the snow and nabbed those four guards at the warehouse. The Koreans won't try another one of their random kidnaps around here again."

"I hope Gary busts that Tech Team. They opened the door for those North Korean cyber thugs. They figure Americans are fair game for their crackpot terrorist plots."

"Gary's tapping Amber's phone, checking out her activities a while longer. Then the agents gonna haul 'em all in."

Dusty took a drink from his cup and looked at Sue in discomfort. "Might be the tip of a giant iceberg. More companies with tech teams and North Koreans, all talking to each other."

"Yeah, I can see that. Worries me, too."

"Anyway, what you did is outstanding. You're one spunky lady. You made a difference."

"I love you, sweetie. I'm really glad you bought the store."

"I love you, too." Dusty stood, drank his last drop of coffee, and rinsed his mug in the sink. "Let's feed the chickens and get going. We got cleanup to do before opening time."

Jim and Beth climbed the stairs to a third-floor conference room for Judy's staff meeting.

Beth said, "I can't fathom why we came into work today." *I desperately need about twelve hours of sleep.*

Jim massaged the skin between his eyebrows. "Ghosting Heenehan is tempting. We could turn around, walk down the stairs and out the door, and cut off communication. Heenehan lays people off with no warning, which is the same thing."

Beth yawned. "Our days at Heenehan are numbered. We might as well leave with a clear record."

In the conference room, Jim, Beth, and Amber gazed at dozens of multicolored helium balloons filling the ceiling, left over from the previous day's teambuilding events.

Judy sat expressionless at the head of the table. "I have been informed that Bomkamp is restructuring Heenehan. You will finish any work requiring immediate attention. You will make a list of your outstanding tasks and provide them to me today."

"How will the restructure affect our jobs?" Beth asked.

"When I receive further details, I will inform you."

"What will happen to the other Bomkamp companies?" Jim asked.

Judy stiffened. "I am not given information regarding other companies. And I can tell you Bomkamp gives no credence to any stories circulating about yesterday's teambuilding exercise. It was a well-planned, fun-filled day. Every employee who took part benefitted from their shared experience."

A blue balloon on the ceiling popped with a bang and dropped onto the conference table. The staff jumped. Judy brushed it onto the floor.

Amber brightened. "I had the best time ever!"

"I'm pleased to hear that." Judy unwrapped a hard candy, tossed it into her mouth, crumpled the wrapper, and threw it into the wastebasket.

Beth frowned. "I've been having systems issues this morning—"

"Bomkamp is doing a server configuration change."

"We can't do anything," Jim said.

"The system will be functioning normally within a short time. I'll discuss your unfinished work with each of you. Do not drink from any water fountains or faucets in the building today. The pipes are being serviced. This meeting is over."

Judy left the conference room with Amber.

Returning to the tax area, Beth said, "I'm so frustrated! This morning my login password failed several times. The whole system is incredibly slow. Error messages when I try to pull up my files. No internet at all. I can work offline, that's it. I don't have the strength to tolerate computer mishaps today."

Jim said, "The accounting system update is running. That's supposed to happen at night. Someone moved reports from my inbox into my spam folder. I found an email in my sent folder that I didn't write. A message from Judy's email address instructed me to click a link, then provide requested information. I didn't click the link. The email sounded exactly like Judy wrote it, but an odd misspelling of her name told me it came from a robot."

"We can't trust Bomkamp's network."

Jim read a news bulletin on his phone. "'A spokesman for Bomkamp Management Group stated its companies are experiencing a network event. An intense power surge caused electronic equipment to overheat. The system overload touched off small fires in some buildings. Bomkamp is working to resolve the situation.'" *Bomkamp is not going to resolve it. The North Koreans are here.*

"The Koreans activated Hwan's code!"

Jim and Beth plodded through dim, stuffy halls, passing figures sitting idly at their desks. As they reached the tax corridor, the garden level grew dark. A smoky smell filled the air.

Jim shouted, "Let's get out of here!" *This building is not going to explode with me in it.*

Beth grabbed her purse from her desk drawer and looped the strap over her shoulder. She and Jim raced upstairs, outside, and across the street. Standing on the sidewalk, they faced the building. Coughing employees carried out their possessions.

Amber came running down the sidewalk, shouting at them, "I broke the glass with the big red fire extinguisher! I just put out a fire! Every office I work at catches fire!" She erupted in shrill laughter, shook her tousled green hair, and ran on.

"Amber's coming unhinged," Jim said. "Let's not slow her down."

"Or she's moving up in the cybercrime world and celebrating her victory," Beth said. "Chang will overlook her mischief since the Koreans' plans succeeded in a big way."

Sandra Young walked toward them, a slim figure in a black business suit, straight black hair swinging lightly. She stopped, leaned forward, and spoke in a low voice. "The authorities will be contacting you. You did the right thing." She hurried along the sidewalk.

Beth said, "I guess that's reassuring. There's more than enough evidence of Amber's misconduct. If she isn't stopped, she'll rise from the ashes of Bomkamp more powerful. I believe a government agency will stop her."

Jim shook his head. "This is another one-way monologue with Sandra. The authorities had plenty of time to contact us and stop Amber. If we did the right thing, why is Bomkamp out of control?"

"The authorities are pursuing the best possible means of dealing with the situation. Or their resources are limited. I honestly don't know."

"The thing is, federal and local authorities didn't keep these foreign criminals in check. On the plus side, our master plan is to save ourselves. The cyber crooks are crushing Heenehan for us. We'll be fine."

"Yes, we will."

Hundreds of employees milled around, talking excitedly or waiting patiently. A group clustered around a woman with a microphone. A man held up a phone camera.

"That's the Heenehan IT group," Jim said.

"The woman is a TV reporter," Beth said.

"The IT folks are briefing the press. Not much the company can do to them now." *Andy's old office buddies. Good on them.*

Jim and Beth moved to a less crowded area farther down the sidewalk. Jim called Andy on speakerphone, turning the volume low.

Andy said, "I listened to a bunch of conversations on Amber's phone and read dozens of texts. A massive failure in the electric grid is knocking out power lines. Bomkamp's backup generators were damaged and shut off. All their companies are in blackout. Their networks are down. They're using flashlights to escort employees out of buildings."

"It's game over for Bomkamp," Jim said.

"I have Heenehan's customer information here. It's not going to save the company. Hwan's code deleted all data on the network. Except for files saved on home computers or hard copies floating around, all the Bomkamp companies' histories are erased."

"So it's impossible to recreate any of Bomkamp's companies," Jim said. "Tough break for the employees."

"They didn't see it coming." Beth coughed, took a tissue from her purse, and blew her nose.

"A company as large as Bomkamp needs huge investments in cyber protection. No insurance company would cover Bomkamp. Its security processes don't meet even the lowest standards."

"Where's Skip Bomkamp?" Beth asked.

"At an undisclosed location," Andy said. "Since the malware damaged the electrical distribution lines, the organizations doing business with Bomkamp are reporting instability. I'm doing network diagnostics several times a day. So far, Analytics' network is clean."

"First class work, Andy," Beth said.

"The Koreans likely drained the Bomkamp companies' bank accounts," Jim said. "Most banks don't offer businesses protection from cyber fraud. That money is irretrievable. Plundered by North Korean bank robbers."

Beth tapped at her phone. "Here's another news report. 'A spokesman for Bomkamp Management Group announced that its operating companies will close indefinitely. The management team will not be held personally liable for any actions of the firm or its companies' liabilities.'"

"Skip Bomkamp will find some poor underling to pin it on," Jim said. "It won't be you or me. Judy will fight any publicity reflecting badly on her group. And Scott can't recall our names."

Jim and Beth walked along the sidewalk near the pond.

"A gold mine of evidence is sitting on Amber's phone," Andy said. "I'll be relieved to turn it over to the authorities. Amber's forgotten it and never mentioned it in her calls or texts."

Jim frowned. "Man alive, that pond stinks!"

"The odor coming from the pond is making me nauseous," Beth said. "A rotten egg smell, maybe natural gas. The water's bubbling like it's on low boil."

"The gas pipelines aren't affected," Andy said. "The crazy Koreans must've used a pump to send sulfuric acid into the pond. That substance is extremely poisonous and causes lasting damage."

"Why would they do that?" Beth asked.

"No reason," Jim said. "Wrecking the Bomkamp companies is their masterwork. Destroying the pond is their finishing touch. At least no vile corporation can hide in an upscale office park on this block again. It'll be just another vacant lot."

"Nature will be slow to heal this ground," Beth said. "The pond is so sad. The acid poisoned everything. I don't want to believe what I'm seeing."

No fish swam below the murky surface. Spring flowers near the pond had wilted. Their blooms lay on the ground. Trees and shrubs had shed their new leaves, leaving bare branches. Grass resembled straw.

"Now we know why Judy told us not to drink from the water fountains or faucets," Jim said. "Talk to you later, Andy."

"It's time for us to take off," Beth said.

At the far end of the parking lot, Beth and Jim stopped at Beth's car. She opened the passenger door, laid her purse on the seat, and closed the door. She walked to the driver's door, key in hand. *How can I say goodbye to this precious friend?*

Jim scanned the devastated office park. "No one will be coming back here for a long time except the cleanup crews."

"I'm already a million miles away from Heenehan. Look at those puffy, white clouds and bright blue sky. I smell summer in the air. I can hardly believe I lived to see this day. My best day ever!"

"You've taken too many whiffs of that pond water," Jim said.

"I'll resist the temptation to burst into song."

"Welcome to freedom. How are you going to celebrate?"

"With a twenty-minute power nap. Then I'm going to my granddaughter Claire's ball game. That's all I have energy for today."

"An excellent way to celebrate. Since I'm short on funds, I'll offer you a low-cost retirement gift. I'd be honored to provide your background music for any future art shows."

"What a wonderful gift! I'd love that."

"Thank you for not bailing out on me," Jim said. "I mean this sincerely. I can't imagine being stranded at Heenehan on my own."

"I wouldn't leave a dog in that place."

"Staying to the bitter end took guts, not knowing what might happen."

"I'm hard to get rid of."

"You're a real pain in the neck."

"I want to experience your wonderful music."

"Without you, it would never happen." He stared at the ground. "I wish we could have done more for the decent employees. After Bomkamp took over their companies, they knew their jobs were temporary. A tough predicament in this recession."

Beth said, "I have immense sympathy for anyone who suffers a loss of their job or pension, especially the long term employees who built their companies. Like Sandra said, we did the right things. We tried to tell the people in charge. We reported Amber to the police and the Tech Team to the FBI. We freed the employees in the warehouse from the North Koreans. And we did all that while carrying the workload of an entire department."

"You're right. There's no grand purpose as to why we landed on our feet and the other Bomkamp people didn't. We all have to navigate our twisted world. We saved ourselves, and that's enough of a victory."

"Someone will open a door for them. They're going to find people like you and Elly and Tom and Andy and Katie to help them create a rewarding life."

A soft breeze ruffled Jim's graying hair. "You view the world through artist's eyes, don't you?"

"I always have, and now I can slip into artist mode anytime I want. I have so much to do, and I'm tight on time. From this day forward my life is my own. I'm going to be intentional about the people I allow around me. I want to get healthy and feel like being alive is a good thing."

"What are you going to do with all your talent?" Jim asked.

"I'm starting a project this week. In accounting, numbers show the real story behind business activities. I'm going to explore pattern designs to communicate my own stories. Gather materials with various sizes, shapes, and textures. Figure out how they align in exactly the right way. It's play, really. The more I play, the faster my skills develop."

"I've created music with rhythm and tone patterns that could fit your artwork."

"Perfect!"

"Let me know when."

"I will! I'm going to hang out with my grandkids for a few days. Accounting has been my life for decades. I need to lay down a hundred percent of my career before I can summon the courage to pick up my artwork."

"Good decision."

"How about you?"

"I called Derek and Elly. I decided to accept both of their offers."

"Oh my gosh! Congratulations—I'm so happy for you!"

"I'm going to take a week off to decompress before I start my job as senior multimedia technician. Derek's relocating his company to the public media center."

"The elegant new cultural arts center downtown? The city approves only the most promising organizations for space in that building!"

"It's an impressive office with plenty of resources available to us. I'll keep on creating music every day, doing what I love."

"You have a future to live for. How's it going to work with two jobs?"

"Derek's fine with my part-time role at Analytics. Elly told me to work any hours I can fit into my schedule. We agreed on a couple evenings a week and one day on the weekend, as you suggested."

"Be careful not to stretch yourself too thin."

"I won't."

"Did you tell Rose about your career change?"

"I told Mom. She doesn't understand. The staff at Sunny Senior Care take good care of her. Doris and I visit her a few times a week. She's still anxious, but she looks a lot healthier."

"It's such a relief not to worry about Rose's safety. My heart goes out to her. Would it be okay if I visited her? I'd like to bring her a cozy, pink blanket like the one I have at home." *A small comfort for a resilient lady facing her final challenges.*

"Rose would love a visit. The blanket's a nice idea."

"What are the plans for your band?"

"Tom and Andy and I are getting together this weekend at my house for a jam session. We haven't played together since high school, so it could be a little unmusical."

"I might sneak over there and listen. I know, not until the band is good enough."

"Fine with us. With time and practice, we're planning to perform at the new media center for a live audience. Imagine that."

"I'll be in the front row."

"Tom and Andy won't have to mess with us troublemakers at Heenehan anymore. They can do their own jobs in peace."

"Those dear guys. They're awesome. I'll miss them terribly." She studied the ground for a moment.

"With Mom in a safe place, along with the band and my new career, everything looks more vivid, like Photoshop punched up the colors."

"Exactly. And there's clean, fresh air. And birds chirping. It's overwhelming."

"Did you know bird songs are more complex than any music I can produce? They sing more notes than are on a piano keyboard."

"That's remarkable." *I just want to keep talking. It's too hard to say goodbye.*

Employees carrying their personal belongings fanned out in the parking lot, searching for their vehicles.

Beth said, "They're strangely calm, as if they knew this was coming."

"We better find the fastest exit out of here," Jim said. "We have to go. The building might explode."

Beth's eyes became blurry. She touched his arm. "I wish you the very best. You're meant for a lot more. You'll be fine." *I'm overwhelmed. My brain is frozen.*

"I'm sad that my new life will happen without you there."

Beth wiped below her eyes with her index finger. "Call me if you ever want me to tell you how amazing you are."

"Take care of yourself."

They embraced for a moment in the early summer sun. Jim took a step back and playfully punched Beth's upper arm. He turned and walked to his car.

Epilogue: Monday, August 14

Judy sat on a guest chair in front of Scott Campbell's oversized mahogany desk.

"I'm telling you, Scott, Vanessa knows nothing about tax."

"The tall blonde woman?" Scott narrowed his eyes. "Are you jealous of her?"

"You're not hearing me. Vanessa's unqualified. Her background is in finance, not tax. She bellows and curses at me because she's frustrated. Says I have no idea what I'm talking about. Never tells me her plans, but demands to know everything I'm doing at all times. She monitors my emails and gives me hell about them. I swear, I can't work with that woman."

"Toughen up if you want to play on my team, Judy. Most of the Bomkamp people are still job hunting, including your former manager, Brad. I hired you as my tax group supervisor, not Vanessa. It's your own fault you were bumped down a level."

"Being demoted is the worst thing that ever happened to me. I learned everything from you. I managed my underlings the same way you manage me. I sacrificed everything for my career. You ruined it."

"Not me. You're reporting to Vanessa because of that little mutiny by your subordinates."

"They're lucky to have my expertise," Judy said.

"I asked you to take a communication skills class. Do it."

"Vanessa is Jim Dennis's ex-wife. She has issues. Sandra Young at Heenehan wouldn't hire Vanessa. You shouldn't have hired her either."

"I don't know any Jim Dennis. Get to the point. I have meetings with six of my team leaders today. What do you want?"

"I want you to fire Vanessa. Terminate her."

"I'm not going to fire Vanessa." Scott made a hand steeple. "She has never engaged in any misconduct here. Work it out yourselves. It's a test of your leadership skills. Brad and I were strong leaders at Heenehan, and we managed to settle our differences."

"Is that so?"

"Look at Amber. Executive secretary is a perfect fit for her talents. She earns a good salary here and gets along with everyone."

"Amber can't write a coherent sentence, but at least you're keeping her away from numbers work. Last week I asked you to approve a software package for my database application to make us more efficient. I haven't received it."

"You don't need any fancy-pants software. Use what's here."

"I can't implement my database without the software. This big company can afford one small software package. You're starving us for resources. You already gutted the daylights out of my staff. The good people are leaving for Analytics Telco. The ones left are racing through huge workloads in a blind panic. I can't take a day off. I should leave, too."

"The choice is yours."

"Fine, I'll buy the software myself."

Scott said, "I told Vanessa to hire a couple of temps. She said it wasn't necessary."

"A couple of untrained temps would be money down the drain. Here's an idea. Pay your staff a living wage. They're putting in hours of unpaid overtime for garbage wages."

"I'm doing the best thing for our company, Judy. I'm maximizing long-term shareholder value."

"You're maximizing short-term value. I wouldn't be surprised if this company went bankrupt."

"Keep in mind you're one lucky employee, Judy. It was my attorney who cleared us of charges from the Bomkamp cyberattack."

"I never did anything wrong."

"Of course you didn't. Let's keep our eyes on the ball and stay focused. I was brave enough to give this new company a good shake-up. That's why I'm vice-president of strategic planning."

Judy stood, glaring at Scott, her face purple. "Brave? I have more balls than you! Nobody can support your vision for this company because you don't have one. Your last vacation cost more money than I made last year. Analytics is eating our lunch." She moved toward the door. "Okay, you won. Now what?"

"Take your class, and I might get rid of Vanessa. No promises." Scott focused on his computer screen. "And lay off the hard stuff. I can smell your breath a mile away."

"Thanks." Glowering, Judy stomped down the hall.

Scott Campbell swiped at a buzzing fly. "Amber!"

She appeared at the doorway, wearing a black minidress with sheer, lacy sleeves.

"Wow, you look very professional today."

"Thanks, boss. What's up?"

"A fly's been circling around my computer screen all morning. It's not a normal one."

"The cleaning crew didn't empty your wastebasket again. Pretty soon we'll have ants and mice." *Get outta here, Scott. Our new fly needs to do its job.*

"Would you please remind the cleaning staff of our standards of cleanliness?"

"You got it. The fly was bothering me, too. Keep your laptop open when you leave for lunch. The blue light from your screen will kill that pesky fly."

The fly came to a full stop. It dropped onto the desk, lying motionless. Scott grabbed the wastebasket and brushed the fly into it. "The only good fly is a dead fly. I'm going to lunch." He rose and left his office.

Amber called after him, "Have a good lunch!"

She lifted the fly from the wastebasket, carried it to her office next to Scott's, and placed it on her desk. She checked her phone. Nothing from Li Chang. She texted: *Li the drone fly died where r u???*

A stocky, middle-aged man with buzz-cut dark hair, a black suit, and a tie stood in the doorway. He held out his badge. "FBI. We have a warrant for your arrest."

Behind him a second, younger man handed him a pair of steel handcuffs.

Amber's voice was shrill. "Gary Hudson, the IT guy? You still mad about the cherry gummy bears? You knew they was weed!"

"You're under arrest for cybertheft. Turn around. Put your hands behind your back."

"NO! I ain't done no cybertheft! Not goin' nowhere!" *Are these guys for real?*

"You have two choices. Be arrested peacefully. Or fight us, and then be arrested."

"This is totally bogus! You got the wrong girl. My lawyer's a tough bitch. She'll beat the living snot out of you in court."

"Put your phone down."

Li would've warned me. They got him. And the Russians, too. I'm screwed. Amber set her phone on the desk, turned around, and placed her hands behind her back.

Gary snapped the cuffs on her wrists.

With a gloved hand, the second agent slipped Amber's phone into a plastic bag and tucked the bag into his pocket. He asked, "What's this thing on your desk?"

"A dead fly, what does it look like?"

The agent picked up the drone fly and dropped it into Amber's empty pencil cup. He placed the cup inside another plastic bag and sealed it. He gripped the bag in his right hand.

The two FBI special agents led Amber, head low and handcuffed, down the hallway. Coworkers whispered and pointed from their workstations in the open office. Judy stood and clapped her hands three times. The group rose, clapping and cheering.

The younger agent said, "Nothing like appreciation for a job well done."

Gary smiled. "Justice is served."

About the Author

Beverly Winter is a retired CPA from Fort Collins, CO. During her 47-year career, mostly in large corporations, she conceived of The Telecom Takeover.